Death and Mr. Prettyman

First he saw the hat and briefcase on the small table and frowned. The room was dingy, with a few chairs obviously originating in some mid-Victorian dining-room and a vast leather armchair which Hearman alleged Sir Jabeez had stolen from the waiting-room on Crewe Station. He peered into the light cast by the twenty-five-watt bulb in its grimy white glass shroud—there were too few clients at night to warrant more watts, Sir Jabeez had proclaimed. There was something there which did not look like a man now but was. Curled in the embraces of the huge chair was a small crumpled form. In death old Prettyman's face was curiously defenseless, the neat gold-framed glasses were not upon his nose. "A seizure," said Greenaway aloud. Then, "Jesus!" as he saw the black haft of the small knife under the small solicitor's left shoulder-blade. Instinctively he gripped it and applied slight pressure. He was revolted at the feeling that seemed to travel along the knife. Besides, he remembered, you let it stay put until you got a doctor. He felt Prettyman's forehead. It was cold and clammy. Dead, dead, dead, he thought, but better get a doctor.

Other titles in the Walker British Mystery Series

KENNETH
GILES

Death and Mr. Prettyman

WALKER AND COMPANY · NEW YORK

First published in the United States of America
in 1969 by the Walker Publishing Company, Inc.

This paperback edition first published in 1984.

ISBN: 0-8027-3086-8

Library of Congress Catalog Card Number: 69-11441

Printed in the United States of America

10   9   8   7   6   5   4   3   2   1

Milton Greenaway, barrister-at-law, stood and peered out into the eddying waves of foul moisture drifting across the large courtyard. A shape appeared ten feet away. Peering, Greenaway saw the swag belly, apprehensive face and general impression of physical disorganisation that reminded him of the art of the late Robert Benchley. He recognised the shape as old Greasing, the publisher, who had made so much money out of controversial books. He'd be going to consult Sir Henry Clayblown. Lucky man, Clayblown! The acknowledged expert on obscenity just at the time when all the publishers were hock-deep in its problems! Greenaway coughed as the fog crept up his nose and wondered what Greasing had got hold of now. Last time it had been that thing about Ancient Greece. Of course, what Greasing liked, and trailed his coat for, was an unsuccessful prosecution: wonderful advertising and two thousand pounds for Clayblown. Briefly he wondered whether he could bone up on it and seek the scraps that fell from Clayblown's table. But by the time he had achieved any reputation it would be something else. Better stick to the Scotch leases. Again he peered out.

Visibility was discernibly getting less by the minute. He could no longer see the shape of his five-year-old Volks, a recent acquisition, parked fifteen yards away. He left the door that led to the grimy stairs of the old building slightly ajar and switched on the stair light. When he finally reached his small room perched under the rafters he found his fire smoking vilely. Scouting, who was supposed to caretake, always muttered that it was when the east wind blew. In fact it smoked when it blew from the south, the north, the west, or even on calm days in early spring when the toffee papers—dropped by people who had given up smoking—lay unmoving on the flagstones. However, as by far the most junior of the five counsel who inhabited the upper reaches of the old building, Scouting treated him with scarcely veiled contempt.

He forced his mind back to work and concluded the document he was writing. His pen dashed over the paper. "Save as is hereinbefore admitted each and every allegation contained in the statement of claim is denied as if set out herein and traversed seriatim."

He read it through and nodded with approval at the final sentence, couched carefully to terrify an outstandingly craven old lawyer. Greenaway had little doubt that his own client had attempted fraud, but his adversary was not known in the profession as The Original Settler for nothing. And with luck he'd screw a hundred for the client. Miss Prout, the typist, had been away for ten days with 'flu, so it would have to go to the typing agency tomorrow via Hearman, the young clerk. Sir Jabeez Lusting, the leader of the Chambers and a Treasury Silk, had a passion for economy and there was no office boy. Not that Greenaway had any urge to own a fifth of an office boy who would become part of an agonising equation involving giving up his car, or forsaking his week-end round of golf, or not taking Barbie out once a week.

He sighed and caught himself. He was sighing a lot these days. Sometimes he thought he should have quit the law. Six years and a room in a pretentious residential club which was really a second-rate boarding house with its execrable food hiding behind restaurant French. But the address was good and the public rooms were cunningly tarted up for the likes of him. Perhaps he should quit and join one of the companies who liked an LL.B. in the higher echelons. A fellow pupil had gone into advertising and allegedly breakfasted on caviar, champagne and sumptuous redheaded women. Still, he had thought he saw a little light ahead. He did not kid himself that he thought quickly enough for brilliant cross-examination, but his paper work was both solid and imaginative, of that he was sure.

Sir Jabeez always pleaded urgent governmental consultations if the weather was bad and was doubtless holed up now in some comfortable Whitehall club with his brandy. Greenaway meditated that none of the other four were less than thirty years his senior. Old Runting, sixty-nine to Sir Jabeez's seventy, had never taken silk, but if you were a publican and in trouble anywhere in England—Runting disliked the Scots and the Welsh—you got to Runting before the other side did, if your solicitor was wise. Margits, a stout sixty-five, slow-minded and studious, picked up Runting's leavings very capably, and Hewson, at sixty, possessed a phenomenal county court practice as well as being an expert on appeals in cases involving traffic offences. Lucky dogs! Old Runting was in Carlisle on a licensing case which had already lasted eight days, at forty-eight guineas a day refreshers. His financial taste buds watering, Greenaway looked at his watch and saw with a sense of shock that it was six-fifteen. He went to the window and peered through the grime. It was dark as hell. Inside, the sixty-watt bulb, authorised by Sir Jabeez, fought lazily with the wisps of fog that crept through the badly fitting window-frame.

He checked his appointment pad. There it was. 'Mr. Pretty-man, 5.30.' He had been in seeing Hewson who had kindly asked him to devil a brief for him next day. It had been at nine-fifteen, a sullen grey-skied morning. Hearman had poked his head round the door. The clerk's relative youth meant that he was cheap, albeit competent. Greenaway had often reflected uneasily that he would soon have to pay more.

"Ah, Mr. Greenaway, is it all right for Mr. Prettyman to see you this arvo?"

"Suggest five-thirty," he said, "to be safe. I don't know how long I'll be this afternoon."

After a minute Hearman had returned and said it was confirmed.

Prettyman, an elderly solicitor with a faint resemblance to a duck, practised in Kent, where his firm, Prettyman, Benjamin, Trotter and Cope, was in fact Mr. Prettyman solo, the others probably having mouldered away in the rambling, dusty old office which housed the firm.

He had come in four years ago and vaguely said he had heard Greenaway was a specialist on leases. Greenaway always thought he had to thank old Runting, who handled matters affecting the twenty-one public houses situated on the three large estates which provided Prettyman with almost all his practice. It was a lovely little business, thought Greenaway. He had no illusions. First, Prettyman knew as much if not more about leases than he did, but with innate caution referred to counsel's opinion ten times a year. Secondly, he had chosen Greenaway because although competent he was cheap. Mr.

Prettyman was frugal about his clients' costs—his own fees from the constant conveyancing keeping the old bachelor happily in his snug Georgian home. When Greenaway increased his demands, Prettyman's business would melt away, together with the small, but very handy trickle of other business. Prettyman was known as conservative and shrewd, and the timid or the indecisive sought to know how he went about matters and followed suit.

Not like the old gentleman to be late! Greenaway looked at his watch again and wet his lips as he got the taste of fog. No good hanging around. He would have to walk home, if you could call it home. But first to check all lights, the standing order of Sir Jabeez. He found himself shrugging. The Q.C. could be very rude when aroused, which curiously came about not from big things but small things such as paper being wasted, overstamping envelopes and lights being left on. He checked the three rooms on the floor below, and turned off the landing light. On the first floor were the archives, library, a small room for Hearman and Miss Prout, Sir Jabeez's massively furnished room and a small waiting-room. He checked the waiting-room last.

First he saw the hat and briefcase on the small table and frowned. The room was dingy, with a few chairs obviously originating in some mid-Victorian dining-room and a vast leather armchair which Hearman alleged Sir Jabeez had stolen from the waiting-room on Crewe Station. He peered into the light cast by the twenty-five-watt bulb in its grimy white glass shroud—there were too few clients at night to warrant more watts, Sir Jabeez had proclaimed. There was something there which did not look like a man now but was. Curled in the embraces of the huge chair was a small crumpled form. In death old Prettyman's face was curiously defenceless, the neat gold-framed glasses were not upon his nose. "A seizure," said Greenaway aloud. Then, "Jesus!" as he saw the black haft of the small knife under the small solicitor's left shoulder-blade. Instinctively he gripped it and applied slight pressure. He was revolted at the feeling that seemed to travel along the knife. Besides, he remembered, you let it stay put until you got a doctor. He felt Prettyman's forehead. It was cold and clammy. Dead, dead, dead, he thought, but better get a doctor.

He stumbled into Sir Jabeez's room. There was one opposite. What was the name? They'd phoned him when Sir Jabeez had food poisoning. "Three 'elpings of his favourite lobster mayonnaise, more like," Hearman had said *sotto voce*. Funny how useless debris kept popping into his mind. He concentrated and flipped open the neat green book on the desk top. There it was under 'doctor'. He dialled the number and spoke briefly and then telephoned the police.

As he propped his head in his hands he noticed they were shaking. His heightened sensitivity registered that the old house was creaking in the heavy silence.

There were footsteps on the stairs. The doctor was a heavy young man with a very long woollen muffler round his throat.

"This way," Greenaway muttered. This was what it would feel like when he was eighty, he thought, as his knees barely supported him.

He gestured towards the armchair and the doctor bent and did things. Quite quickly he straightened. "Poor old chap's been gone two hours or so. A bad business. Who are you, by the way?"

"Name's Greenaway, work in the building. He is—was—a client named Prettyman."

"Not now!" grunted the doctor. "Here," he caught Greenaway's arm. The barrister saw that the worn carpet had slightly tilted. The doctor lowered him expertly on to a chair and removed his coat. "Put your head down, steady, that's fine." He rolled Greenaway's shirt-sleeve up, fumbled in his bag and there was the sting of a hypodermic.

"You're in slight shock. This is the bomb, but better intravenous. Just stay put."

In what seemed seconds, but was probably two minutes, Greenaway felt vigorous life flood back into him. His head was clear, his hands steady. Only his mouth felt parched. He looked up. The doctor was handing him a crystal glass from Sir Jabeez's silver tray.

"Mouth seized up? Drink this. Good stuff, water!"

"Sorry about the womanish weakness," Greenaway noted that the burly man kept between him and the armchair.

"Have to send you a bill, I opted out of the grand national. Oh, not for the old fellow, but for the injection!" he con-

9

tinued to talk soothingly as he shepherded Greenaway out. "Let's see the old hands." He imprisoned them in his and peered for a long minute.

"I'll vouch you're no Lady Mac, but we want some cops."

"I telephoned."

"Good oh, but God knows how long in this fog. I wonder if . . ."

There was a short silence with heavy uncertainty in the air.

"She is up in Liverpool. It was on the news."

"Had a swine of a day, no time to read or listen."

"Police here!" The voice was a pleasant tenor.

"Come up. Doctor here!"

There was the noise of tramping footsteps.

Greenaway saw a mousy-haired man emerge from the stairwell. He was a trifle taller than Greenaway, perhaps five feet nine, neatly dressed, with a canary-coloured waist-coat and a curious look of . . . his mind hesitated . . . diffidence, lack of confidence. But there was no weakness in it. His voice was quiet when he said, "My name is James. Acting Chief Inspector. You would rate higher, but we have much 'flu and troubles. This is Sergeant Honeybody." Honeybody looked like an ex-N.C.O. and his moustache was spiky and waxed.

"I am Greenaway. I telephoned the police. I am a barrister in chambers here. This is the doctor." He introduced them, noticing that Honeybody was large, cauliflower-eared and slightly running to seed. Although there was no odour Greenaway sensed a patina of stout and whisky over the Sergeant, whose eyes were nevertheless what Greenaway, in his new sense of observation caused by the injection, classed as beady and sharp.

"I'd like you to meet our police surgeon. Perhaps you two medical men can get together, but for five minutes we must do photography and measuring."

Three quiet men stood together, one holding a Linhof camera with telescoped tripod and flash attachment.

"Perhaps you would come into Sir Jabeez's office, gentlemen?" asked Greenaway.

"Sir Jabeez Lusting?" James sounded half amused.

"The same."

"I've met him two or three times and of course have been examined by him. Is he here?"

Acting Chief Inspector James looked around as if expecting to see the pear-shaped figure of Sir Jabeez.

"No, but take his chair," invited Greenaway. The Acting Chief Inspector and the Sergeant seated themselves, James in the red-plush-covered throne—"more like my old grannie's commode," Hearman used to comment—which normally contained Sir Jabeez.

The two doctors stood in the corner talking in low voices.

"Better search the building, Sergeant. Now, sir, what is the corpse's name?" asked James, a notebook on the desk.

"He is—was—a solicitor named Charles Prettyman, of Windlesham Parva, Kent, a small town . . ."

"I know it. So he was a small-town solicitor. . . ."

"Not exactly. He administered three large estates, one very large. He was seventy-two and still vigorous. As far as I know, no family at all. . . . He had a good income from the business and donated a lot of time free, hospital boards, poor persons' aid, that sort of thing. Plus a lot of the county families getting quiet bits of unpaid advice. 'I say, old man,' stuff. Good bloke! Harmless!"

"He was consulting you about what?"

"Dunno. The clerk made the appointment. But it would be an opinion on a lease. About ten times a year, ten guineas a go. I specialise in repairing leases."

"Just a minute," it was the young doctor. "Mr. Greenaway was in shock, I gave him an injection. He may be a little light-headed."

"I'm all right."

"Very well." The doctor crossed over to the desk and whipped out a quarto sheet of Sir Jabeez's cherished Turkey Mill Bond, reputedly reserved for the Solicitor-General and counted twice weekly. He crumpled it. "Two pills here for bedtime. If possible no alcohol, if not possible the less the better."

One of the quiet technicians looked in at the door. "The cadaver is ready, sir."

The doctors left.

"Now look," said Acting Chief Inspector James, "I don't want to ask questions. Just tell me."

"I'm light-headed from the dope," said Greenaway, "but here goes." He talked for fifteen minutes.

"Hm," James rifled through his notes. "There was nobody else in the building?"

"Everybody out or gone home except me."

"Is that usual?"

Greenaway sounded defensive. "It would not be unusual for one of us to be working alone. In the law you sometimes find you've worked a seventy-hour week. So when a break occurs, hang on to it. Once you lose it it's gone for ever."

"Same with us," said James, "although the hours off do seem to me to get fewer. Now look, the Sergeant will take you down to the police car which will drive you home. No, no, these men are the best drivers existent. They'll get you home. I've seen a lot of shocked people. I prescribe a couple of boiled eggs and bed. We would appreciate if you would give the driver the clothes you have on; he'll come to your room while you change. Then we can knock that possibility right off the board."

Greenaway had noticed the Chief Inspector gazing at his hands. He spread them out.

"The doc had a look at them."

"You are most helpful." Swiftly James produced a bottle and a swab and anointed Greenaway's hands with a spirit-based liquid. "If it turns brown we must talk some more. Nope, positively no berlud, but we'd better check the clothes."

"In case I drove the shiv in with my navel?"

Greenaway saw the Inspector's white teeth flash as he laughed. "The legal repartee, one cannot match it! The Sergeant will take you down."

The Inspector went to the door and called. Honeybody appeared. "Nobody on the premises, sir."

"Take Mr. Greenaway to the car; he will give his apparel to the driver."

Greenaway felt an odd dreamlike feeling, as though he were floating, as he followed Sergeant Honeybody's great buttocks downstairs, coughing as the sulphurous air hit him.

The doctors had joined Acting Chief Inspector James.

"No disagreement," said the police surgeon, "not longer

than two hours and a quarter, not less than seventy-five minutes. Apparently a knife with a specially pointed tip. Usual cheap carving knife."

"Where was he killed?"

The surgeon shrugged and his stubby hand came round the Inspector's rib cage and pressed. "Just there, into the heart and practically no external bleeding. Done by an expert, say me or young Timothy here," the surgeon, an old cynical-looking man, leered, "it's foolproof and the funny thing is that you might not know. Of course you'd suddenly feel unwell, but there have been cases of people walking a hundred yards before, *bonk*. But if you put that up, you would really see the forensic circus contradicting each other."

"Thank you, sirs both."

"My fee," said the big young doctor, "how do I collect?"

"Not from my frugal purse. It's covered under Section 280 (c) of the natty health, along with post-mortems and accidents."

"I opted out."

"Why do I get the troubles?" James demanded of the ceiling.

"That's the boy," said the police surgeon, "bill for ten—with the odd bobs attached. Worth that to examine one of the Blue Lady's corpses."

The Inspector's face became rigid and his eyes cold. "She's working up north."

The surgeon shrugged. "I saw her Brixton job. She missed the heart, blood spraying like a fountain, but the knife was identical."

"And pictures have appeared in the press."

"Take an old sweat's advice and blame her, close the file and hop back to the indecent exposure."

"Send your bill to me, Doctor, room 309, thence to the Auditor-General, then back to me, but with luck one day a pay clerk. Again, many thanks."

He waited for the creak of Honeybody's brown boots, anchored below stout blue serge legs, and feet with curious little mountains on them, produced by a patent machine in the area of the Sergeant's corns.

"Sorry to delay, 'Arry," their relationship was friendly

enough for the Sergeant occasionally to condescend to unbend, "but Superintendent Hawker came over the squawker. Most upset. Wanted to know if it was the Blue Lady. I gave him an outline and he said what about Greenaway?"

"I doubt that he's a homicidal female."

"But there's that doubt, sir."

"Based on graphologists examining the letters to the *Sun*. Masculine cast of vowels. My guess is a les. who hates men."

"I wish sex was simpler, sir," said Honeybody. "When I was at the Oval thirty years ago, I remember . . ."

"I am in no mood for libidinous anecdotes. The caretaker, one Scouting, lives at 37, please fetch."

Honeybody creaked away. The Chief Inspector wished he would oil his damned boots. There were other sounds, a stretcher arriving for the last of Mr. Prettyman.

"Taken all the shots, sir," said one of the technicians. "Dabs all over that room, but nothing on the knife. Here's his briefcase and his wallet, all his own prints."

"You and the boys get a lift back in the ambulance."

"Very good, sir."

The man Honeybody returned with was very tall, with very thick black hair and a plastered-on scowl, graven around a great nose and fierce black eyes.

Harry introduced himself.

"I don't know what Mr. Bottle will say." His voice had a certain, inbuilt whine under its gruffness.

"Who the hell is Mr. Bottle?"

"The managing clurk of the agent. I dunno how to tell him the Blue Lady is around."

"Have you seen a Blue Lady?"

"I don't go out no more, sir, at night, what with the polis not givin' a workin' man no protection."

West country, thought Harry, and watched Honeybody's bulk heft up from his chair and the massive forefinger prod the man's sternum. He heard a wheeze of pain.

"You give my guv lip," said Honeybody, "and I'll take you out in the fog and you'll wish you was with the Blue Lady."

"Now, now, Sergeant, I'm sure Mr. Scouting means well."

"No offence, sir, it's just that it gets on a man's nerves what

14

with Mrs. Scouting having her two aunties in the kitchen all the time."

"Just tell me who inhabits this building."

Scouting obliged. "You have no ideer, sir, what these legal men are like. Always on about smoking chimneys, though I tells them it's board coal, not like the old days when you got washed Brighton nuts what burnt solid red," he concluded.

"Nobody on the ground floor or basement?"

"It's progress, sir. When my dad came here the old gents had top hats and some of 'em slept in. Now they like those glarse offices with steam heat, though it's unhealthy and dries a man out so he can't have children. Mr. Bottle advises rebuild, but old Sir Jabeez do have another fourteen years on the lease. Cunning old effer is that one."

The Chief Inspector saw Scouting's eyes swivel and his spine jerk. The door had opened and small green eyes in a mottled face surveyed the room. "I am afraid we have taken over your room, sir." Harry got to his feet, noting that somebody had spilled ash on the immaculate blotter.

"Cut off home, Scouting," he said.

"I'm greatly feared, sir, of bloody great knife."

"Escort him, Sergeant."

Scouting surrendered like a bride to Honeybody's clutch on his wrist.

Sir Jabeez was short and pear-shaped. He sat in the master chair and absent-mindedly flicked away the ash.

"The Commissioner phoned me. I was with the Attorney. A bad business. How is young Greenaway?"

"A slight case of shock. Twenty-six looking at sudden death for the first time. Now at his home."

"The Blue Lady?"

"I'm not on that case, thank God."

"Hawker is."

"And three other superintendents," said Harry quickly.

"Um."

"Did you know Prettyman, sir?"

"He seldom consulted me professionally. I knew him slightly. Good conservative firm, three generations. Of course he had the Redapple estate."

"I'm not with you, sir."

15

"Oh," Sir Jabeez smote his bald pate. "I learned it as a student. Redapple was one of the classic purgers."

"Forger?"

"Victorian purgers. It was a national industry, the equivalent to a million-pound trade. All of them bound up. It was Redapple's Great Heart, Liver, Lung, Kydney, Bladder and General Irregularity Pill that made his money. He claimed to cure the lot. God knows what was in it. Somebody told me cantharides and soft soap. He retired in Victorian magnificence. Funny will, but the Prettyman of the time avoided Chancery, shrewd old devil, taking the bread from our mouths! Very wealthy estate, my own maternal grandfather, a Chancery judge, lived in Herne Hill—low now—but he had seven lavatories and one small bathroom. All the household—eight girls—perpetually purging, queues outside each door, even the servants eating pills by the handful. The age of the old queen was the age of purging."

"Would he make enemies?"

"I don't boast about it," said Sir Jabeez soberly, "but I do not suppose any man has appeared in more cases of violence than I, and I have learned a man can have unsuspected enemies, but an elderly solicitor seems improbable! He had a nice cellar and liked Mozart. On visiting terms with the county."

"All right, sir, I'd better get along."

"I'll stay, I'll stay. All the lights on I see," Sir Jabeez's green eyes flickered. "Always danger of fire—all our archives here. And the way the cost of services rises! I'll be here tomorrow at nine."

Harry closed the door as Honeybody loomed close.

"Worm-eaten lot around here. You ought to see the wife and her aunties. Coo. He's got his hell on earth."

"Got your bearings?"

"I got indoctrinated, as they say, in the old pea-soupers. You could get a girl in the family way and she wouldn't know 'oo it was. I'll be your guide, sir."

"Across the court, one-o-two." He felt Honeybody take his arm.

One-o-two possessed a shining brass plate with two names, topped by that of Sir Henry Clayblown. The Chief Inspector's finger stabbed the bell.

"We're seeing Mr. Greasing of à Becket and Laud, publishers."

The Sergeant, who seldom read anything but his Sunday
papers, grunted.

The door opened and a tidy young man appeared. It was as
different as chalk from cheese from the chambers they had left.
Red carpet glowed on the threshold: he could imagine the fine
old port and a bit of Stilton.

"I am Sir Henry's clerk, sir."

"I am an inspector of police. I want to see Mr. Greasing
rather urgently."

The young man's face did not stir. It might have been an
hourly occurrence. "This way, sir."

The small anteroom was elegant, with large chairs on
wheels. Honeybody sat heavily and only by using his boots as
brakes avoided crashing into a sideboard. He got up carefully
and scratched his left buttock, a sure sign of discomfort.

"Leave these fancy chairs alone. The Super got jammed in
one, took two men to get him out," advised Harry.

A tall man who exuded charm from his thin, ascetic face
bustled in. He was beautifully but casually dressed. The place
was air-conditioned, the atmosphere pleasantly warm and
faintly redolent of leather.

"I'm Henry Clayblown. My clerk says you want to see Mr.
Greasing."

"If it's convenient, Sir Henry. I'm Inspector James and this
is Sergeant Honeybody."

"Glad to meet you. As it happens Mr. Greasing is just about
through, so come in."

Sir Henry's room was large and almost inordinately comfortable. Apart from the rows of books on the walls, the only
concession to business was a small table drawn up in front of
the two glowing logs in the grate which reinforced the central
heating. Sir Henry sat down on an upright chair at one side of
it.

"Please draw up chairs," his white hand waved towards the
collection of small comfortable-looking armchairs. The Inspector and Honeybody pulled two nearer the fire.

"Mr. Greasing, this is Inspector James and Sergeant Honeybody."

17

Greasing clumsily hefted his bulk from a large club chair. The Inspector remembered he had several publishing companies, all named after former archbishops, the principle being that the public vaguely remembered the names in a respectable connotation.

"A leak, I suppose. No good asking who!" The publisher had a querulous voice. "But here it is." He held up an ancient-looking book. Gold lettering so faded it was nearly brown proclaimed, *Three Great Whores in Babylon*.

"Ah, a religious book," said Honeybody, his huge thighs spread towards the fire.

"Are you insane?" There was coldness in Greasing's voice.

"I 'collect them tellin' us about Babylon in Sunday school, and my mum used to sing something. Let's see," the Sergeant's singing voice was frankly beery, " 'ow many miles to . . .'"

Mr. Greasing fairly shouted. "This is the most shocking book the eighteenth century produced."

"Please qualify that." Sir Henry's actor's voice somehow floated above the publisher's.

"Allegedly written by a byblow of the Earl of Sandwich— although some people say the father was Charles James Fox— it takes the lid off the teeming stews of that period."

"Very fond of a good stew myself."

As Greasing boggled, momentarily speechless, Harry thought he had never been able to decide how many of Honeybody's gaffes were planned.

The publisher turned his face firmly towards the Inspector. "You have heard of Professor Crutching and Dr. Donald Cry?"

"After my time, I'm afraid."

"You may take my word they are top of the tree. They state no one can hope to understand the eighteenth century without reading this book."

"That was, as it happens, my period," said Harry. "I would have thought that the fact that London was as whorey then as now was not particularly relevant."

"That a jury can decide. I had seven eminent academics, four famous lady authors and two rural deans offering to testify after just a few hours' telephoning. You cannot, sir, in your Victorian backwater take away from the British public the key to understanding. At least à Becket and Laud will defy you, yes, defy."

"I'm not on smut," said Harry.

"What!"

"I think we should listen a bit, Mr. Greasing," said Sir Henry quietly.

"A solicitor named Prettyman was knifed over at number sixty-three, that's the third house to the left as you enter the west gate."

"Prettyman, Kentish man?"

"I understand so, Sir Henry."

"Good God! Old Prettyman!" said Sir Henry.

"You knew him?"

"Briefed me once on a defended divorce case. It wasn't his line of country, but, well, he liked the gentry and the husband was titled and of an old family."

"What's this got to do with me?" Greasing's eyes flinched away.

"You arrived here at what time?"

"Four," said Greasing sullenly.

"When you passed that house did you see a man?"

The publisher's eyes roved about. "Should I answer that, Sir Henry?"

"You need not, but an innocent man has a duty to help the police."

"There was a shape in the doorway. I was keeping fairly close to the building line because of the fog. I think it was a man. That's all I can say. Was it a Blue Lady killing?"

Harry shrugged.

"Why can't you get her?" whined Greasing.

Again the Inspector shrugged.

"The depravity of this age. Too much welfare, too many idle hands."

The Inspector remembered that Greasing had shares in a magazine and frequently wrote with leering relish articles on the decadence of England, which was obscurely linked with the nameless vices of the later Roman emperors.

"I won't trouble you further, sir."

"But what about protection? I have to get home."

"Now," said Sir Henry, "I and my clerk will take you to

the tube and you live practically outside the Hampstead exit."

"But maniacs have the strength of ten," muttered Greasing.

"I think the analogy is wrong somehow," said Harry, "but anyway one cannot do more than one's muscular development allows. Some drugs and some manias release inhibitions, but three men should be a match for a stout lady, Russian discus throwers perhaps excepted."

Sir Henry laughed. "I should add that the Blue Lady has never been known to kill two persons in one night. Doubtless her shop steward forbids it."

"She could change her mind." Greasing sat down heavily.

"What you want, my dear fellow, is a drop of my special old Glenlivet. I'll open one of my last two dozen bottles; twenty dozen originally, a gift from a financier I defended. Can I tempt you two?"

"We must be off, Sir Henry."

Honeybody sighed audibly.

"To a long night's work, doubtless. I'm pleased to have met you." Sir Henry's shrewd blue eyes raked the Sergeant. "Dorset man?"

"The dad was, sir," Honeybody looked pleased.

"Some of it rubbed off. I come from there. Good night to you both. Tom will let you out."

They crept along in the darkness, the Sergeant's flashlight rebounding from the fog.

"Fine gentleman, Sir Henry," said Honeybody.

"He gets his living out of it. Round the profession he is known as the head waiter and that isn't entirely due to his habit of delaying until the opposition gives up."

"Ar," said Honeybody, thoughtfully. "That Greasing and his Babylon. Could he be the Blue Lady?"

There was a theory—the Blue Lady had produced various opposing camps—that 'she' was in fact a man.

"We'll check, but I remember reading in my paper the morning after the third murder that he had spent the night in the chair at the annual meeting of the Total Sexual Freedom Society. There was a row about flagellating minors in public which went on to midnight. The murder took place around ten."

At least these days you saved a bit of time! Harry often

wondered how his Victorian predecessors sweated their long reports out in longhand. Those tens of thousands of words re Jack the Ripper! At least the Blue Lady was taped! He used the telephone in the police car to dictate his report on to a recorder at Central Records. So slowly did one have to drive that he had finished it before they had covered half a mile. Thence it would be played to the semi-permanent committee 'managing' the Blue Lady case and finally twenty copies would be struck off on an electric typewriter. The tape itself would be filed. Finally he called the Kent County Police.

He turned to Honeybody. "See that Greenaway's clothes have gone to Forensic, Serg. If they have not phone me at four twelve, but if everything's okay knock-off. Seven ack emma tomorrow if you can manage."

"Night, sir," Honeybody lumbered off. The Inspector thought that if he knew Honeybody his departure would be to the nearest pub. The Sergeant never missed an occasion which could alibi him with his dour Scots wife.

In room four twelve the fluorescent lighting seemed abnormally bright after the fog. At the head of the heavy table presided Superintendent Hawker. Winter was usually Hawker's best time of the year; he thrived on frost and fog, declining as the warmer weather descended at last. Now he looked dyspeptic.

Harry glanced around. Richman, newly promoted Superintendent, and classically handsome, sat at Hawker's left. In addition there were two inspectors, one a recent promotion, two sergeants and a plain-clothes constable.

"Sit down, Mr., er, James." When furious at the world old Hawker affected dubiety about the Inspector's name.

"Thank you, er, Superintendent," said Harry. You had to spit back at Hawker if you wanted to survive.

As it was, the Superintendent remained impassive. He practically never rose to the usual run of baits.

"We heard the tape, Mr. James. Is this the so-called Blue Lady?"

"I've been on these smashings at the docks, sir. All I know is what I read in the morning bulletin. Modus the same and the knife looked like the others."

"What steps are you taking?"

"Waiting on the lab. Tomorrow we'll sift through all the neighbours. Useless tonight with the fog. Besides nobody would be out because . . ." he shrugged.

"Yes," said Hawker. "Ten murders, a knife in the back. Plus one other in Liverpool and this one tonight. Imitative?"

"She, if it's a she, could have nipped up to Liverpool and nipped back. British Railways."

"In this fog," said Hawker, "British Railways retire to their teapots and the public can go and hang themselves in station buffets. But it doesn't fit the pattern. One a night, intervals from four days to one week."

The Superintendent lived and worked by patterns.

"You know," said Hawker, "the killer may have moved out because of lack of opportunity. The cinemas, the bowling alleys, the pub keepers, they are all howling because the custom has dropped. You can pass by streets that are dead. All indoors, frightened to answer the bell."

"Could be imitative!" said Harry.

It was proper that the press should report things, but if somebody was strangled with an old bicycle tyre there was the possibility, that the news aroused another potentially demented brain to do likewise; on a lesser scale if a gang of young men, intent only on a little brawling outside dance halls, wore magenta leotards and the fact was reported, in four weeks' time every young teenager was buying them and the middle-aged manufacturers of leotards looked forward to early retirement in Mallorca, whilst bemoaning the folly of youth.

"The kill was neat, according to your two quacks. The previous have been haphazard, two through the lung; they died in hospital. One was conscious but didn't know what or who hit him. He was walking along a road in Wembley worrying about his hollyhocks." Hawker looked older than ever.

"When I started I met a retired station sergeant. He'd served in the old Whitechapel Station when 'Yours truly, Jack' was about. His Superintendent arrested on suspicion about thirty innocent men, mostly street traders. Sheer desperation. If Jack had not committed suicide, as the departmental memo said, he could have carried on for years, or until somebody blundered on him while he was dismembering the corpse. Whitechapel, fog, gutter-warrens, bull's-eyes lanterns!"

Hawker coughed and continued: "To a point, the same here. You get a maniac in the dark winter, stabbing men at random in the back. How can you stop it?"

Hawker glared at Richman, who gave his Roman emperor look at the ceiling, and continued:

"We will not catch this mass murdering maniac who has already knifed at least ten, probably two up on the Ripper already, unless we fluke it. All I can do is what I have ordered. Spot checks. We cordon an area and sift everybody there. Needle in a haystack but a haystack is what we are in. My calculation is that he could go to thirty before somebody barged down an alley and said, 'I say, old man!' "

Hawker belched dismally. He was a noted statistician.

"The Ripper case is somewhat on all fours," said Richman puffing his pipe, "disguised handwriting in the letters, perhaps faked illiteracy, and some evidence of personal disguise."

"The law again," murmured the young deputy inspector.

There were some grins and Harry remembered the old legend that deadly Jack had been the son of a barrister, member of the Establishment, and that the result had been hushed up after the young man's suicide.

Richman ignored the interruption. "My team have been round every coat manufacturer in the country. Now there have been three people who saw the Blue Lady, five feet eight, bulky, blue coat, floppy blue hat and blue scarf. Always seen in the shadows. The best witness was Bronstein, forty years in the rag trade. He said five foot eight and forty-two bust." Richman waggled his hands, " 'Superintendent, it gets so that Bronstein sees a bust at a hundred yards and he says to himself the inches and I want you to realise it's professional and even the wife doesn't mind.' Good fellow! The other two, well, one had been in a pub for three hours, a soak from way back, and the other is a mousy little lady with a weak voice. I got the idea that the coat might be reversible; the usual idea of disguise, one moment you're blue, the next, for God's sake, brown. We put our resources into it. Two years ago a Bristol firm named Sottling and Nephew brought out a range with," Richman looked at his notes, "Royal-blue-coloured cloth and black-and-white rainproofed fabric on the inside, so you could reverse. Somebody got the bright idea that big women would go for it, so they put up fifty prototypes in forty plus bust measurements. The stores bought the small sizes, but these big affairs they shunned. There is a store in Brixton that started as The Big Lady and failed, but they changed the name to Fine Figure Store, all outsize, and are doing well. They took these outsize samples as a job lot and sold them over a period of four months. The point is that of the fifty only three were in the ultimate forty-two size. Now there are two ladies on coats. We got them hypnotised."

"Christ!" said Hawker, dropping his cigarette on to his blotter.

"Now just wait. One purchaser we identified easily, a cook in the local hash shop, eats her own wares. The two women readily signed waivers, and we had two doctors and a registered medical hypnotist."

"And not possible as witnesses *per se*," snarled little Mr. Middle, the Treasury junior, who was sulking in one corner of the room. "A jury and hypnotised witnesses!"

"I had the Commander's approval," said Richman smoothly and Harry saw Hawker's thin lips momentarily tighten, but then the old man said, easily, "Better an unwitness than no witnesses, Mr. Middle."

"Precisely," said Richman. "And I have no opinion about credence. Hypnotic recalls, according to the doctors, who quarrelled violently over detail, can be influenced by fantasy, suggestion, God knows what. But it came out that both recalled (a) somebody with dyed blonde hair and an Irish brogue who said she was going back to Dublin the next week, and (b) a hirsute—slight moustache—powerfully built woman in her forties who they did not like. She was 'dearing' them a little. Very powerful woman! They said, 'a lidie'. Close-cropped black hair, funny eyes. About five feet eight. They could not recall what was funny about them. However, during the second session, while they were still controlled by the hypnotist, we tried them on identikit. Here is the colour print."

He propped up a full plate photograph of a woman's face. Rather coarse black hair cut rather noticeably short and with a slight curl in it. The eyes appeared greenish with a slight, rather attractive, squint. The nose was straight and the jaw overly firm. The general impression, however, was of roundness and a very white, coarse matt skin. The trouble was, thought Harry, that there was a slight feeling of unreality, as if it had been thought up by an artist rather than carved out of flesh and blood.

"And here's the dyed blonde. She was a big woman, rather fat than powerful. 'Very busty and big-tailed' were the words used."

Under the very obviously dyed hair, the face was broad with lines of humour on it. The eyes were very blue and the mouth large and generous. One felt she had had a lot of food and drink in her time, and would be good fun.

"About forty-five, they thought," said Richman. "The other, they could not agree about. One said thirty-five, the other went as far as fifty."

"What are you doing with them? The press?" asked Hawker.

"I was going to ask your advice. It might deepen the panic."

"I think you are right. In fact any woman who looked like them would be lynched by the mob."

"I have circulated prints to every station in the British Isles, and Eire."

"That was a bright idea of yours," said Hawker, who never grudged praise to his equals, but withheld it from underlings or superiors. "Just a moment." He went and dropped the blinds. "It's impossible, but I always get the feeling that London fog can get through windows, like termites through a log."

When he came back Hawker remained standing, resting his weight upon his large mottled hands, with their long, spatulate fingers, palm downwards on the table. He grinned at Richman.

"I must say your technique is Porterman rather than you."

"I prefer the 'my dear Watson' gambit," said Richman amiably, "but mass murders require mass measures."

"At the moment," said Hawker, "Porterman is taking Liverpool apart. The police of four counties, by the Home Secretary's orders, are providing him with three hundred men on a three-shifts basis. At this moment you could steal the whole of Manchester without anybody noticing a thing wrong. If there is any suspicious character, with rolling eyeballs, and a knife or two in evidence, he will be taken. It's not knock at any door, but hammer at every door. So far he has nicked ten people on the wanted list, including a bod dating back to the train robbery who had got himself a job with British Railways. But you see, suppose the killer has a car. We have presumed he— or she—hadn't because the ten London killings were in the vicinity of a tube station. No identification, and as at least six were messy, the supposition is that the killer had some additional outer garment to hide blood splashes."

Richman started to speak, but Hawker waved him down. Nobody interrupted the old Superintendent unless he wanted to be.

"No, let me recap. Today is November twentieth. The first killing, a Mr. George Knapp, part proprietor of a hardware store, got it in Kennington Palace, near the Oval, when he was going home at eleven at night after spending the evening stock-taking. That was on the night of September eighth. Today we have either Mr. Prettyman, solicitor, in London, or an apparently equally harmless man named Shoulder, a lavatory attendant on shift work in Liverpool, who was due to unlock the convenience at seven a.m.

"Of course, a clever maniac could disguise herself. You note that *both* these mock-ups have short hair, one very short, the other shorter than seems to be the fashion. Once upon a time people who bought wigs were remembered by the wigmaker. Now, so my old housekeeper says, they're all at it wholesale. A wig, a dab of this and that round their chops, and Porterman doesn't know whether he's Arthur or Martha."

Hawker produced a white handerchief and blew vastly into it. A widower for many years his attitude to women was one of rather awed dislike.

"I once read a story that very much impressed me," said the youngest inspector and flinched as he caught Hawker's eyes over the expanse of handkerchief. Harry appreciated his dilemma, forced to continue, but with the risk of being turned into stone or a pillar of salt at any tick of the clock.

"I mean," the youngest inspector slightly stuttered, "there was this series of apparently maniacal crimes, but all staged because one, only one, benefited the killer. I mean ..."

"I know what Miss Christie meant," said Hawker. "She's responsible for every little tea-leaf wearing gloves these days. Until she told 'em they didn't *know* about crime detection. She should have been locked up years ago. I'd have *all* authors locked up, journalists too, except the critics." Momentarily Hawker brooded, his wattles flushed. The youngest inspector gave a little sigh, as if a thunderbolt had missed him.

"I know that the Home Secretary . . ." said Hawker and checked himself. "Now, young man, when you were at police college I think Superintendent Porterman was doing the homicide course, eh?"

The youngest inspector was rather red. "Yes, sir."

"And what was his first precept?" Hawker looked like an elderly jackal under the fluorescent lights.

"Who benefits, sir."

"Precisely." Hawker's voice rose two octaves. "And if you persist in thinking we do not obey our own rules you'll be the top-ranking officer inspecting ladies' lavatories in Hyde Park during political rallies. In each of these ten killings we have obeyed this rule. In only one case could any beneficiary have been involved in one of the other cases. There was one exception, in the Marylebone killing, who could have been in the vicinity of Paddington on the night of *that* job, but it was a question of 'ten pounds, my set of bowls and my hunter watch' in the will. And that was that."

"Sorry, sir," the youngest inspector was humble.

"No, no," in victory Hawker was magnanimous. "There has been no financial pattern. The victims were mostly lower middle class, the perennial victims in fact, apart from the first one and the seventh, a property developer who cut up for fourteen hundred thousand—I use cut up advisedly. They were relatively poor men. No pattern there."

"Women?" Harry dropped his penny.

"No," said Hawker, "nor could anybody have coveted somebody's ox. Toothcomb job. Now what we know are only a few things. One is that the victims were of relatively small stature, and of course all male. From five feet five to five feet nine. Of the recorded ten, the age group is between twenty-five and sixty-two. That may be significant. On the other hand, if we predicate that the killer is short he is also muscular, because the examiners have said that on at least four occasions the knife was driven in with tremendous force even allowing

27

for the sharp point." He opened a folder. "They measured Prettyman at five feet seven."

"Now, what I am doing concretely is to set in motion a series of spot checks. The killings have occurred between five p.m. and, possibly, seven-thirty a.m. We are going to use squads of two hundred and fifty men on foot, two cars and a public address system. We'll search a thousand people at a time and anybody with anything more than a penknife will be taken to an interrogation centre."

"Christ," said Richman. "Civil rights, conscientious objections, you crazy?"

Hawker smirked. There was a slight edge between the old man and the spruce, fortyish Richman.

"I was summoned to the Home Office, not to the incumbent but to the man who runs it. You saw yesterday's election result, the opposition candidate, if not in a canter by a long neck."

"It always was pretty marginal."

"The back-room boys said that the public were venting their spleen on the Government."

"Pish," said Richman, "and they in Scotland!"

"The streets of Edinburgh are deserted at nights," said Hawker grimly, "apart from people in groups. Nobody strays out of the lamp-light. But as for reaction, we called in the advertising boys. If we present it properly, it will become a kind of national crusade. 'We need the Churchillian touch,' a little man in what appeared to be a suit made of red satin told me," said Hawker distastefully, "but they'll do the job so people *want* to be searched. It will be a something or other symbol, so this loathsome little man said. There's not enough policewomen and matrons to go round, so we are tapping the hospitals. We start tomorrow night. The press and T.V. are most co-operative, of course."

"But won't a lot of people refuse to be searched?" rashly asked the youngest inspector and flinched at Hawker's sneer.

"You take a thousand people, dear boy, who have been wheedled and hypnotised into thinking that it is a patriotic duty to be searched and you proclaim yourself odd man out. You get a smack over the chops, and the beauty of it is that *we* don't do it but your patriotic civilian friends."

"You won't catch the killer," Richman tapped the dottle out

of his pipe, "and you'll stir up a blazing row in the Commons."

"I *know* I won't catch him, but I want to scare him or her so he does not operate. As far as the House is concerned the Big Feller has his majority and any man stepping out of turn better reconcile himself to trying as candidate for Stonehenge. He said, 'The Blue Lady must be stopped period'. Otherwise he'd call down his Yorkshire Moors same as Franco." As usual yellow teeth were displayed as Hawker laughed at his own pun and as abruptly became serious. "I saw the medical committee under Sir Bradbury, who as you know specialises on head injuries and general daftness. They say that, man or woman, the killer is suffering from a rapidly progressive degeneration which within four months must lead to total disintegration of the whatsits, higher faculties I think they meant. Then 'it' may suicide, openly attack somebody, remove its clothes and proclaim itself Queen of the May, but in any case the secret will be out."

Richman made a slight bow. "Ingenious, but we have to trust Sir Bradbury's word for it."

"Nobody's met more loonies than Sir Bradbury," declared Hawker, "they say he even gibbers to himself when he thinks he's alone. But, now, wait one minute." Hawker walked to a grey iron cabinet, unlocked it and produced a flat case, for all the world like paterfamilias preparing to carve.

Ten knives lay upon the green baize lining of the case, their blades stained with the distinctive brown of blood and rust. They were neatly labelled.

"The first four are of French origin," the old Superintendent said, pointing. "A bright lad spotted the shape—there was no mark of origin. Sûreté told us that they are part of a line manufactured for the largest French chain stores—you know, twice as big as us on kitchen utensils and canned food, but only a third on cleaning materials." Hawker leered at Richman who frankly winced. The old gentleman was in one of his trying moods, thought Harry, dismally, which meant he was worried.

"I got on to Customs," said Hawker, "hoping somebody's phenomenal memory might just click, but, alas, the British bring back, *bring back*, Scotch whisky, English cigarettes, and French culinary apparatus. I remember when it was almost solely dirty books and postcards. Times change and whirl an old fellow like me about like a top. It's the journalists who are responsible, with their travel articles.

"The other seven knives are our own superior domestic product. But none of them are stainless. Your skilled cook will not work with stainless steel, or at least not the good ones, and a knife is dispensable once it won't take an edge. They are small carving knife or restaurant kitchen drop-outs, except one small mass production general purpose knife. They all have blades between five and five-and-a-half inches long, mostly second-hand, the kind of thing you get in a mixed tray in a street market, and have been given a needle point with some kind of sharpening machine.

"I'm getting old, of course, but yesterday it occurred to me to ask Paris if they had had any murders with such knives. Last March they had a stabbing in Marseilles, into the back in an alley. I asked for a depth report—it had been written off as one of those dock brawl things. The victim was a Russian, a young deck officer on the *Frederick Engels*, changed in transit from Vladivostok from *Nkrumah*, as it happened. The Soviet authorities, after the initial coyness, were forthcoming. The boy—he was twenty—had the desire to read Charles Dickens in the original, to see what England was really like. He was quite good at English, but he had the habit of wandering up to people and asking if they knew the language to get practice. The ship's political officer had his eye on him, but, according to the French, admitted that he was just an uncomplicated youth who wanted to read the Odhams edition of the immortal Charles in the original. He had spent three hours trying to understand a couple from Newcastle who were waiting on a ship to London. They had some incomprehensible conversation and six beers and a bowl of bouillabaisse each. The sailor started back for his ship around eleven and somebody knifed him."

"Are you saying this was part and parcel?" Richman's voice was cool.

"A lead," Hawker sounded very tired. "A possibility. The knife was identical with the four French ones. The French police are reopening it. Now I've got to go and monitor the first T.V. release."

"Not appearing yourself? I would have thought it would have been right up your alley!"

In a way, thought Harry, Richman was right. There was a streak of flamboyance in the old man's nature, a fondness for production numbers.

".Take a good look at my face," said Hawker simply.

"Well. . . ." Richman hesitated.

"I selected a young constable. He looks rather like a god and hasn't got a thought in his head, but the words will be written up and he can read them. I told him that if he fluffs he'll be directing traffic the day before he retires. They will have all the T.V. detectives on the programme, 'mass identification' as the loathsome little man said."

"Commercial as well?" Mr. Middle, the Treasury junior, sounded horrified. "Surely not commercial?"

"Well," said Hawker, "that was difficult, but they rang the Big Feller, who quoted John Maynard Keynes to the effect that mass prostitution was automatically commercial. It fair upset the bearded man from the Third Programme—he wanted to argue—but it's the first time all branches of T.V. are co-operating, plus the press and the radio, even the pirates."

Mr. Middle, whose sense of humour was entirely professional, moved his dentures uneasily.

"I suppose you've thought of the probable action for molestation, wrongful arrest, interfering with lawful activities and perhaps battery?"

Mr. Middle, thought Harry sourly, never advised going into court unless there was a full confession and three independent witnesses. Even then he hummed and hawed like a man in anguish.

"I reached Sir Jabeez after chasing him round Whitehall. He thinks we are right, but if necessary an enabling act would be rushed through or an Order in Council."

Mr. Middle pursed his lips; it was well known that he considered old Sir Jabeez too dashing by half.

The intercom rang. "There's a long report from Kent police oozing over the teletype," grunted Hawker. "Nothing you can do here."

Thus ungraciously dismissed, Harry exchanged nods and

31

went to his own room to wait until the stack of pasted tape was brought to him by a messenger.

Windlesham Parva was a rustic village off the main road eight miles from Windlesham, a town of fourteen thousand people, much noted for its fake stockbroker's Georgian houses erected forty-five years ago and now very fashionable after their period of eclipse. It was a wealthy area—'stinks of money' said the writer. Charles Haversham Prettyman had been born at Windlesham Parva, the son of the third Prettyman to be a partner in Prettyman, Benjamin, Trotter and Cope, but, in practice, since 1885 it had been Prettyman senior alone and on his death his son Charles.

It had always been a good practice with an immense reputation for shrewdness. People often preferred to journey to Windlesham Parva to consult Mr. Prettyman than to go to Windlesham or Dover. Prettyman senior had eschewed civil courts or assizes, but his son was a force to be reckoned with at the county court. Occasionally Charles would act in divorce. But in the main the money came in from three sources.

One, the estate of the late Sir Ebenezer Ethelred, which the firm managed. Lady Ethelred was aged and rather spread the story that the family dated to Ethelred the Unready and people went along because she was kind, if eccentric. In reality the late Sir Ebenezer had been a jerry builder in Tooting whom Lloyd George had baronetised for war services. In fact, the teletype had clicked, Sir Ebenezer had bought up a rundown knitting mill at Bradford and manufactured an astounding number of green balaclava helmets and cholera belts for sale to the War Office, which reputedly still possessed warehouses filled with them, the British Government having unsuccessfully offered them to Stalin in the spring of 1944 as part compensation for the lack of a second front.

The second, the Benting Estate. Most of the present generation of Bentings, a very old and inbred family, were in private lunatic asylums and Mr. Prettyman had accounted to the Commissioners in Lunacy.

The third, the Redapple Estate, one of the largest private estates in the country, representing a trust first made in 1858. Charles was the third Prettyman of his line to be trustee, the others being Lord Redapple and the Manager of a Windlesham bank. Prettyman did all the very profitable work. The report said: "Something strange about the trust. The present and first Lord Redapple is reputed to be trying to break it. He received a barony in 1945. Said to have been a very brainy member of the economic warfare ministry.

"Charles Prettyman was married in 1922 to an orphan, Mary, who died in 1942. No issue. Charles has no living relative. Office staff consist of a managing clerk, Peter Winding, sixty, a younger man of twenty-four and a typist.

"I questioned Winding who was very shocked. He had been with the firm forty years. He said Prettyman had no enemies—optimist eh? Prettyman lived in a charming two-hundred-year-old house with an acre of garden, housekeeper and gardener-cum-chauffeur. Winding estimated that the estate would cut up around a hundred and fifty thousand, all to charity except generous bequests to employees. The housekeeper gets five thousand, and Winding admitted that he would fall in for his bungalow, which Prettyman owned, the old man's car and five thousand. More than enough temptation, but the young man and the typist say he was in his room all afternoon. The housekeeper has no alibi. Blue maybe? Signed Sergeant Biddling."

Harry remembered the sergeant, a young fellow with a passion for knowledge and an encyclopaedic memory.

He looked at the clock; getting on for eleven. There was a knock on the door and Honeybody entered.

"You look redder in the face than I remember," said Harry.

"It's the cold, sir!"

"I see it flies straight to the nose."

"Yes, sir. Any calls for me, sir?"

Dodo Honeybody, the Sergeant's helpmeet, was on the formidable side, and Honeybody, after a couple of hours in a pub, got unpleasant premonitions that she might have phoned and been told that he had gone home.

"Your wife has not called, neither has your daughter." Mrs. Honeybody occasionally resorted to subterfuge.

Honeybody wheezed gustily in relief. "The time flew, sir. I met an old friend, a bloke I nicked in 1940 for relieving himself in Piccadilly. He pleaded the blackout, but the magistrate wasn't having any. We talked of the old days. Ar, I remember one night . . . what are you doing?" The Inspector's hand had reached towards the telephone.

"I'm going to phone Dodo. You need collecting!"

"Sir, sir, sir, I'll be concise, sir. I saw the lab boys"—the medical alcohol again, thought Harry—"and they report that the first stage showed no trace of blood on Greenaway's clothing. They run three stages but if the first is negative it's odds to onions that that will be the result. And here," Honeybody looked down, "is his briefcase and wallet, all itemised. You note that all there was in his briefcase was a box of ten cigars. It had his name on the box; one of the chichi jobs, your own humidor at the dealers."

"You get into a habit of carrying these things, feel a sense of sudden shock when you find there is nothing in your right hand," mused the Inspector. "I looked into one of mine the other day. Change from a quid note, bus tickets and a quarter of Stilton I'd bought for Elizabeth three months previously. That's why I looked in it."

"Ar," Honeybody had the tendency to sway on his chair, but the Inspector, aware of the Seageant's powers of recuperation, was not alarmed.

"And the wallet, a notebook, with names typed inside, headed London addresses, and containing two hundred names. At seven ack emma we set you off with a squad to establish relationship."

"Cor," said Honeybody, "mostly lawyers but some of the upper crust. Old Baroness Grinling for one. You remember we had a complaint about all her cats and she bashed the constable with a disused parrot cage?"

"You'll have to take it personally and spend a preliminary hour admiring them. And remember she *is* Grace and Favour."

"I'd rather face Dodo," muttered the Sergeant.

There were three pound notes and a book of sterling area travellers' cheques, originally for two hundred but reduced to one twenty-five. A deck-chair ticket issued by Margate Corporation and a receipt for nine pounds five from Mrs. Hentrotts Hotel for the previous night.

"Mrs. Hentrotts Hotel. In God's name what?"

"A prudent old gent, knew the weather, I'd say. My old

34

dad'd look at the sky and say, 'Fog tomorrow', and always right. So he came up the day before."

"But what is Hentrotts?"

"I went there once when I was at Bow Street—it's in that area. Four big gloomy Victorian houses knocked together, ugly as hell." Harry recognised the loquacious stage.

"Get to the point!"

"Sir, sir, sir, let me tell it my own way."

The Inspector resigned himself.

"There was a pugilist, sir, called Game Chicken. His real name was Hen Trott and he could lick twice his weight of wildcats. When he retired he bought one of the houses and opened a kind of private club where the gents could spar and have a sup of brandy and a cold collation. Get it? 'Hen Trott's.' When he died the widow just called it Mrs. Hen Trotts Hotel; by that time letting rooms was the profitable side. She enlarged it. Sometime in the last century it changed into the London snug of wealthy old professional men from the country and the old aristocracy. Very few women there, just comfortable old fellows who're in the money. Best plain food in the country, best wine cellar and although it's central heated—and you ought to see the carpets—you can have your private fire lit any hour of the day or night. And expensive! I saw one old geezer paying the bill and nearly collapsed. Phew! Was old Prettyman warm?"

"Warm enough!"

"Ar," said Honeybody.

"Who owns it now?"

"Well, there were a pair of Hentrotts when I was there."

The Inspector sighed. He felt a longing for a quart of beer, the central heating of his flat and slippers, but he said: "I'd better go out there. I'll tell you what, I'll drop you off afterwards. You know them."

Honeybody brightened, "Er, d'you think you could have a word with my Dodo, sir? Working my head off, like."

Harry dialled. Over the years the raw-boned Dodo had become, if not a friend, at least an accomplice to the legend of Honeybody.

"I suppose he's sober, Mr. J.?" she said.

"My dear Mrs. H.!"

35

"But just tell him if he comes home with his breath stinking he gets no supper."

Harry hung up and looked at the Sergeant. "Necessary, chlorophyll."

"Ah," Honeybody tapped his hip pocket. "I'll wait until we've done Mrs. Hentrotts. Last time she was free with the drink. Very nice. They have a notice in the bar. Let's see: 'One of the last outposts of civilisation'. 'Course if they heard about it the Gumment'll put it down."

"Get your coat. Refrigerating outside. And get a car."

One thing, thought Harry, the 'Acting Chief' appellation meant you ordered, not asked, about cars.

Mrs. Hentrott's hotel, dimly visible through fog—which had slightly eased—and darkness and the street lighting which had a curiously pallid quality, possessed all the repulsiveness which Harry remembered attaching to the boarding houses he had stayed in as a student. Inside—through a plain glass swing door with '37' on it in gilt—one went fetlock-deep into carpet. There was a slight smell of rosewater and a small table with a discreet man seated at it, staring into vacancy. He rose, with a smile which managed to compound caution, affability and respect, the latter quality fading slightly as Honeybody's boots squeaked above the deadening medium of the carpet.

"Police," said Harry, his voice becoming hushed.

"Quite so, sir," said the man, as though confirming a surgical diagnosis, "and we should see the missus."

Behind the desk was a door that was scarcely visible in wallpaper that simulated a rose garden. It swung open at a touch.

"The police, ma'am," said the receptionist. "Please enter, gennelmen."

"Mrs. Hentrott," said Honeybody, professionally effusive, "we met in 1954. Name of Honeybody."

"Half a bottle of Hennessy!" said the large woman behind the desk.

"I well remember the hospitality, ma'am, and those crisp little pancakes, blindis they were."

"Ah, well," she was a comfortable woman, "live and let live. Hentrott's in Germany, tasting the wine."

"This is my boss. Acting Chief Inspector James."

The Inspector's hand was enveloped in a warm palm.

"Pray seat yourselves. Inspector. No, Sergeant," Harry had seated himself on a delicate brocaded chair. "No, Sergeant, that one over there. I keep it for the fatties, like old Lord Priddlesham, who tips it at twenty-two stone." Honeybody dragged over what looked to be a gutted commode. "Now let's be comfy." She pressed a bell and a small maid appeared. "The number two for three persons," Mrs. Hentrott said. She winked at Harry. "The number one has special black caviar, but the two has smoked Spanish swordfish and New Zealand toheroa patties. I keep the one for Dukes and senior members of the peerage. I suppose spirits, Mr. Honeybody?"

"A drop of Scotch would go nice, ma'am," said Honeybody.

"But for you, Inspector, my husband sent back a case of a Spätlese, six years old, light on the tongue as Epsom salts, just the thing with a bit of smoked fish. I usually have a bite at this hour."

"In your hands," said Harry, as the maid returned with a tray. Mrs. Hentrott repaired to a large refrigerator.

The wine was excellent, although the Inspector found the hors d'oeuvres on the rich side. Mrs. Hentrott watched him keenly.

"A nice bit of Cheddar and a plain biscuit, dear," she said and went again to the refrigerator.

They munched in silence. Finally Mrs. Hentrott pushed her plate away. "Frankly, we get the coroner's officer, Constable Bunce, here three or four times a year when the old parties have their final attacks, but police, if you know what I mean ... not often here."

"Mr. Prettyman got a knife in his back."

"Good God, old Prettyman." Mrs. Hentrott's broad country face went white. "My ma-in-law knew him first. I don't usually, sir, but there's an old brandy in the cupboard. I'll take a drop."

"Ar," said Honeybody, swiftly draining his whisky.

Mrs. Hentrott summoned the maid and ordered coffee.

"Was he . . .?"

"I said he had a knife in the back."

There were small beads of sweat on the landlady's face. "The Blue Lady, dear?"

Harry shrugged.

"Oh, dear. You know we've been down twenty per cent on last year. They're not risking it."

"Most everything's off," said Harry, "pubs, bowling alleys, the lot. And housebreaking. People stay at home listening for a suspicious noise and the Burglars' and Pilferers' Union has sent a deputation to the Trade Union Congress."

Mrs. Hentrott gave her rich laugh, but sobered abruptly.

"Mr. Prettyman was such a regular, little old fellow. He would never allow himself to be pushed or hurried. In a joking way he would say his old grandad died at eighty-three because he kept rushing about Kent in a pony and trap so that he wore out quick. He did not eat greatly, but what he took was the best. I'm famous for my chops and a sauce that's in the family, and he invariably had two of an evening. You see, Inspector, he always came up the day before. Like a lot of the old gents he didn't like the morning rush, but a train after a nice lunch and a bag of work in a first compartment and nice and fresh next morning."

"Didn't he have a lot of friends in London?"

"Oh, he knew all the big Kentish families. But he was independent and used to say the best way to lose a friend was to lend or borrow money or be a guest too often. All the old gents feel that way, I've noticed."

"How was he yesterday?"

"I did not see him personally, dear. I'm like the conductor of an orchestra. Those phones"—she indicated a large intercom box—"go all day. I run it, but my orchestra plays it. I don't think much can be done tonight. Higling, who always valeted him, lives in Twickenham and the waiter . . . just a minute." She talked into the intercom. "I thought so," she told Harry, "Ginn is checking the cutlery."

"Sorry, not quite with you."

"Ever since I took over, we have numbered tables and the same numbers on the cutlery and tableware. That way I *know* exactly where I stand. He'll be in. Oh, I should have told you he's in charge of the dining-room."

But for his professional impassivity Ginn would probably have been a very knowing-looking gnome, thought Harry. There was a tiny hint of a sardonic personality. For his size and spareness Ginn had a very deep voice. He absorbed Harry and Honeybody without appearing to look at them.

"All correct, madam. One bread-and-butter plate broken. The kitchen boy set a cauldron on it."

"That boy!" Mrs. Hentrott's face was hard and businesslike as she made an annotation. "He did the same to a sauce boat three weeks ago. Should cook give him his cards?"

Ginn wagged his head. "He's a willing lad and does the hard work without complaint. Cook thinks she can make something of him."

"Keep your eye on him. However willing, a smasher is something I won't stand in my kitchen. Have a cigarette." She pushed forward a box, and for a moment Ginn looked faintly startled. He lit up and stood there in his shirtsleeves, puffing away. Harry had never overcome a youthful awe of head waiters and it was strange to see the demigod, so to speak, undressed.

"Mr. Prettyman has been found stabbed. These gentlemen are detectives."

"My God! Not . . ." Ginn's eyes slewed to Harry.

"We don't know."

"I suppose you want to know what mood he was in last night?" shrewdly asked Ginn.

Harry nodded.

Ginn stared at the glowing end of his cigarette. "It feels as though I'd known him since I started here in '37. Courtesy itself. Some of the gents are a bit testy, you might say, but Mr. Prettyman always thanked and never complained. But last night he was out of sorts. Almost invariably he'd join one or two of the other gents, but though there were a number in the room he knew, he just said, 'Get me a small table on my own, Ginn'. He had the mulligatawny, a piece of turbot, charcoal-grilled chops and peas, and the orange soufflé. Small portions, he couldn't stand large portions. Said they took his appetite away. But, an unusual thing, he drank a full bottle of wine— a nice Moselle. It was his habit to take a half-bottle and perhaps not finish all of it." Ginn half chuckled. "Many a glass I've had on Mr. Prettyman, back in the kitchen. Well, he drank the last of the wine, initialled the bill I took to him, and went over to the lift. I presumed he'd gone to his room."

"He had ordered a fire," said Mrs. Hentrott. "He disliked central heat, so we turned it off for him."

"Did he go out?"

She shrugged, flicked a switch on the intercom and spoke briefly. "My clerk says not."

"He could be mistaken, I suppose," said the Inspector.

"No," Mrs. Hentrott shook her head, "this is almost a club with rather old members, a lot of them at the possible keeling-over stage. So my desk men watch them. If old Lord X doesn't come back we worry and maybe instigate a 'discreet enquiry', although, dear, what some of those old boys do get up to . . ." she gave her rich chuckle, "but not here, of course. All right, Ginn, you can go."

"If you don't mind, ma'am," said Ginn, "I'll stay the night. We're a third empty. I'd like to phone the wife."

"Nervous?" asked Harry.

"A nervous man doesn't get to be a head waiter," said Ginn, coolly enough, "but it's the silence and the fog and the feel of the paving stones and the thought that the effing old bitch, pardon me, ma'am, might be standing round the corner in her blue hat."

"That's all right. See the housekeeper."

"Thank you, ma'am. Good night, sirs."

"They're all rattled," said Mrs. Hentrott as the door closed, "like a lot of old women, but it's natural. Between you and me, I wangled it so that my old man had to go to Europe."

"Tell me," said Harry, "were there any—I know I sound melodramatic but we encounter the strangest situations—any sinister strangers, so to speak, in the hotel?"

She smiled. "I don't take people without introduction off the street and it's 'sorry we're full', unless you mention a name. Last night there was only one 'new boy', an elderly American who had been staying with a lord in Derbyshire who rang up to book him in. I took the call personally."

"Could I take a look at Prettyman's room, just in a vain hope?"

"Oh, dear, General Stanhope's in there. I really do not encourage regulars, dear, because of the responsibility, but the General—he's ninety-three and led some famous charge in the last century—has got nobody. His own little suite is being redecorated so we moved him into 917 this morning. He goes to bed at seven, dear. Of course, we could go up...."

"I'll arrange for a man to take a look tomorrow. He'll phone you," said Harry quickly.

"Very well, but we clean the rooms thoroughly. If he had left anything it would have landed on my desk."

"He was wearing a grey pinstripe suit when he arrived?"

"No, a country-type blue check."

"What about his luggage?"

"Oh dear, I keep forgetting that everybody doesn't know us. If you want to, Inspector, you can keep a wardrobe here, for a small yearly sum. In the basement we have a kind of huge wardrobe, catering for two hundred odd gents. Just a minute," she produced a card index. "He keeps two suits, the grey pinstripe, and a blue double-breasted, plus a dinner suit. When I say two suits I mean that my index is not up to date. Now it is the blue check plus blue double-breasted. And there is a toilet case—I see he used an electric razor, most of 'em don't—six shirts, underwear, pyjamas, dressing-gown and slippers. We wash anything they leave and store it. If they notify us in advance, and you get the rushers-in, blast 'em, and the old steadies like Mr. Prettyman who sends a postcard five days before, we dry-clean, air, etcetera."

Harry noticed that Honeybody had slyly refilled his own glass.

"Perhaps the Sergeant could have a look."

She pressed a button and a weary-looking youth appeared.

"This is a police sergeant," snapped Mrs. Hentrott and the youth flinched.

"She were willin'," he whined, "and it wasn't on the premises."

"Wretched boy," intoned Mrs. Hentrott, "I do not wish to know your state of grace. Get the key and take the Sergeant to the wardrobe, station eleven."

Reluctantly, Honeybody put down his glass and assumed the classical police-versus-youth expression. "All right, my lad," he snarled and ushered the youth out of the door.

"A little drop more?" asked Mrs. Hentrott, already pouring.

"This must be a nice life," said Harry.

She shrugged her plump shoulders. "It's been the women,

dear, all through, ten generations. The men'd give you the shirt off their backs. But it's partly staff, dear. Without the West Indians we would have been out of business ten years ago. Still, there's the problems. The hall porter was a clergyman back in Jamaica. Of course, they won't have him here, although he keeps writing to the bishops. But the old gents will call him 'bearer' and he keeps threatening to quit. Frankly, if he did I'd go mad. I give him another ten bob a week and the bit about rendering to Caesar, but . . ." She shook her head.

Harry accepted another drink. There were compensations. "But a good business," he suggested.

She laughed. "All good businesses come to an end, dear. In five years they will tax us out, us and the public schools, not with a nationalising bang but with a weak tinkle on the cash register. Oh, we've had a good innings! My kids run motels in Australia—horrible places from all accounts—but times change. Hentrott and me will follow the sun."

Presently Honeybody appeared.

"He liked socks with crimson clocks, sir, and his undies, very sporting I may say." The Sergeant was swaying.

"And this wee book." Small and red-leather-covered it reposed on the Sergeant's vast palm.

The Inspector took it. He judged there were about fifty pages edged with gilt. On the cover was printed in green foil, 'Memoranda'. It was the sort of potty little book one was likely to get at Christmas. It was three-quarters filled with very small precise writing; dates and figures. "April 14th, 1860, Orion 4 p.m. £25" was the first entry. He flipped through the pages. The rest was simply dates and money, sums ranging from five pounds to thirty-seven pounds. The last entry, dated June sixth 1872, was for fifteen shillings.

"Some kind of abstract of outgoing payments," he grunted.

"Tell you what, Inspector, Mr. Prettyman was in here during Whit week. He had brought me a little present back from Portugal. He mentioned he was writing a little history about one of the estates he managed, the red something or t'other estate."

He slipped the little book in his pocket. "You've been a great help, ma'am. Get going, Sergeant!"

Outside the fog was clearing and he found he could see the fuzzy outlines of street lamps.

He told the driver, "Drop me first and then the Sergeant." Honeybody was already snoring gently.

The Inspector's wife was in a dressing-gown and to his annoyance the door opened only two inches at his push and then stopped.

"What the devil?"

"It's a chain. The nice boy from the store put it on for me. If you'd been the Blue Lady I'd have been able to get to the phone."

"Open the ruddy door and stop bawling nonsense," snapped the Inspector. It was the second year of marriage.

"You'll have to shut it first."

"Great God of battle," moaned Harry as he complied, "a man can't get into his own flat because a pack of old women...."

The door opened and his wife looked faintly amused and replaced the elaborate chain device as he took off his overcoat.

"I'm twenty-nine and not a pack, sir, just one woman who gets nervous at being alone. All the women in these flats have installed these chains. The boy was working all day."

"But, dear girl, only men are killed."

"She's crackers, isn't she?"

"Obviously."

"Then who can say what a maniac will do next?"

"Oh, well." He went into the kitchen.

"Thick kidney soup and an omelette. In bed," suggested Elizabeth.

"I think I don't need it. I had bits and pieces."

She sniffed as she kissed him. "Some of the bits were liquid, I see."

"In the hexecution of my dooty."

"Trouble is you always get the spiritous hexecutions."

He showered and went to bed. As was his habit he told Elizabeth of his day. He found it clarified his thoughts.

"Obviously that ghastly old publisher is the Blue Lady," she snorted. "Nutty as a fruitcake. Stews indeed!"

That was one he could cross off the list, thought Harry as he slipped off to sleep. Elizabeth's first impressions were inevitably ill-founded.

2

Honeybody did not deserve to look so well, thought the Inspector dyspeptically next morning as he found the Sergeant waiting for him at half past six in the largish room temporarily assigned to him, with the ritual six feet square of tatty looking Axminster which was a badge of rank. The large expanse of red skin was cleanly shaved—Honeybody used a cutthroat razor—whereas, Harry caressed his chin, his own neat electric never did a close job when he'd taken drink the night before.

"The Sergeant would cut his right hand off for you," Elizabeth had said over the coffee pot.

"I do not want his bloody great right hand," the Inspector had countered, coldly. "All I want him to do is to cease these constant manoeuvres to obtain free drink."

"Don't swear," she had said, at her primmest.

Honeybody was a great one to sense moods, and now he remained silent and demure, if six feet two and seventeen stone can be demure.

"All right," said Harry, with a briskness he did not feel. "I want statements from everybody in those buildings, exactly where they were from two o'clock to seven yesterday. You and four constables."

"I thought you would, sir," said Honeybody smugly, "so I nipped in at seven and got four, sir, and hid them in the library. Staff is that short, sir, you've no idea. I heard Mr. Richman asking for an extra constable and being knocked back."

"When are they off duty?"

"Eleven a.m., sir, but four hours should be plenty, what with me at hand." Honeybody assumed a look of insufferable virtue.

"I want where they were the afternoon of yesterday, and where at eleven p.m. on September eighth, when the first killing occurred at the Oval."

44

The double-checking made it pretty foolproof, but the cost in labour and feet was tremendous. The official chiropodist, an innocent-faced man, had succumbed to a nervous bout after a session on Hawker's big toe, the Superintendent having had to plod to Whitehall several times a day after many sedentary years. Plasters, sinister fluids in small bottles and steaming bowls of washing soda were a commonplace in the little offices of the staff.

His own left foot hurt as he got his car and waited for Honeybody, who presently loped along in front of the constables with his ineffable conspiratorial look.

The Inspector said he would take number sixty-three himself and entered as the bell of the tower clock struck nine-five. He went up the worn stairs and hesitated on the landing.

"Hallo, you're Watts and Willowing, I think."

"Acting Chief Inspector James!"

Harry looked at a tall young man, perhaps twenty-eight, with a mop of auburn hair and an open smile, made more attractive as it sat crookedly on a rather ugly face.

"Oh, and me thinking you were a solicitor from Worthing. Ten to one he won't come because of you-know-what. Sir Jabeez is in Whitehall, sir, Mr. Runting is finishing up in Carlisle—verdict this arvo—so it's Mr. Margits who's senior. All paper work this morning unless Watts and Willowing turn up for Mr. Hewson. This way, sir."

Margits was an elderly man whose moon face and great sloping shoulders—like a bison, thought the Inspector—conveyed a great feeling of solidity. You would not incline to doubt what he said. He spoke slowly in a mahogany voice polished with port wine.

"I understand, Inspector," he said after listening. "I finished before Judge Fennel at two-thirty, went home to Ealing by tube, and at four-thirty was eating crumpets and anchovy paste with my wife and my brother-in-law. He is in holy orders, in fact a bishop. And on the earlier date you mention I was at Bodmin Assizes, junior in the towpath murder case, if you recall it."

The Inspector did.

Mr. Hewson was younger and briskly thin, with a slight

45

nervous tic in his left cheek, but with a pair of eyes which seemed to hunt you like a stoat after a rabbit. His voice was buzz-saw.

"Yesterday, County Court until five and then went to his home with a solicitor, Mr. Pogling, of Bailey and Pogling. I was with him until twelve, waiting for the fog to lift. And on the evening of September eighth, just let me check"—he opened a desk diary—"I was at a lecture held by the Tropical Fish Society, I find them soothing. I got there at nine, and left around midnight after a drink in the Committee Room."

"Is Mr. Greenaway in?"

"He's devilling a county-court case for me. Nothing to it; two toilet bowls broken, but a matter of principle on both sides. We make our money from principles, Inspector." Hewson gave the thin smile that did not touch his eyes. "Greenaway is concentrating on repairing leases, so sometimes we put a little something in his way. When you are starting out you have to get noticed."

"When will he be back?"

"Say, three hours at most. He hoped he might get a couple of last-minute briefs when he got to court."

Harry thanked him. It was going to be one of those cases, he thought, everybody eating crumpets with old clergymen when it happened and a disapproving sniff from the staff commander when the whole mess went into the permanently pending file, where it remained for sixty years, by which time somebody, probably old Hawker, had calculated that murderers passed to what the staff commander, a great believer in divine retribution, referred to as 'the higher court'.

He found Hearman behind a small desk in the alcove, loudly sipping a cup of tea.

"Can't offer you one. Old Sir Jabeez allows one teabag per person per day and ten minutes of the gas ring. Horrible stuff, but it's cold as hell in this old place. The lady typist's away, so Sir J. collected back the three teabags remaining out of her weekly ration. Mean old bastard, but worth every penny in court." He grinned at Harry, who found himself grinning back. He thought that Hearman would probably be one of these men you could not help liking.

"Keeps you on a short rein, eh?"

46

Hearman shrugged. "On the whole I rather prefer working for a mean man; at least you know he'll keep going."

"A lot of business?"

"I've been here six years. Yes, the four old folk do well. Of course, Sir Jabeez means a lot, a doyen, etcetera. When he goes we'll lose a bit, and of course Runting's sixty-nine, so these chambers will fall apart. But by that time I'll be able to get a better job easy." He glanced at Harry shrewdly. "I'm not fool enough to think a good clerk is half the battle, as you hear the fellows boast in the 'Grapes', but he's twenty per cent of it."

"What's Greenaway like?"

"He's a gentleman, but of course this is a hard profession unless you're a genius like F. E. Smith, which he is not. Sir Henry over the road can destroy a witness in his first question. Greenaway always says, 'Do you mean to tell me that . . .' which antagonises everybody. But he works like a packhorse and never lets a client down. If it is a question of law for the judge to decide, he's as good as most of them. He's specialising in leases, although there are three senior men who get most of the work. When he's fifty-five he'll be earning more than you or me ever will, put it that way."

"I'd rather have my bit now."

"Me too."

"Now yesterday, you went off early?"

"This ruddy fog. It's like this, there's no overtime, so when it's slack I push off. The old folk were well and truly holed up, except Runting who is up north."

"You went home?"

"Sure, I live in one of these one room and find your own lavatory jobs in South Ken. I opened a tin of soup and cooked it in the cupboard they call a kitchenette and read until about ten."

"And on September the eighth at eleven p.m.?"

"Ah, that Oval business, the first of the murderings! Let's see." Hearman produced a small diary. He sighed and got out his pen and wrote on a scratchpad.

"From nine until two I was in this night club in Hampstead with five other people, whom I have listed. They are solid citizens. The fifth is married and counsel don't like their clerks

47

being co-re's; much too good for 'em! Can you keep her out, or at worst be so very discreet?"

"Sure," said Harry, "we mayhem blokes disdain adultery, discretion itself." He glanced at the list. "Isn't the second one ... ?"

"The actor? Yes. He was between shows and had landed his present part, so we had a little celebration."

"Four men and two women."

"The third male is doubtful," said Hearman, "nice but doubtful, like the Blue Lady. Ah, I'm sorry, forgot that name must be anathema."

"We don't get excommunicated easily," said the Inspector. He snapped his notebook shut, and paused as he heard the sound of creaking shoes.

Honeybody paused on the landing. "Nothing, so far, sir." He stood at attention. "But when I went back to the car to send the early report, Mr. Hawker came on the blower and asked you to ring him urgent."

"Would Sir Jabeez mind if I used your phone rather than going to the car?" asked the Inspector.

"Not if he doesn't know," said Hearman.

Hawker was at his gloomy worst. "You know a house called the 'Barbary Ram'?"

"Near the Bank?"

"I wish your other professional skills equalled your knowledge of licensed premises," grated the Superintendent. "A man named Spoon wants to see somebody there at ten-thirty opening time. I would send the village idiot, but he's out looking for the people who have escaped from gaol over the last year."

The Inspector suppressed his groan. One could not do anything with Hawker in such a mood.

"He hinted it was about the Blue Lady. And good luck to you!" The line went dead and Harry, in spite of the cold, wiped his brow.

"It's his feet playing up!" said Honeybody. "Lor, I had a governor once with bunions. You should have heard him!"

"Perhaps you'll carry on, Sergeant," said Harry tersely. "Get the reports in every half-hour. When the men knock off, if you haven't finished you'll have to process what's left yourself."

"It's not an easy job, sir, they flit about so much. Court, etcetera. There's a Master in Chancery that is practically never in his chambers."

"Over to you," leered Harry. "Thanks, Mr. Hearman. Tell Greenaway I'll try to see him today."

He took his time and had coffee and a bacon sandwich en route. He recognised it as a bad sign. When things were going well he had little desire for anything but very good food, but on a cold scent he hankered after things like sausage rolls.

The Barbary Ram had at one time been a sleazy pub which boasted no lavatory, in which the glasses were sloshed around in a tin bucket in cold soapless water, but nevertheless where the draught mild was perfect and the huge portions of oxtail and dumplings sold at rock-bottom price. A bob, Harry thought he remembered from student days.

The hand of time and the brewery had erected toilets adorned respectively by paintings of Madame de Pompadour and Louis XV, in whose style the place was redecorated. There was wall-to-wall carpet in the only bar, the public and jug-and-bottle having made way for the plumbing. The atmosphere was hushed and refined and at this hour there were only three people at the bar, being attended to by a ladylike barmaid. The manager was rather ostentatiously reading *The Times*.

Standing by himself was Mr. Spoon.

He was a small man with an immense spiked moustache. Inevitably the fact that he ran restaurants—of the type referred to as caffs by the inmates—had attracted the nickname of Greasy, although in fact his premises were clean enough to pass the health inspector. At his ten emporia, strategically placed near tube stations, were sold the cheapest egg, sausage and chips in London. The reason was that nearly all the raw materials were stolen.

He had been a fence specialising in lead filched from building sites when a friend, over a cosy glass of stout, bewailed the fact that with the abolition of price maintenance plus the decay of the back street grocer it was impossible for an honest thief to dispose of a lorry load of stolen eggs, let alone the stuff that workers in sausage factories smuggled out in the legs of their pants, plus the carcasses that vanished off wharves. It was

49

then that a blinding flash of genius illuminated Mr. Spoon and he opened his first café.

He had six adult sons and four teenage—and ravishingly lovely—daughters who spent their days in the cafés. For the evening shift—Spoon kept open until two a.m.—he had ten superannuated burglars, old gentlemen whose failing sight and congealed joints made it inadvisable to practice. Spoon spent his own evenings driving round in his Mercedes making spot checks on the cash position. He always said he bitterly regretted that Mrs. Spoon had not produced several more pledges of affection—mainly due to his seven years in Pentonville—as he could not risk employing strangers during the critical hours when the food was being brought in.

Mr. Spoon's suit probably had cost him eighty guineas, and in fact created the illusion of having a life of its own with Spoon crawling around inside in some kind of parasitic relationship.

"A double Scotch?" suggested Spoon.

Harry nodded.

"Chin chin," said Spoon, downing half of his.

"Health and strength," said Harry.

Spoon's eyes were grey and cold and too far apart. They met the Inspector's.

"I got some info."

Harry could not refrain from raising his eyebrows. The men who fenced jewellery and furs often turned their clients in for favours or money, but not fences who handled perishables. Besides, Spoon probably declared ten thousand a year and made as much again untaxed.

"I'll buy another round, Mr. Spoon," said the Inspector, "just so I don't faint from shock."

"I know what you're thinkin' and you're right. Why should I grass? I'll tell yer, I'm runnin' at a loss."

Harry gaped at him.

"Nah, nah, you know and I know that you know. But there hasn't been nobody in to see me for a month. Nothin's being sent orf. Partly it's because every copper's peerin' like his eyes was on stalks, and if he sees a bulgin' coat he wants to know what's under it, partly because the boys don't like going out at night. Yellow bunch of bastards! Fer the first time in six years I placed an order for sausages and, damn my eyes, the eldest boy goes up to Smithfield each morning just as though we was squares."

"Heart bleeds," grunted Harry, squirting soda.

"Coppers ain't got 'earts," brooded Mr. Spoon.

Harry knew that Stolen Property more or less had resigned themselves to the fact that Mr. Spoon would pass away in liberty as well as the odour of sanctity. Raids produced nothing conclusive, the position being governed by the fact that Mr. Spoon had purchased a small wholesalers, placing it under nominal charge of a completely deaf uncle. It ran legitimately and unprofitably, except for the fake invoices it supplied. The goods themselves were never handled personally by the little fence, but reached his cafés through middlemen who constantly changed.

"Well, let's have it," the Inspector said.

"This blue old bitch, could she be a man dressed up?"

"I suppose so. Look Mr. Spoon, I warn you, don't you start coming any nonsense, not on this one. We're not in the mood and if you make me mad, really mad, God help you."

"Oright, I'm giving you it straight. There's a boy I know. No names, no pack drill. It was on the night of September eight—remember, she done a bloke in outside a station? Well, this here cove was staying in a lodging house. He don't normally, but 'e 'ad reasons." Mr. Spoon shook his head as if to reassure the Inspector that his associates stayed at first-class hotels, which they probably did, thought Harry mournfully.

"Now he gets back in at three ack emma. You know these places, with walls jerry built. Now this cove 'as sharp ears. I'll level with you that it's 'is lay."

A Listener, thought Harry, one of the men who sat in crowded transport cafés seemingly concentrating on a meat pie, or mingled with employees leaving banks and shops. Practice made their powers of hearing phenomenal; some were reputed to have the power of cutting other conversations out of their range so that their hearing could, so to speak, reach out and snatch what was particularly wanted. Sometimes they sold information, more often they were leader of the gang.

"He's sitting on his bed massaging 'is plates of meat when 'e hears this noise. Uncanny is 'is word for it, like Batman. 'E

51

creeps out in his socks. The doors 'ave transoms, see? Very powerful is my friend—he climbs, too. 'E pulls 'imself up and takes a dekko. The light was on. There was a thickset cove, wiv great shoulders and a mop of black curly 'air"—Mr. Spoon's aspirates came and went like surf on a thirsty beach. "'E had 'is back to the door, but he was kind of giggling. My friend said it was like," Mr. Spoon threw his head back and gave a kind of moan, "tee hee hee.

"I don't know whether it frightened him, but by God it . . ." Spoon stopped as a Campari bottle slipped from the barmaid's hands.

"Now look here," the manager had a red tooth-brush moustache and a tie with a lot of stripes, "this is a respectable establishment and I must ask you . . ."

"Eff you," said Mr. Spoon, showing his false teeth. Harry remembered that the man had an ugly reputation when he was first starting.

"Police here," said Harry producing his warrant.

"Well," said the manager with a bright smile, "bottles don't grow on trees, you know."

"Suppose you get back to fawning on the gentry." The Inspector leaned over the counter and the manager smiled weakly and went away.

Four years ago and he would not have behaved like that, thought Harry uneasily, and took it out on Mr. Spoon in the shape of a menacing snarl. "Quit the histrionics, Spoon."

"'Istory?" said Mr. Spoon, nonplussed.

"No horrible noises, no taking off your pants and doing the highland fling."

"Oright, Mr. J. Oright. But—let's 'ave another. Miss, two large Johnnies—but it made an impression on me, like. You know my youngest daughter, Flo? She fainted clear away when 'e done it. Even my friend, 'e turned green when it come up past 'is tonsils. Never 'eard anything like it, he said, but," Mr. Spoon's plump hand pawed the Inspector's sleeve, "but on the bed were two knives and he had two more, one in each 'and and waggling them like he were conductin' an orchestra. My friend was in 'is prison band—they used to 'ave one to play when one of them Parliament ladies came down to take a look, the triangle 'e was on because he was willin' but can't read music, like. But the knives, with the points to 'em, were dead ringers to those they 'ad in the press as the Blue Lady's."

"So?"

"'E dropped down and went to his kip."

"For Christ's sake, why not the police?"

"Now, now," said Mr. Spoon, "we all know about the man who turned Queen's ev. and got twenty years from old Justice Spottle."

"That's a myth," said Harry, "he got the twenty because he hit his brother too hard with a beer bottle, after he had given the evidence, two months after in fact."

"Well, we don't know about that!" said Mr. Spoon.

"I could find him," said Harry. "Listens, climbs and played the triangle."

"Wiv four witnesses that 'e was with a bird in Leeds on September eight, and me denying we ever 'ad such conversation!" said Mr. Spoon.

"All right, all right," said Harry, cocking his finger at the bridling barmaid.

"It's on me, I earn a trifle more," said Mr. Spoon, "keep the change from the fiddly, miss. Now there's one more bit. My friend thought the man playing knives might be a seaman."

"Any reason?"

"'Is mum ran a 'ouse in 'ull when 'e was a nipper. He says he can tell the way they sit on beds, kind of waiting for the roll of the waves." Mr. Spoon, overcome by the thought, drained his glass.

"Pish, tush and general corruption," snarled the Inspector.

"Parm?" said the little man, politely.

"Now," said the Inspector, glaring at the manager so fiercely that he disappeared into a small office, "was he drunk?"

"Now look, 'e was doing his work, sober as, parm me, a Judge."

"Reliable?"

"Nah, look, I told you. You could prove nothink. Everything denied, and me with two Q.C.s and all the witnesses money can buy. Plus police brutality—I give generous to the election funds and it'd come up in the 'Ouse, you bet, bashin' people in little rooms. But 'e's reliable. 'E used to do the Fat Chap's smashin' jobs."

You had to be sober and reliable to work for the Fat Chap, whose ramifications were wide and criminal. The Inspector thought it would be Croucher, a 'tradesman' as the underworld would label him. Croucher was educated and since his twenty-second year would have averaged six thousand a year, even taking into account four years inside. He was not the kind of man to have hallucinations.

"You told me too much or not enough. But I'll crawl right out and guarantee we don't want to know about the smashing. One, it was Croucher!"

Mr. Spoon looked at the ceiling and whistled. 'Rule Britannia' while the barmaid's eyes rolled and her hand shook as she poured out a small Russian stout.

"And the address?" said Harry. "Now, don't muck about if you don't want real trouble. And God love you if you're lying."

Spoon looked coy.

"You'll drive me insane," said Harry.

"Insaner," suggested Mr. Spoon.

"Now," said Harry, "I promise you I won't badger your boy, but I want the address."

"You'll remember the favour?"

"If there is anything to it you'll get tipped off if the Stolen Goods traps are closing in."

"The Morning Star in Rotherhithe, a private hotel."

"A private . . . er!" The Inspector controlled himself with difficulty.

"The car's nearby, I'll drive you," said Mr. Spoon smoothly, "not insane but to Rotherhithe."

The Inspector hesitated, weighing subtle pros and cons, seeing in his mind's eye old gentlemen in silk gowns asking embarrassing questions in a nasty way. Finally he said, "I'll take you up on it and thanks, if I can make a phone call first."

"A pleasure, I'm sure," leered Mr. Spoon as Harry went towards the telephone which reposed in the innards of a plaster cast sedan chair.

He got on to Records and asked about the Morning Star Private Hotel.

An anonymous voice reported, "Superior type of lodging house for men. No meals. They use the hotel designation for legal reasons. Nothing known. Occasionally a man has been arrested there but no suggestion of complicity. The owner is a Commonwealth immigrant named Baker. Nothing known."

"Thanks. Transfer me to Pillaging, please."

"Ah, hallo, Harry, have you found the Lady?" said Pillaging in the person of a fat inspector named Ponting.

"She's modelling for *Vogue* at the moment," snarled Harry. "What went off on September eight?"

"Arf a mo. God knows it's more than my feeble mind can record." A notebook rustled. "Two lorry loads of artificial fertiliser; whoever listened got it wrong because two others carrying lead ingots were in the next bay. A doctor's car with dangerous drugs, not recovered. Ah, a lorry load of tinned steak. Commercial gallon size destined for a Yankee base, product of Chicago."

"Give me Receiving, old pal," said the Inspector.

"No need," said Ponting. "Greasy Spoon started running a special at his places—meat pie and chips. Delicious and a lovely buy. All the lads in the manor dropped in for a cheap nosh at it. The annotation says it was Croucher's boys who knocked it off. Croucher himself was on the job, at least we got a partial identification—thick-set man with a bad lisp."

"Croucher—he climbs as well as listens, doesn't he?"

"He listens. Now he's in the money he leaves the hard work to his stooges."

"Thanks!"

Mr. Spoon's driving was expert and relaxed.

"How's Croucher?" asked Harry abruptly as they were crossing the Thames.

The needle of the speedometer, immobilised at twenty-five m.p.h., dropped to twenty-two, shot to twenty-eight and steadied again. As good a lie detector as any, the Inspector thought, but the fence did not glance round.

"Two and two don't always make four, mister, not with us."

"This is big stuff, old boy. I wouldn't say that the kid gloves are aired today."

"I'm a business man," said Mr. Spoon, "it's what they call a seller's market. Peter Sellers, like!" He wheezed at his own joke.

"All right, funny man, I hope you choke on your own pinched baked beans."

"I could do with twenty cases right now," confided Mr. Spoon. "I don't carry a big inventory of hot stuff because of the risk—your people know it. From thieving 'and to mouth, as you might say, and I'm levelling when I tell you the last nosh of stolen grub in any of my places was 'ad Thursday week by two bus drivers off duty in young Marleen's caff in the Stockwell Road. Frozen hamburger meat—not very popular, but I 'ave to take the slow-moving stuff along with the good."

"Can't you put the prices up?"

"What and lose me clinteel? And what about some nosey old bitch in Parliament gettin' up and sayin' I didn't give no early warnin' and so am undermining the economy?"

Harry shut his eyes and thought about some golf clubs he wanted to buy but his wife didn't.

"'Ere we are," presently announced Mr. Spoon.

Surprisingly the Morning Star was a newish three-storey building with a neon sign and a glass entrance door.

"'Is name is Snowy Baker," said the little fence as Harry pushed open the door. For some reason the Inspector had expected an Indian, but Baker was a tall, rangy man with a face made of crinkled leather. When he heard the voice, the Inspector thought of a painting he had once seen of a gaunt man somehow balanced against the wooden verandah of a tin-roofed pub with the skeletal remains of cattle in the foreground and blazing sun overhead.

"Yair, I'm Baker," the voice grated, "don't get many demons around here. I'm a colonial migrant so I got to be careful until there's another Tobruk and you want me." He smiled without much humour and showed white dentures. "I could be sent back to Brisbane any tick of the clock."

"Didn't I see you firing at me at the Eureka Stockade?" asked the Inspector innocently.

"Aw right, aw right, let's stop the jokes. Wadgerwant?"

"The night of September eighth. There was a thick-set man staying here with a lisp."

"I remember that joker," said Baker, "at least I think I do."

"Do you keep a register?"

"Like I have mink covers on the bog seats! They're either too drunk, or they haven't got a nime, or they call themselves Smith. So I haven't got one."

"Let's see, you been here long?"

"Summers three. I got the idea of starting a chain of these places. We got 'em back home, for blokes without much hoot and wanting a clean bed for the night. But clean, not like you poms with a pot under the bed. Here we got plumbed wash bowls in each room and no pots." He stared solemnly at the Inspector. "I've got another one being built."

"You have permanents?"

"Nah, transients. I don't encourage regulars. They're a responsibility and I got a social conscience. Money on the knocker, a clean bed, pee in the wash bowl and a sanitary block on each floor which isn't much used."

"Are you mad?" wheezed Mr. Spoon. "Baffin' in winter, weakening yer back! You strines are crazy!"

"You kippers—no guts and two faces—are only strong under the armpits," said Baker truculently. "What about the east of Suez caper, eh?"

"Now," said the Inspector, "this is murder."

"Who got done over?" said Baker, interested, lifted as it were from the scent.

"We thought the Blue Lady might have been here on September eighth."

"A woman?" growled Baker. "Me run a drum? I never done over a demon yet but there'll come a day."

He was very tall, albeit stringy, thought Harry.

"This is men only," said Baker, restraining himself with difficulty. From the corner of his eye the Inspector noted that Mr. Spoon had picked up a huge brass ashtray and was toying with it. He felt relieved.

"Now, look, we think he could be a man."

"A poofter," said Baker horrified, "don't come the raw prawn on me. I should let a room to a poof? I kick the glass door open with me foot and throw 'em out."

"I do wish," said Harry, "you had not visited 'The Summer of the Seventeenth Doll'. The argot gets trying."

"All right, all right," said Baker suavely. "But I pick up a bit of money on the T.V. doing it. They think we speak that way. I have to practise it."

57

"I have no intention of closing you up."

"You couldn't, but you could stand over—pardon, persecute —me," said Baker, "but believe me I'm clean. If I can help you get that bloody old bag count me in."

"A certain person was in two-o-four," said Mr. Spoon. "'E 'eard the noises in two-o-three. The night of September eighth."

"Jesus," said Baker. "I told you, this is a transient stop. Oh, I have regulars, but generally it's a one-night stand. Most of 'em on the skids, but a bit above the common lodging house. Of course there's the occasional commercial, coming here to tickle a bit on his expenses—I don't mind giving them a false receipt. In fact I got a special receipt book, 'The Morning Star Hotel, Jermyn Street'. Then there's the blokes a bit down on their luck, and the gamblers who've done their roll."

"What staff have you got?"

"Me," said Baker. "I'm into the bank and it's a case of every post a winner if I'm going to make a go of it. There's a young fellow who comes in to help. We do as much in four hours as ten gossiping sheilas would do in a day. If I get a job on the T.V. there's a retired seaman who backstops for me."

"You must work hard."

Baker shrugged. "I'll have me own yacht in ten years and challenge for America's Cup."

"Now, about September eighth."

"I just got a mental feeling about this joker. Not a regular, but he's been here off and on over the three years since I built this place. Thick-set and a lisp. Not effeminate, though, looks tough."

"But next door, in two-o-three."

"Ar," said Baker. "This total recall calls for rum. Sit down." He produced three sturdy, small chairs from behind the desk and a bottle.

"This comes from Bundaberg, a pal off a ship smuggled me a dozen. Beautiful smooth dark rum, not like that nancified white stuff you poms put in your cokes."

"Ever tried undiluted naval rum?" asked Harry.

Baker poured the second glass and stopped, interested.

"Try it sometime," said the Inspector.

"Not for me," Mr. Spoon said. He reached back and produced a silver flask.

"What's that, gnat's pee?" asked Baker eyeing the golden fluid.

"Made by a French prince," said Spoon, "at seven pounds ten the bottle. My wine merchant keeps it for me special. 'Ave a nosh."

Baker drained his rum and reached for a fresh glass.

"At seven ten a go *anything* must be good." He sipped. "Hair oil but with a kind of quality about it, like the dandruff on a millionaire's eyebrows."

"Joker!" growled Spoon.

"If you don't mind, begin the ratiocination," pleaded Harry.

"Meaning thinking. You think we're ignorant! I went to Xavier where they teach you football. Give us another swig of the hair oil, sport, and you'll hear the brains gettin' meshed. Trouble is that the faces run together into about ten prototypes; long and thin, moon-faced and slack-bellied, powerful and chunky, little and wizened, usually with goggles, etcetera. Let's look at me diary." He immersed himself in a folio ledger. "Yair, day before I had a bit with the commercial T.V.; sheep shearer, me who never saw a bloody sheep till I came here and saw 'em in Hyde Park. Yair, then I had a five bob winning double at Cheltenham, forty-five bob back. I only bet small these days. A friend called by to bot a swig of rum, Sydneysider of course. Now I'll close my eyes."

Harry slowly drank his rum, reached for the bottle and refilled. After perhaps four minutes he said, "Have you finished the maiden's prayer, cobber?"

Blue eyes looked at him. "It's a blank. I remember the chunky cove with the lisp, that's all, plus a tall red-headed Irishman on the ground floor because he washed his feet in the hand basin and it and him smashed on the floor. Crouched on it like an effing monkey he must have been, the sod. The troubles you get!"

"Try a lubricant." The Inspector shamelessly poured out a measure from Mr. Spoon's flask.

"Thanks, but it won't help. I know when I'm stonkered. I put it on record that I want to help, but there it is." He sipped. "This old hairy oil gets you in. Where does the hoot come from, sport? Seven ten the bottle!"

"He runs restaurants," said the Inspector as Spoon looked mystified.

"Didn't know there was that money in the tucker," said Baker, "though I knew a guy who made a mint out of poys."

"Boys?" said the Inspector, professionally scandalised.

"Poys, with tomato sauce so it runs down your chin. Our national sport, apart from racing. But restaurants ... with what you have to pay the eyetie waiters and the chef these days!"

"He has a lot of kids, no waiters, he cooks the stuff himself and the raw ingredients are stolen."

"Hm," Baker scratched his chin and blinked. "Come to think of it I'd guess most of the stuff that went into this was pinched. Lot of little men like him," he nodded towards Spoon, who stared back amiably, "came along to see me. One bloke wall-to-walled me at a fifth less than cost. Oh, I checked! He said he didn't pay selective payroll tax on account of he stole lorries. Oh, there y' are!"

A large pimply face had appeared uneasily round the partition wall. It emitted a startlingly deep voice. About seventeen, thought Harry.

"We'll 'ave to get the plumber in for four-o-two, Mr. B., the connection is leakin' all over somethin' terrible."

"Get him! That's the way the money goes!" snarled Baker.

"Half a mo," said the Inspector. "Come here, my boy, and what's your name?"

"Bertie Snow." He was tall, but in a few years would be very powerful, although just now his body was slim. Baker noticed Harry's glance.

"He's paid well, eats like a horse, always cramming stuff into his gob. Might be a tapeworm."

"Works for you?"

Baker hesitated. "Self-employed."

"And no tax."

"A kid of seventeen pay tax? You're joking!"

"I'm not the Chancellor."

"It's the working class what pinch and fiddle, thank God," said Spoon, who had finished the flask and was in a philosophical frame of mind. "There's more of them, you see!" he said darkly. "How would I be selling savoury mince to them lords?"

"Well off," rasped the Inspector, with the intimation that this was going to be one of these alcoholic mornings so deplored in the annual Auditor-General's report. "Nowadays that's all they can afford. The other day I saw a life peer noshing jellied eel."

He swung round, "Here you!" and beckoned.

With the aid of long practice Bertie Snow had begun slowly to recede into the landscape.

He stood there, gangling, his spotty face arranged into the cockney's first line of defence, bewildered blankness.

"Do you remember the night of September eighth?" asked the Inspector.

Bertie Snow allowed his lower jaw to droop slightly while perplexed ridges furrowed his forehead. "Uh?"

"Now, Bertie, we got nice little cells for people who obstruct the police. I am an Inspector, by the way."

Bertie's dull eyes questioned Baker.

"Tell the truth, Bert," said the Australian, "always help a demon in distress and he'll kick yer teeth out afterwards."

"Wait a minute." Bertie produced a grimy notebook and leafed through it.

"He's an ornithologist," said Baker, "in his spare time, that is. I can't allow it here."

"Wendy May," said Bertie Snow. "Yes, I remember the night of the eighth."

"Look here," said Baker, "he clears off at five and I don't get much custom until well after that. Ten to one the cove wasn't here. But Bert gets here at eight a.m.—unless he says the alarm didn't work which is always after a night's ornithology.

"Now, Bert—the boy's like a son to me," added Baker in a patently false aside, "now, me boy, did you see the cove in two-o-three?"

Bertie's eyes glazed even more and ogled the ceiling. A smart cookie, thought the Inspector. Perhaps a note to the local division might be in order.

"How many convictions?" he said quickly.

Bertie did not stir, only his lips moved.

"I never been nicked, not once."

"I *thought* you were smart."

"Don't 'ound the lad," Mr. Spoon was a trifle merry, "and

61

seein' I'm wastin' me mornin' in the public weal, as you might say, I'll 'ave a drop of that rum."

The Australian filled the glasses. "Bertie doesn't drink, except that horrible fizzy muck. Back home he'd be quaffing his schooner with the best of 'em."

"Do Aussies quaff?" asked Harry. "I thought they swilled."

"In my State they're open till ten and on the back verandah all night. And six o'clock closing's out all round."

"I might go there."

"They put the boot into coppers," said Baker. "But as far as I'm concerned Bertie and I do alternate floors, starting at five past ten, and we alternate each day. Anybody in a room either gets or pays for another twenty-four hours. If they give trouble I throw 'em out. Now I've been doing my mental arithmetic —didn't know we can count, did you, sport?" he eyed the Inspector truculently, "and on September ninth Bertie would have had floor two."

"There was a party in the room," said Bertie sullenly, "siting on the bed doing up 'is boots. They were light brown leather things up around 'is ankle. Soft like. I wished I 'ad a pair. Wot would an old man like 'im want wiv Carnaby Street gear, eh? About forty 'e'd be, very dark face. I thought 'e might be 'alf a nigger. Only Mr. B. always says 'e's full if they turn up, except Chinamen who'll pay double. I said, 'I 'ave to do the room, mister'. He took up a green duffle bag, big thing it was, and muttered away as he walked out of the door."

"What did he mutter?"

"Effed if I know. I remember 'aving 'alf a mind to sing out for Mr. B. Ugly kind of effer 'e was."

"Tall?"

"Short but powerful like and fat-arsed like a bird. Very fat-arsed," Bertie added judicially.

"Could he have been a woman?"

"Could 'e 'ave been a woman?" Bertie gaped for a moment. "'E 'ad no bust but," he hesitated in perplexity, "I mean you don't look for it in a man. A bird now, you look at 'er legs, and then up . . ."

"Quite, quite," said the Inspector. "Now at the Yard we have something known as an identikit. You pick out a nose, say, and then some hair. . . ." He was conscious that his voice had assumed the horrid jocularity of a departmental store Santa Claus.

"I'm not comin' to no Yard." Bertie's voice was quite flat.

"Now my lad, I told you, it could be a serious offence to impede the authorities."

"In the buildin' there's an old squirt wot runs the commos 'ereabouts. A friend of me dad, except my dad don't 'old with the reds because of that 'Itler," said Bertie obscurely, "so 'is friend talks abaht civil rights. 'E's on the committee. When I was a nipper I used to sit listenin' for hours before we got the T.V. because 'e's got a 'are lip and it's as good as 'Ancock when 'e dribbles. But I know me rights. You can't take me blood or bits of me epiwhatsit wivout me permission and if you take me in the Constitutional Society wiv Dame Alice Grittle at the 'ead will 'ave your uniform."

"I don't wear one," said Harry.

"The shirt orf yer back, then."

Mr. Spoon, in the midst of filling the glasses, sniggered.

"Thanks so much," said the Inspector, "you are both right and appreciated. Back to your plumbing supervision."

Suspicion, fear, calculation all merged in Bertie's face as he hesitated, turned and scuttled away.

"At home," said Baker, "he'd get the back room and a mouthful of teeth."

"I don't believe it."

Baker laughed. "Taking you on, sport, eh? Let's have a rum." He poured.

"Seriously," said Baker, "he retreats faster than the English army. Withdraws into himself, you might say."

"You bore me!"

"I'm telling you one thing, sport, you handle these cockney people on a long line."

"We must go," said Harry to Mr. Spoon, who rose and staggered sideways, his tan shoes performing a kind of fandango across the carpet.

The Inspector clutched him.

"Nonshense, I can manage a straight lion."

"Use a machine gun," advised Baker, imperturbably pouring another rum.

"Thanks," Harry glanced back to Baker. "I'll drive, Mr. Spoon."

Mr. Spoon quietly went to the Mercedes and stretched out on the back seat while the Inspector, inwardly cursing, drove to the smart part of Camden Town. Mrs. Spoon was a large woman whose raven hair was spotted with grey.

"Police," she said resignedly, with the shrewdness of years.

Harry supported Spoon, who was mumbling about the price he paid for stolen Yugoslavian tinned kidneys.

"Just friendly; a few drinks, loving-cupped."

"You're sure?"

"He's whiter than white. He'd better lie down."

Mr. Spoon sat down heavily on a strange, but obviously fearfully expensive, octagonal settee and shot back several yards.

"Why do they 'ave to put wheels on everythink?" asked Mrs. Spoon querulously.

"I heard they're goin' to put little engines on the two-hundred-quid models," said Harry, inwardly counting his input and happy that the last three rums had gone on to Baker's floor.

"When 'e's like this 'e 'as Bitter Lemon, Fernet Branca and pepper. In 'arf an hour it makes 'im bring it up orf 'is stummick. Would you like one, luv?"

"I think I can walk."

"'E don't often get pissed of a morning, and never drivin', but 'e's got 'is business worries. This here Blue Lady gives 'is customers and suppliers the trots. 'Is bank manager says the rate'll 'ave to go up and the seamen is bound to go out again. 'E says . . ."

"Thank you, thank you, goodbye, goodbye," said the Inspector scuttling professionally for the door.

3

Having been drugged, divested of his clothing by a very large man whose leather breeches creaked and whom he dimly remembered calling Brother Moss, Milton Greenaway had spent a nervous night in the twilight of unnatural sleep, sweating under the ex-army blankets provided by the management.

Thank Christ it had not been his best suit, the one he reserved for bastardy cases—astonishingly profitable, but needing rather natty dress—he thought as he shaved, dressed and decided not to eat breakfast.

Mrs. Garbell, the landlady, had the nose of a bloodhound, the mind of a private detective specialising in unsavoury divorce cases, and, apparently, the ability to survive without sleep.

"Good morning, Mr. Greenaway!" The old lady was ensconced behind her desk in the foyer, a stale cup of tea by her side with a biscuit disintegrating in the slopped saucer. It was this habit, almost a trademark, that got on Greenaway's nerves. Usually it betokened that somebody had not paid the weekly bill. Once in fact he had worried ten days in his most impecunious period. Not that she ever said anything, at least not to him, but you had to pass the boiled eyes and slopped saucer within a foot in order to go out of the small gilt and glass door.

"Good morning, Mrs. Garbell!" He was paid up, thank God.

"The porter"—she referred to a small adenoidal youth who was supposed, but never did, to clean shoes; but his talent for spying on the guests and the other staff made him Mrs. Garbell's joy. "The porter says the perleace brought you home yesterday." She had a curious accent, compounded of cockney and refined gentility.

"Have you seen the paper?"

She held up her *Daily Sketch*.

"There was a murder in my chambers yesterday, a man stabbed. I found the body."

Nothing could really affect Mrs. Garbell. Her eyes flickered and her lips pursed. "This has always been a respectable residence, I'm sure. We can't have the perleace around all day, Mr. 'Um."

"I'm a barrister, as you no doubt know, and I have no objection to conducting my own case for damages arising out of slander."

Mrs. Garbell gave the impression of closing her face up. He turned to go, but her inflexible voice came again. "There's a woman to see you in the Brown Lounge."

Barbie, he thought. Mrs. Garbell knew who she was almost

as well as he did, but it was part of her skill to introduce scandalous overtones into the word 'woman' and put those who visited in the Brown Lounge, otherwise seldom used and a vestigial memory of what the place looked like before the process of tarting up.

He turned and walked through the foyer. The first thing you noticed about the Brown Lounge was that its paint was in fact turning blackish and that one knocked one's hip against the vast, curlicued old sideboard which stood next to the door.

"That bloody sideboard! Morning, darling!"

"Why don't you take an axe? I mean they wouldn't miss it."

"They say the old hag keeps her money in it."

"Fine, steal it! Look, there was a bit in the paper about . . ."

"I found the body."

"My poor darling." She kissed him. "Would you like not to talk about it?"

She was his own age and height, with green eyes, shining black curly hair, wonderful teeth, conveying a slight, indefinable feeling of excessive muscularity which stopped her from being a raving beauty.

"I copped a brief from Hewson, bless him, so I must dash. I might get a couple of last-minute jobs. Look, suppose we eat at one-thirty at the Gamecock and Feathers?"

"But, dear. . ."

"And a to-hell-with-it-all day."

"I'll pay my share."

"Dispute later. I'll be in fine form after arguing about two cracked toilet bowls."

They went past Mrs. Garbell whose face did not move; only the boiled eyes slewed on to the back of Greenaway's neck as he went out of the door, waved to Barbara and sprinted for a seventy-seven bus.

He had been fortunate literally to stumble over Barbara. The small park in North London had been very quiet on the Sunday morning. He had glimpsed a girl in an orange dress coming down the grimy steps of an old house. Afterwards, walking fast, he turned a corner, felt his feet slide sideways, clutched something human and found himself lying winded with a substantial pair of female knees in his ganglia.

"You're hurt!" She got up. "There was nothing I . . ."

"Winded," he gasped. "A minute."

He got to his feet and looked at her. "It's assault."

"But I have no deadly weapon, kind sir."

"Your looks and charm."

"Am I to be knocked down and then picked up?"

He looked at her hand. "Unless you've left the gold and diamonds on the kitchen stove. I'd like you to pick up a bit of lunch with me. I'm a penniless barrister of great respectability."

"I always understood that penniless barristers ate buns."

"Ah, but the clerk, the one I own a fifth of, persuaded me to put five bob into something I don't understand, mixed doubles on one Breasley. By some mysterious process it returned me seven quid and ninepence."

"No rings! There's a place not far away if you like Italian."

She designed swimming suits. Probably well, he thought, as she was a conscientious worrier. Her fault was a kind of diffidence, a lack of confidence in her work. As she earned rather more than he, Greenaway had never attempted to tell her that she needed more push.

He had understood that her boy friend of some years had abruptly married the daughter of a very busy undertaker— Greenaway felt himself smiling as he sat in the bus.

When he had proposed six months before—they had known each other sixteen months or so—she had said they should wait until the next year.

"I shall have saved enough to furnish a small flat," she had said. "If I continue working, which I guess I shall, I want things like a good vacuum cleaner, a first-class stove, things like that, so it's easier and not so depressing as coming home to some dirty old implement that doesn't work."

"I should be doing that," he had demurred.

"You concentrate on getting a second-hand car, a decent hi-fi, the T.V.—Lord help us—and two weeks where there's sun and sea."

She was eminently practical, mused Greenaway, like himself without any family and educated from the provisions of a tiny estate. Her father had come from Australia, his own from the

United States. Funny how these old decisions influenced one's life. He sighed and got out the brief wherein one John Gladstone Higglestone sued Charles Edwin Hale for the cost of two cracked lavatory bowls, Mr. Hale pleading that (a) the lavatory bowls had been cracked since 1951—a plumber was to give evidence—or (b) it was fair wear and tear. Mr. Higglestone alleged that Mr. Hale had stood on the bowls and jumped up and down, a fact to be deposed by a Mrs. Burdon, described as a lady house-cleaner.

Hewson's angular writing had annotated: "The two have been suing each other in the County Court for ten years. Higglestone is the landlord, but the original grievance is lost in time."

He sat thinking, changed buses almost without knowing it and, still engrossed in thought, was almost into the courtroom when a hand plucked at his elbow.

It was an elderly clerk whom he knew by sight, faded and harassed-looking. "Sir, I thought it was to be Mr. Hewson."

"I'm devilling."

"It's my Mr. Jones, sir, his wife rang. Laryngitis. He can't speak."

Greenaway rather welcomed the news. Of Jones it was said that he could extinguish any fire by a few well chosen words.

"How many?"

"Two, sir, if you'll take them I'd be grateful. I have to be at the Bailey in an hour, sir. Here they are, one tenancy which you'll win and a dry-cleaning which nobody could win."

Greenaway sat down and studied them. The clerk was right, he thought. They usually were. Two hours later he found, to his surprise, that he had won all three. The dry cleaners were represented by a young man with twitching nerves who had seemingly lost all knowledge of the law. First case, poor devil, thought Greenaway. Although county court judges perhaps intervene in the cause of justice rather more than their brethren, in this case the incumbent seemed disposed to resign the young man to his fate.

"Bad luck, old boy," he said as he filled his briefcase.

"I think I'll try something else." The young man's face had oily sweat on it.

"Give it three years if you can eat."

68

"The old man makes coats so I eat, but do you always feel like I did?"

"First time up they had to carry me screaming out of the gents where I'd locked myself."

Several solicitors nodded to him as he left the courtroom and at the door two were waiting for him.

"By the way, Mr. Greenaway," said Rattle, of Coke and Rattle, "could I bring a client in this afternoon—embezzlement?"

Greenaway waited two seconds. "Would two-thirty do?"

"Certainly and I think our friend . . ."

Little Mr. Scobie of Scobie, Bishoping and Nust grinned and bobbed. "A partnership claim arising out of arson."

"Four, perhaps."

"Splendid," intoned Mr. Scobie.

He'd get a cab, thought Greenaway without elation. Life did that to you. You studied, you sweated and people ignored you. Then you fluked a case against a beginner and you got two briefs in an afternoon, something he'd dreamed of.

Outside his chambers he doubletook for a minute at the unassuming man in the blue tweed overcoat. It was only by association with a towering, mustachioed man with him that he recollected—an Inspector James, that was it.

"Blanco," called James, "all whiter than the snow, which speaking of I fear may fall."

Now he thought of it, Greenaway noticed there was a nip to pinch one's ears.

"No go, Inspector?"

"Nobody saw nuttin', nohow, but that's always the case until the impossible happens. Wouldn't like to confess, would you, and save us trouble?"

"Ply me with drink," said Greenaway, "and see what veritas is in my vino. Oh, hallo, Hearman."

"How did it go, sir?"

"I won three straight off the reel as they say. And Rattle at two-thirty, embezzlement, plus old Scobie at four, partnership troubles."

"My, sir, we'll have you in ermine yet. Old Scobie doesn't pay well, you know. But Rattle—justice-at-any-price Rattle, he's known as."

"If Scobie gets mean, tell him to go and get another boy."

"That's the spirit," said Hearman. "When I hear that, I know a man's arrived, sir. That's the spirit."

"Where?" said the Inspector.

"Eh, oh, the spirit," said Greenaway, "there's a pub called the 'Gamecock and Feathers'. I'm to meet my young woman at one-thirty. That gives us thirty minutes of bawdy conversation."

"Follow me," said Honeybody, "I know a short cut."

"Better come along, John," called Greenaway to Hearman, "to celebrate my putative judgeship."

Honeybody did know a short cut, involving three alleys, a right-of-way mysteriously passing through a licensed premises, a perilous trot across a one-way street and finally the pub. It was, Harry knew, celebrated for its plain English cooking which included fresh vegetables, normal—if one could apply the term—capons, field-raised calves and bills of astonishing magnitude.

The Inspector had not intended inviting Honeybody, now perched on a stool which seemed in danger of collapse. The Auditor-General had become increasingly critical of expenses and the Inspector, unbeknown to his wife, commonly only put eighty per cent of them in unless he held special authority.

He ordered a round, three double Haigs and his own half of bitter.

The Inspector climbed on to the stool and winced as the fleshy growth on his left big toe hit the ground.

"Trouble?" said Greenaway.

"Occupational disease. We all get bad feet. I take this to Mr. Harold Grunting at St. Isaac's. Sometimes he sees me and says 'Ah, yes, an interesting but non-malignant growth', orders a dab of pink stuff and there we are. Trouble is I have to buy two pairs of shoes, one eight, one broad nine. You can't bloody well get a mixed pair. I even tried a man who pinches them and he wouldn't play. Said it was unethical."

Probably a very deceptive kind of fellow, thought Greenaway as he sipped his whisky, a throw-it-away, with-it guy.

"Have it out," he advised.

"What the hell do you think I want? Old Grunting has a

70

backlog until the turn of the century. There's a man—a grouchy old bank manager with what he calls galloping piles, although it's not in my medical dictionary, and he's been on the waiting list since 1956."

"Pay, man, pay!"

"You see," explained the Inspector, "once I've started in the free, Mr. Grunting can't switch me on to the guineas side. There's a man named Sir Hubert Bultitude at St. Balsam's who does it for thirty guineas on the posh side, plus ten quid for the room, eight for the anaesthetist, and calls you 'sir' when he brings in the cup of tea and the bill. But it means going through all that machinery again . . . and the wife . . . she says why pay when you can get it for free. . . ."

"Feminine logic," said Hearman.

"Ar," said Honeybody.

"The trouble," said Harry, "is that I can draw for three pairs of shoes per year, but it now means I consume six. The Auditor said he could not sanction six pairs. If you want twelve singles, as they currently are, of left foot number eight shoes see me any day after ten at night."

"'Ave one on me," said Honeybody, unexpectedly.

Harry looked at him suspiciously. It was reputed that, in defiance of regulations, Mrs. Honeybody had a share in a cosy little fried fish shop in which Honeybody had invested his savings. Private enterprise was definitely on the banned list, but sometimes Honeybody exhibited little signs of affluence which, when officially pressed, he attributed to a system of picking four draws.

"Get 'em through the Treas.," said Greenaway. "Now you buy a pair a month, won't cost you more in the wash-up. You send the receipted bills—if you know a man in the business who'll double it so much the better—to Inland Revenue. They'll squeal and you squeal louder. Look, I'd take it for nothing . . ."

"Sir, sir," said Hearman.

"A couple of good dinners. We'll put the fear of God into the bastards and Grunting will get the lash so he'll eviscerate you if wanted within forty-eight hours or be put down to Skegness Ladies' Maternity Clinic for the Wives of Lighthouse Keepers."

"You've got a point. I'll press the income tax, but you're cheerful!"

"Use existing channels," said Greenaway, "blind 'em with science. But I had a good day," he said soberly, "tomorrow you will see a sad Greenaway, no doubt."

"He'll be a judge yet," said Hearman, "I've seen—no that's not true—I've *heard* of them coming suddenly, like a thoroughbred at the eleven-furlong post. That makes us clerks happy. A libation, sir." Hearman drew a note from his wallet.

"Hallo Milton, hallo John."

The Inspector looked round. Very nice, a bit tensed, and, well, a trifle hefty, but the Inspector liked them a bit that way. And very good teeth, and real, he thought.

"Oh, Miss Redding, my intended spouse come a council house, Inspector James and Good Sergeant Honeybody."

"I'm in the chair," said Hearman. "A final noggin. Your young man won three in a row this morning. You'll have a title yet."

"But money!" Miss Redding draped herself with dignity on a stool, an effort which the Inspector had noted the current affectation of short hem lines made difficult.

"Gin and tonic, one says ladylike. I don't like it, but I may as well be taken for a wealthy American as not."

"Ta," said the Inspector taking his bitter, "no further thoughts?"

"No," Greenaway fingered his glass. "Old Prettyman had been a bit of a doer in his time; but you'll find that out. I would say possibly imitative homicidal mania, small old party in the fog, follow him in."

Miss Redding looked a trifle green.

"Sorry," said the Inspector, looking at her, "lawyers and coppers get used to these things." He drained his glass. "I'll leave you to the cow's heel at thirty bob a go. Last time I was here the cod and parsley sauce fair bankrupted me. Come, Sergeant."

"Seems awfully nice for a policeman," said Barbara Redding, "and a bit ineffectual."

"I saw him giving evidence on the headless man trial," grunted Hearman. "Old Jabeez made his usual muck-up and the bloke would have got off if it hadn't been for your ineffectual young Inspector. He gave his evidence like a maddened viper. Crowley led for the defence, and he's smarter than a pepper pot, but dear little Mr. James was a match for him."

Barbara said, "I wonder why he wears a canary waistcoat, I mean there's always something wrong with men in canary waistcoats."

"What extraordinary pieces of conversation one hears in pubs."

Dapper in his expensive overcoat, Hewson nodded to them. "Good morning, Miss Redding, your young man's court triumph has reverberated to me. Morning Hearman. Didn't know you stooped to such places."

"I stepped in to order Sir Jabeez's lark's-tongue pie, sir."

Hewson allowed himself a faint smile. Sir Jabeez ate the cheapest dish in the bar mess and drank mild ale. "Perhaps I may buy a round in celebration of that dry-cleaning case, a forensic triumph."

"My opponent was twenty-three, sweating, tongue-tied and clueless, poor devil."

"Always take the credit, laddie, because you'll get the blame. Such reputation as I have originally rested on three monstrous coincidences, a doting judge, a senile witness and the fact that old Bromley—before your time—broke his upper plate a quarter through his final speech."

"I've got two conferences this afternoon," said Greenaway, "on the never but it pours principle."

"Splendid." Hewson sipped sherry. "I had Runting on the phone. He's still tied up, lucky devil. The trouble is that he is Prettyman's executor and as the old gentleman was a one-man band, so to speak, he thinks somebody should go down to his practice, what is its name?"

"Windlesham Parva."

"And spend a few days there. There's the practice, though from all accounts it was mostly trust work. But it'll have to be sold and accountants had better verify all trust funds. I thought you might take Hearman for a few days—providing your afternoon clients aren't that urgent. It'll be a profitable little jaunt, and we'll get a sub for Hearman."

"Old Percy Riddle, sir, 'im who was Justice Foster's clerk.

Lives at Tooting and likes a few days harnessed up again. But whether Sir J.'ll like his fees is another matter."

"I imagine part of them will be chargeable to the estate," said Hewson dryly. "No lack of money there, I understand. Well, I must pop along. Stuffed cabbage in the mess with Sir Jabeez whose turn it is to pay. I must say I bought him rissoles on Monday. Have a good lunch."

"Better have a bite with us, John," said Greenaway, "as from now we're on expenses."

"But there's me," said Barbara, "do I pay for my own?"

"Co-opted on the sheet as temporary stenogging," said Hearman, "a hundred words a minute."

"You know what?" said Greenaway as they were seated. "I've never had their carpet-bag steak. Just worshipped from afar."

"That's the one with a dozen oysters shrewdly stuck in the middle of about two pounds of grilled fillet," said Hearman to Barbara. "Melts between the fangs. And a Moselle with it, eh?"

"I think I'll have lamb cutlets and vegetables," she said. "I've never been a great lover of blood sports."

Not much was said whilst they ate.

"When I become a judge I'm having that three times a day," Greenaway finally said, conscious that his collar had suddenly grown a trifle tight.

"You'll be like old Dyspepsia—charcoal biscuits and dry toast. They said he 'anged a man because he said he was eatin' pork chops at the time the victim was done in. But say we take your car? It'll be first-class fare each way, and taxi fares in the way of business. A good few nicker involved. Pay for your honeymoon, sir."

"You'll be careful." Barbara had a thing about cars.

Greenaway felt a familiar flicker of irritation. "It was you who suggested a small car, miss. I'll drive at a steady forty-five, completely sober, and give every bloody signal in the handbook. Hearman will stride ahead with his red flag. Sir Jabeez will be on the bonnet waving a writ of habeas corpus. . . ."

"All right. Surrender," said Barbara. "Just remember to call me tomorrow night. And now I have to stagger my bloated way to a studio in which four unfortunate girls will proceed to model two hundred bikinis. It's as draughty as the Antarctic and the big boss has installed a twenty-watt electric fire he got in Petticoat Lane when he felt generous."

"I'd like to come and see those birds one day," said Hearman. "Couldn't I be a fitter? A friend has a friend who designs theatrical costumes and the friend 'as a tape measure, see? He goes around and . . ."

"Cease these libidinous desires, Hearman, when the smell of the late Prettyman's money is around," said Greenaway.

"Besides," said Barbara, "they all seem to have six foot nine husbands with bad tempers. Bruised all over where you can't see it."

"Which is precious little," said Hearman. "Seriously, you might remember old Hearman on your travels."

"From what one hears old Hearman travels not hopefully but too well."

"Talkin', eh?" The clerk's jovial eyes looked at Greenaway. "We better get back and lie in wait for Rattle. A good time you chose. Very free with the port when a client's payin' is old Rattle. Scobie now . . . he drinks barley water for 'is kiddidilies and is never known to tip the waiter."

Barbara buttoned her coat and swiftly kissed Greenaway. "Bye, I'll fly through the east gate. Phone. Love."

4

Inspector James had despatched Honeybody on three small chores before going to see Superintendent Hawker.

Hawker's large, splay feet reposed in a solution of strong washing soda. He looked at Harry malevolently.

"I got the dame," he said, laconically.

"Oh! Gawd," said Harry.

Dame Alice Grittle, M.B.E., had entered the mother of Parliaments on a landslide majority of thirteen thousand four hundred and eighty-one—her detractors said it was partly the product of sheer terror and partly her determination to abolish all ranks of the armed forces above lance corporal. At any rate she had so intimidated the Whips that within four days she had received an under-secretaryship and her rather nasal accents zealously supported the Prime Minister on all occasions and to his manifest embarrassment. Small, faintly gingerish and bony, the Dame had the quality the French call *formidable*.

"How tall are you?" said Hawker with an air of distaste.

The Inspector flushed. It was a sore point.

"Five ten."

"Don't lie. I can have you demoted for that."

"Well, blast it, five nine."

"I looked up your record," said Hawker, coiling his six feet three in the swivel chair. "The doctor said you only made it because of the calluses on your heels and balancing a bit on your toes. If you hadn't been white and with a degree you wouldn't have got in."

"Yes, sir."

"Grittle wants to lower the height to four feet seven," said Hawker.

"Sir?"

"The Commissioner told me to rebut her. I nearly asked for my pension, but I got her in and said what about the physical side and showed her Lofty Jones."

"My Gawd," said Harry. Lofty had been brought in by seven rather badly mauled officers after pouring petrol over his *de facto* and touching her off.

"In the strait jacket, of course," said Hawker. "She said, 'My poor man, are they giving you psychiatric treatment?' We had the screw-gag ready, but she just listened with relish to what he had to say and told me to see he got vitamins in his food."

"She surely didn't think a man of four feet seven could take Lofty, sir? He's killed four men in his time."

"Well!" Under Hawker's gaze, Harry felt himself shrink.

"It's mainly the helmet, sir," he said defensively. "If you're short you feel a nana in it, a bloody great flower-pot on your sconce. Your backside seems to creep up to your neck."

Hawker hardly listened. "The Dame said that the Japs bash their hands on stones until they become like steel. She told me to get bits of old concrete from the Ministry of Works and have them bash their hands on it for a couple of months at police college. Then they could swarm up people and hit them. She was thinking mainly of ship owners, I think."

"The P.M. couldn't allow it," said Harry.

"It was the aircraft industry. When we had one there were four thousand men under five feet who used to creep around the fuselage riveting and wiring. Now they haven't got jobs. The Professor says they've got to be trained as telephone mechanics—less wear and tear on the poles—but that will cost one million quid, so the Dame thinks she can (a) save the money; (b) solve the recruitment problem."

The Superintendent looked at Harry without much hope. "All suggestions received."

"The American Army won't take recruits over six feet four or under five feet."

"You know what the Dame thinks about America!" said Hawker, gloomily, "we'd be giving her ammunition. She'd go on about freedom of choice."

Harry pondered. It was important to him generally to placate Hawker.

"Do you know anybody in the Treasury, sir?"

"I've got a godson named Percy Potting. I blenched at the font, but my late wife was a friend of the mother. He's in charge of all Government charladies and workhouses."

"Important?"

"Good God, yes! Knighted last year and works out chess problems all day. Lunches with the Professor on Wednesdays."

"Perhaps you could have a word with him, sir, pointing out the insurance risk. A man of four feet seven would be likely to sustain incapacitating injuries at an early age.... Compensation, pension. . . ."

"'Incapacitating injuries'," said Hawker with relish, "that's good civil service prose. If Percy wrote a memo he'd do himself a lot of good, perhaps a life peerage eventually. He was knighted because of the savings when he suggested putting plastic pots instead of china in the workhouses. They used to break the china ones out of spite. Thank you, Mr. James, I won't forget it."

"I had a conversation this morning about my feet, which brought the Treasury to mind."

"I'm not interested about *your* feet. Tramping about at my

77

age!" snarled Hawker. "Constable, bring me more hot water and Mr. Porterman."

The constable with the unfortunate rostered duty of being runner for Hawker departed rapidly. Porterman had probably been waiting nearby; he was in some awe of Hawker. In any case his burly, bustling presence came in within seconds. He grunted at Harry, and watched Hawker wriggling his feet.

Curiously, Porterman was not reputed to have the occupational disease, although slightly gone at the knees owing to three years of capped rugby.

"I think you should have a chiropodist, Mr. Hawker."

"They haven't the nerve any more," Hawker said. "I remember years ago in C Division you'd give this man half a crown and he'd cut down to the bone so you felt you were treading on air, but now they just get out a nail file and scrape. Richman's found a bottle of paste, but the Deputy Commissioner got blood poisoning out of it, so I stick to the washing soda."

"Well, you got *my* report. Complete coverage. Three possibles. Two women and one man, no alibis on all relevant dates. Contra, no knives, no bloodstains, no identification." Porterman looked at Harry distastefully, so that the Inspector wished that his wife would not insist on his wearing fancy waistcoats.

"It impresses your personality, such as it is," she had said the last time he had complained. He sighed.

"You may well sigh, Inspector," said Porterman. "At Liverpool the prime requisites of the Blue Lady were observed; darkness, the open, a deserted street. She—or he—has never slain indoors."

"The doctor said Prettyman could have walked with the knife in him."

"Present that to a jury. Bosh and balderdash, cock and hokum. Take a look at this."

This was a photostat of a note addressed to 'Mr. Cecil' at the *Sun* newspaper. "'Another. How he squills when he feels it. Yours the lady.' Dated Liverpool twelve a.m. yesterday. Handwriting the same. And from a similar paper pad from Woolie's."

78

"You got my report!" said Harry, wearily.

"Croucher's filth," said Porterman, "no truth in him that a jury with moderately good eyesight would believe. Plus a record of violence when he was starting. He used to run with Big Bertie Strout, that animal, and a girl—I forget her name. She used to get a respectable-looking mark into an alley and Big Bertie and Croucher would do the rest."

Porterman mused. "A good living they made. We worked it out that about eighty per cent of the marks were too embarrassed to complain. Then he got a scare. There was a mêlée over in North London—a welsher got his head stove in. It was Croucher, so we felt sure, but it was so confused there wasn't a case. But after that he cut out doing anything rough personally. Went in for listening."

Hawker paddled his feet audibly as the constable bent and topped up the plastic bowl. "That'll do, that'll do, trying to boil me alive. All right, suppose she knocked off this Liverpudlian lavatory attendant and drove back here."

"Well. . . ." suddenly Porterman looked old. "I lunched with Richman. We're damned if we know. You saw the *Standard* mid-day?"

"Yes," said Hawker, "funny how water gets cold. 'When respected members of the judiciary may not go about their duties . . .' Oh, they're justified, though they give the impression the Privy Council were knocked off. My spot checks are my only hope. Dame Alice Grittle wants to go on the first screening—lot of publicity via T.V. Now you, Mr. James, I can't think of anything more productive than for you to poke around Prettyman's pad at Windlesham something."

"Parva."

"You're pardoned." Hawker gave his leer. "The point is that I got Sir Jabeez on the blower. He'd been scuttling around the law courts, a word here, a word there, like some ghastly old . . . Christ, what does washing soda do to carpets?"

"Takes the pattern out," said Porterman with an air of resignation.

"Don't hang about, constable," roared Hawker. "Get a mop, sponges, or the Auditor-General'll have your guts for carpets."

"Yes, sir."

"It's these plastic bowls," grumbled Hawker. "Where was I?

79

Oh, yes, Sir Jabeez hinted . . . you know how he goes on, like a virgin on her first heavy date. Talked about the weather and how equities have dropped, then via the sterling situation to old Prettyman. Still waters run deep, to coin a phrase. See how deep!"

"Did he mention any particular millpond?"

"He hemmed and hawed. It might have been women."

"But he was seventy-two!"

"Are you seventy-two?"

"No, sir."

"When you are you'll know, but not until then. You go down and fish. No cars, the train."

"But, sir."

"You read that bit about the Dame saying the police drive up lounging in Humbers and bash the working class. She's always on about it. Hire a car. It'll cost double but Sir Arbuthnot'll sleep quiet of a night. You first class . . . the P.M.'s own instructions, all M.P.s and coppers of inspecting rank go first. Your man . . . Peebody . . ."

"Honeybody, sir."

"Anybody I bloody well want," snarled Hawker. He was in a bad mood, thought Harry.

"It works out the same, sir, because he overflows over two of the five a side. Some guards say he should pay twice."

"Tell him to stand in the corridor."

"People can't pass him, sir, without indecency."

"Tell him to lock himself in the toilet, then. I once . . . no matter, get going. Watch the expenses. The Dame is like a lynx."

When the door had closed Hawker looked at Porterman. "I think he might do."

"Those waistcoats!" said Porterman.

"That's his wife. Almost but not quite a copper's wife. He may make it. Now, about these reports . . ."

Harry James eventually found Honeybody inevitably emerging from a public bar, chewing chlorophyll tablets.

"A trip to Kent," he said.

"Good. I'll phone my Dodo and get a car."

"Train. Change twice. Eight-o-six, platform eight, Victoria."

"Cripes, in this weather."

"Dame Alice Grittle! We hire a car there."

"Oh, well," said Honeybody, "I'll get four of stout and have a bottle of cheer for the way down. Halves, sir."

The Inspector arranged to meet Honeybody at seven-forty-five and caught a taxi home.

"I'm going to join the League of Modest Maidens," Elizabeth announced as she opened the door.

"But," Harry stopped; the Maiden bit was strictly alliteration's artful aid for the League welcomed sturdy grandmas and even great-grandmas. Its aims were, one, a patent system of calisthenics called joy through dancing, two, the introduction of flogging for (male) sex offences, three, the badgering of M.P.s concerning television programmes.

Almost inevitably it was a creation of Dame Alice Grittle, or rather the founder, a Welsh nationalist and a vegetarian, had been eased out by the Dame and was currently muttering in Carmarthenshire.

"Oh, dear," said Harry, "they'll get you on to health foods. I know you, Elizabeth!"

"If you're craven enough to want your womenfolk at the Mercy of Beasts, as the Dame says. . . . Anyway we patrol in packs with bludgeons and a walkie-talkie per seven. The Dame will direct from her wireless car."

"Dear, I've got to go down to Kent with Honeybody. You come!"

"Money?"

Elizabeth had a yen, unsatisfied, for bludgeons.

"I will pay, your funds precluded. Three days maybe. Get the dog to the kennels, pack and to Victoria. Make sandwiches as Honeybody bears drinky."

As his wife flew to the kitchen, making tongue sandwiches while telephoning the kennels and the nextdoor neighbours, the Inspector packed, a job at which he was not good, impeded by the huge mongrel hound, Mr. Bones, which somebody had given them for a wedding present and which habitually lounged on clothes.

"Sandwiches," eventually gasped Elizabeth, "and, you crazy fool, I haven't worn that for three years. Where are we going, funerals?"

"For myself there are three drip-dry white shirts, three pairs of underpants, six vests, ditto plus socks and hanks and pyjamas. Choose your own poison."

The Inspector spent the rest of the time choosing paper-backs. He had a feeling that the future might have holes in which both Elizabeth's and Honeybody's conversation would become redundant.

The kennels, in the shape of a laconic man with a way with dogs, and heavy leather gloves as the second line of defence, if love failed, collected Mr. Bones.

At Victoria, Honeybody, vast in his blue overcoat, was waiting near the ticket office.

"Three firsts to Windlesham Parva, sir."

"Christ," said Harry, "I forgot. Hawker said you were to go second."

"Dodo gave me six of the best fried Dover soles and some frozen prawns," said Honeybody. "Lovely grub, but second . . . everybody complaining! When the account gets in, sir, they'll be so muddled they'll pass it. If it's queried it's my error; they can 'ardly throw me out after thirty-two years. I got a porter, sir, four years the last time I took him in, what will get us an empty compartment and 'ave it locked with a NATO card on the door. I brought a pack of cards; so it's a friendly glass and a happy voyage down."

"I said you will get me hanged," said Harry.

"They said Mr. Hawker after the war turned off a couple of the Hitler boys just for fun," said Honeybody, reflectively, "but he lacks what they call spatial relationship and the 'eads come off. Too much drop!"

"Here's your porter," said Elizabeth, who rather supported flogging but flinched at execution. Honeybody enjoyed tormenting her.

"What happens about the lavatory?" said Elizabeth practically, as the porter, an old man with a long neck and curiously thin head, affixed a grimy card and with sidelong glances whipped out and turned a key.

"We fixed it with the guard," said Honeybody, "he takes a dekko at us every twenty minutes. If wanted he'll let us out. Not that . . . well, I got used to it on night duty. They should give us hard lyin' money."

Honeybody's opinions on this subject were a byword among his colleagues.

"Don't be beastly." Elizabeth passed round the tongue sandwiches and accepted a glass of the stout which rested in one of Honeybody's two bags.

Honeybody was the only person the Inspector knew who carried a gladstone bag, one so ancient that at first sight it resembled some curious and battered old animal. It smelled of fish from Mrs. Honeybody's shop, but generally contained four bottles of stout and a bottle of whisky, with the fish, as it were, packing.

"The glasses are in my case," said the Sergeant, reaching upwards to the rack. Harry glimpsed the long underwear which Honeybody affected winter or summer and was alleged to have worn when he journeyed to Mozambique to arrest an embezzler.

"Now, a swig of stout, to settle the nerves, and a munch of plump Dover sole. I had 'em salted and peppered with just a touch of lemon."

Apart from wishing he had brown bread and butter, Harry enjoyed the meal. His wife had provided tissues for hand-wiping and presently the Inspector read while Honeybody taught Elizabeth an apparently ruleless card game called 'Down to Hell'.

The stout had gone before they changed trains and Honeybody's influence did not extend that far. The only first compartment was non-smoking, said a joyful youth with a red tie and a copy of the *Labour Front* ostentatiously peeping from his inside coat pocket, and inside the compartment was a lady of such awesome aspect that even Honeybody could not bring himself to broach the whisky. As it was, their fellow traveller kept sniffing as though choked by stout fumes.

The stout and Mrs. Honeybody's soles were lying heavily in the Inspector's craw. He realised he had forgotten his soda-mints—best friend of those who work odd hours—and groaned as a further thought struck him.

"'Ave one of mine. Brings it up like thunder." The Sergeant favoured a much more expensive patent nostrum. The fish parlour must be doing all right, thought Harry as he saw the price.

"Thanks, I will, but the thought struck me that I forgot to do anything about booking in and God knows when we're going to get there, at this rate." The train was inching its way along a cutting.

"Rest quiet, sir," said Honeybody. "I phoned the Dendles. Remember eighteen months or so ago? It's three miles from Windlesham Parva and Mrs. Jewel said they're about empty. I booked two singles, but she'll be able to manage a double."

The second and final change was on to a small station, surely forgotten in the campaign of scrapping such amenities. It seemed to rest at the bottom of what might be a dried-up moat.

"Br, they must be goats in these parts." Honeybody huddled into his overcoat.

A few feeble lights cast an anaemic glow which barely reached a derelict-looking packing case stencilled: 'Fresh food, urgent'. In what looked like a disused potting shed was a window with a holland blind, behind which blazed light.

"Come on," said the Inspector. He rapped at the window. The holland blind rose, revealing a scrawny man. The window was raised a couple of inches and a gust of warm stale air smelling of kerosene caressed them.

"What now?" said a thin voice.

"When does the train go off to Windlesham Parva?"

"This platform in 'arf an hour—if it's on time. If it is I'll give you my old pipe free of charge."

"Is there a waiting-room?"

"There was, but the old doctor sold it. 'E didn't believe in no cosseting. My cousin bought it, flogged the furniture, and 'as it as a 'en 'ouse."

"Thank you!" said Harry bitterly.

"Welcome I'm sure." Window and holland blind popped down, only a whiff of kerosene remaining hanging in the freezing air.

"Better walk up and down," said Honeybody.

The train was seventeen minutes behind schedule, so the skinny man kept his pipe. There were no first compartments but this hardly mattered as the carriages all appeared deserted. There was no heating, or none obtainable as Honeybody wrestled with a small brass lever.

"Let it alone and broach the whisky. Three stations, one at each!"

They drank at Snellbury, at Lower Plucksgutter and at Effingham. Then the old engine gave a sigh and bashed into the buffers of Windlesham Parva. Abruptly the lights went out.

"Hallo there!" bawled Harry.

There was no reply to the Inspector's call. Train crew—if indeed there had been one, the Inspector thought eerily—had melted into the night. Only the hiss of tired and overheated metal could be heard in the blackness.

"Must be a phone," said Harry, fumbling and thanking the ordinance that provided that a torch be carried at all times. "Get your torch, Sergeant," he said as he flashed the beam of his own, "and take Elizabeth. I'll go ahead."

They went through a dismal little gap in an iron railing.

"Probably a box outside," said Harry veering left.

"Christ," said Elizabeth, "a bull."

"Steady!" said Honeybody as Elizabeth clutched him.

"Her's a cow," said a beery voice.

"She shouldn't be out in this weather," snapped Harry.

"I just bought her. She's been snug as an owl in the public bar. I told ol' Mrs. Jewel there weren't no rule against 'aving a cow in the public and the dart team took my side. Put out she was, but I told 'er nothing could 'urt that old lino she's got."

"Where's the phone?"

"They took 'em away. The ol' doctor what makes the Beecham's pills 'ad it done when 'e owned the lot. Line closes next month. 'Ow'll you get 'ere then? Giddup, Daisy...." They saw the gumboots under a thick brown coat, and heard a crow of compounded malice and self-satisfaction.

"Not for the first time," said Honeybody, "I thank God I was raised in a city slum. We had manners there. If we have to walk I think I can find it."

There was a road of sorts. Harry cursed whoever the nine-teenth-century squire was who had sufficient influence to keep the station away from his village. Now the position was reversed, he mused as they trudged along, all sorts of influence from modern-day commuting squires to keep their ruddy stations. He was conscious of headlamps.

"Can't be anywhere without a car coming . . ." he started to say.

"Can I trouble you please?"

My God, he thought, and walked into the headlight's beam.

"Am I seeing things?" said Milton Greenaway.

"Only me, the wife and the Sergeant."

"Do you know a pub called the Dendles?"

"Can you give us a lift?"

"Try cramming in the back."

Elizabeth sat on the Inspector's knee, while Honeybody, with difficulty and haunches first, eased into the little car.

"Straight ahead, sir, there's a main road, turn left," the Sergeant said.

"We had trouble with the timing, waited an age to get it fixed plus advice about a short cut," muttered Greenaway. "Thank God there's no fog."

"Queer you going to the same pub!"

"Hearman says it's the best nosh for fifty miles around, plain but scrumptious. We ordered goose for tomorrow. I may as well explain that we have been employed to look into poor Prettyman's estate, hence the luxury."

Peering past his wife's tawny head, the Inspector made out the outline of Hearman rather slumped in his seat.

"Well met, Mr. Hearman, but you look travel worn."

"I hate car travel," grunted the clerk, without his usual good humour. "A pullman now, respectable, neat waiters pouring brandy into balloon glasses, steak and mushrooms and a bottle of something in the dining car, back for a nap. That's something else."

"You're joking!" said the Inspector. "Apart from the Sergeant's sagacity in stocking up with grog and fried fish, plus our own little contribution of tinned tongue," the Inspector squeezed Elizabeth who nuzzled his ear, "our journey would have been hell on earth. No heat, no light, imbeciles in gardening huts, demented cowmen, old engines, crews that vanish, disapproving passengers. . . ."

"That's why I hate to travel," said Hearman. "My great-grandpa, now, mostly first was above his touch, but he did all right in third. If he wanted a hamper he threw a note through the window going through a station and there it was, napkin round the cutlery, at the next stop. And good civilised drinking."

"My gran said the soot dust got imbedded in her navel," argued Harry.

"But in those days," said Hearman, "you just pulled a bloody great piece of wire with a nob on the end and the landlord sent up the boots with a hip bath and chambermaids with buckets of hot water. You had your bath in front of a roaring fire and damn the carpet."

"I remember the waitin'-room with the roaring coke fire and the big old settees," said Honeybody. "It was a night like this I met this red-headed bird and we got off for a drink at Carlisle. I was twenty and 'ad been in training for three months. We got engrossed and suddenly the barmaid said she was closing and the train had gone two hours ago. So . . ." Manoeuvring Elizabeth on to his left knee, Harry directed his elbow well into the Sergeant's now fleshy ribs.

"Silence," he said, "except for the radar job."

It was striking midnight from some public clock as they reached the Dendles.

"Well," said Mr. Jewel—the door opening a fraction before Harry's knuckles could register on it. "Inspector James and the Sergeant. Oh and Mr. Hearman, thought you were never coming, we did. Here's the missus."

Mrs. Jewel was as stout and comfortable as the Inspector remembered. He introduced the landlord and landlady to his wife and Greenaway.

"We'd just better get to bed, Mr. Jewel."

"I must admit I'm famished," said Greenaway.

"I put out a bit of ham, glazed you know, and some pickled walnuts, stuff like that, in the snug," said the landlady.

"I suppose a steak is out of court?" smiled Greenaway.

"You'll find the cold collation and a bowl of Jewel's Bishop very good, sir, and since you were here last, Inspector, we put in electric blankets. If you'll come this way."

Jewel huffed in with Hearman's and Greenaway's luggage. Honeybody effortlessly heaved up the rest.

"I'll carry it up, Mr. Jewel, you get to bed."

"Well, it has been a long day—been out buying. You're just up the stairs, the first four rooms. The last is the double. Made this morning for parties that cancelled, and the bed aired."

They took their seats round the dying fire in the snug, warm and cosy with the smell of ale on the woodwork.

The meal was good, the pickled walnuts, Honeybody opined, being of a five-year-old vintage. Sweat stood out on the Sergeant's brow as his dipper repeatedly plunged into Mr. Jewel's Bishop. Greenaway and Hearman did themselves well, and Harry saw Elizabeth dig into the glazed ham and pineapple and a bottle of light ale. For himself he toyed with the cheeseboard.

"I suppose you'll be burrowing around Prettyman's remains," said Greenaway, "like us, only for different motives."

"I suppose so." The Inspector had no great relish for work being discussed in the private area of his eating.

"As you haven't a car, you and the Sergeant—and your charming wife if she goes along—are welcome to cram into my old crate."

"I'd better hire one." The Inspector speared a piece of Stilton. "Just in case it develops into a cops and robbers chase, me pursuing old Prettyman's staff along Kent side roads. Let's see, he had a managing clerk named Peter Winding. How is it pronounced, like the elements or a watch?"

"I was told like the wind that blows. I'll try to intrude on your investigations as little as possible. I'm interested in drawing a plan to liquidate Prettyman's estate as advantageously as possible."

"Parm me, gents," Harry noted that besides her night robe Mrs. Jewel wore something rather like a turban swathing her hair, "but his lordship . . ."

"Thank you, Mrs. Jewel, thank you. Now which is Mr. er, Greenaway? I'm Redapple."

He was a tall lank man in a grey coat and hat. His voice was a high tenor and there was a drawn, flickering expression about his face that the Inspector registered as 'nervous'. Oddly, in the adverts they were solid, squat persons, but in life the twitchy person tended to be thin.

"I'm Greenaway," said the barrister, "and this is . . ."

"Quite, quite," said Lord Redapple, events obviously seething in his bosom, "I heard it on the news last night and was straight away on the blower to my accountant in Ramsgate. He started work first thing this morning. Some trouble with the clerk at Prettyman's. Impertinence! I rang up your chambers and they said you'd be down. I thought you should know."

Harry saw coldness creep, perhaps involuntarily, into Greenaway's eyes as he said, "You have no reason, Lord Redapple, to believe the trust accounts are not accurate?"

"Oh, no, no, no, but he was a strange fellow, and with money, you never can be sure." His lordship twitched.

"Good night all." The Inspector rose and shepherded Honeybody and Elizabeth out. Somebody darted up the stairs and he thought it was the landlady.

"'Ot on the job before the body's cold, like some good undertaker," grunted Honeybody on the stairs.

"You get frightened when you get money," said Harry. "Prettyman might have been a deep one. We'll see."

5

In a way the Inspector was relieved that both Greenaway and Hearman were at the mouth-wiping stage when they got down to breakfast. Whilst at home he was relaxed in dressing-gown and slippers, he found the formal hotel occasions trying. And if Elizabeth was eupeptic at breakfast, which was her inclination, Honeybody resembled nothing quite so much as a large grinning, mustachioed bear, its stomach almost audibly welcoming the day's promise of food and drink.

He buried himself with porridge and black coffee behind a paper, smelling Elizabeth's kedgeree and Honeybody's inevitable kippers.

"This is very good, Mrs. Jewel, I didn't know it could be so good," he heard his wife say.

"It's pepper, dear. You young girls"—he almost heard Elizabeth purr—"don't get to understand about pepper till you're an old lady like me."

"By the way, Mrs. Jewel," said the Inspector putting down his paper, "is there a car for hire around here?"

She pursed her lips for a moment. "There's Mr. Cockling— little garage a hundred yards away—has one but," she hesitated, "well, like all of us Cockling has his own funny little ways, and, well, he won't have nothing to do with policemen, sir, so if you go, keep mum, as they say."

"What's his gripe?" The Inspector was professionally interested.

"It's a long story," the landlady's mouth closed for a moment, "but suppose you was tourist, love, down for the point-to-point on Saturday, and Mr. Honeybody could be your uncle," she blinked at the Sergeant, "no, perhaps your wife's uncle, you being on the skinny side, without offence."

Harry burst into laughter. "I haven't enjoyed a breakfast more in years. Thanks, Mrs. Jewel. By the way," he said to Elizabeth, "have you got your driver's licence?"

"Of course." Elizabeth did not sound in too good a temper and the Inspector allowed himself the faint ghost of the smirk which he knew annoyed her.

"You'd better do the hiring, love, mine's a police licence."

"Oh, I'll help you in your piddling perfidy."

When she talked like that she was nearing combustion point. The Inspector was experienced enough to make a note to back pedal. Honeybody, victor and victim of twenty-eight years of marital battle, seemed to have faded into the landscape, not even making the loud crunching noise on his marmaladed toast that was his wont.

A woman in what looked like an old ski suit minded Mr. Cockling's petrol pump. She jerked her thumb at the shed at the back on which faded blue paint proclaimed 'Jas. Cockling repairs'.

The interior was festooned with old pieces of machinery, some hanging suspended from the roof. There was a smell of rusting iron and old grease. Mr. Cockling, a tubby little man, was between a smoking kerosene stove and what might have been the remains of a very old motor bike.

"Car for 'ire, yus, two quid a day, no extries."

"We're here for the point-to-point, me and my wife and her uncle," said Harry, fetching out his wallet, "I'll pay a week in advance."

Damn them, he thought, depriving him of an Acting Chief Inspector's car. So they would pay for a week.

"Gotcha licence?" asked Cockling, obviously hoping they had not one.

"My wife will do the driving." Elizabeth produced her licence.

"Wimming drivers!" Cockling surveyed it doubtfully. "'Alf my slavin' away comes from them."

"I guarantee that wasn't a woman." Elizabeth pointed to the motor bike ruins.

"Gave four bob for it at the jumble sale. Built things to las' then. I'll make out yer receipt I suppose."

While Cockling searched among the grimy paper on a kitchen table, the Inspector's gaze alighted upon a vehicle in a corner, where a fanlight allowed a greasy beam of sunlight to illuminate what he thought might be a motor hearse.

"Here we are," said Cockling, proffering a dirty piece of paper. "One week, fully insured but you up for the first ten quid, no extries. There she stands, with two quid's worth of oil in 'er wot you can pay me now for, ta."

"How old is she?" said the Inspector with a quietness which surprised himself.

"Well," Cockling shuffled, "she gets the regular tests, goes like a clock."

"How old is she?" From the corner of his eye the Inspector saw Honeybody move forward.

"Well, say 1928," said Cockling, hastily stuffing the pound notes into a kangaroo-like flap in his dungarees. "Take the receipt. You 'ave her for a week."

"What does she do?"

"Well, say fifteen per gallon, taking her kind and sweet, and say a pint of oil every twenty or so. But I 'ope the little"—he looked at Elizabeth appraisingly—"I mean the lady can double declutch."

"I learned it at school." Elizabeth had a disconcertingly cold eye when she wanted.

"Well, 'ere's yer licence susstificate back and 'ere are the keys. Simple one, two, three, four on the change and right forward and back for reverse."

The car had bits attached to it with brass screws. It looked as though it had a private chapel and toilet concealed among the slabs of mahogany coachwork. It smelled, not unpleasantly, of very old leather, like a decent club.

Harry got in the back, feeling the old upholstery envelop

his buttocks. Nostalgically he was reminded of his grand-father's funeral and the slow procession up a winding provincial lane.

Honeybody sat beside Elizabeth, his hand gently flapping the gear change. "That's the self-starter," said Mr. Cockling, "and there's a starting 'andle in the back. Good job you got two 'ealthy men, though. Mind the 'and brake. With the best will in the world—two linings this year—she's 'eavy to 'old."

Elizabeth first pressed the brass knob, but as Mr. Cockling smiled pulled the brass knob and jumped in her seat as a great snarling throb came from the old car's innards. "Clutch and the gear forward left," muttered Honeybody without moving his mouth. "Keep her in first, you've two feet either side of the door."

Elizabeth crawled out conscious of Mr. Cockling estimating the first ten pounds' worth of damage.

"Round the bend," said the Sergeant, "then stop."

By the side of a rotting haystack the Sergeant and Elizabeth changed places.

Honeybody's thick neck twisted in deference to protocol. "I had my first hernia in one of these jobs, sir, driving the Deputy Commissioner around. I reckon the knack will come back quick."

"Go with God," said Harry.

The Sergeant's first change-up produced a dreadful grinding of metal, but gradually his heel-and-toe technique came in smoothly. "That fat little bastard knows his work," said Honeybody. "Listen to that engine. You don't hear that nowadays."

"Only near London Airport," said the Inspector, with a shudder.

"You need soul to appreciate these old crates," said Honeybody. "I did my courting in a 1924 model a friend loaned me. You have no idea of the comfort."

"Get a move on," snarled the Inspector.

"I'll proceed gently, sir." The Sergeant's great hands massaged the wheel as they bowled for a few minutes between hedges.

Honeybody slowed as they approached what was evidently the main, indeed the only, street of Windlesham Parva.

He stopped. "The foot brakes are all right, but I don't know about the hand. Look here, sir, these yokels are a nosey lot of devils. When I joined I got an emergency stationing near Reading. There was a barmaid there who came from Putney, so both being from outer space as you might say . . ."

"Get to the point," rasped Harry.

"Well, no need to emphasise our trade, sir. We could slip this old battler into the pub yard—there's the sign ahead, 'The Duck and Gaiters', give 'em some kind of cock story and say we'll be having a drink around twelve. Then discreetly to the soliciting."

"And assuring your great throat of a nosh of boilermaker's mate!"

Honeybody's eyes were bland as he craned round.

"He's right, you know," said Elizabeth, poisonously.

"All right!" said Harry, "all right!"

The landlord of the 'Duck and Gaiters' was agreeable, even faintly curious.

"Down here for the point-to-point," said Harry.

The landlord gazed at the oppressed skies and said, "Waste of time. Sir Henry'll cancel."

"And I've always thought of a little bit of property in this pretty spot," said the Inspector, glimpsing the green slime of the village pond underneath a clothes line which seemed to hold a great many flesh-coloured elastic undergarments.

"Ah," said the landlord, "I might have just the place for you. A sweetly pretty little bungalow out Frottling way, three beds and a built in hi-fi with records thrown in."

"We'll have a talk over a glass," said the Inspector.

It was going to be one of those mornings, he thought, as they walked away. "Why the hell is the population of these islands perpetually dealing in real estate?" he said. "It was always my cover—looking for a house to buy. There was never anything *to* buy, but now I suffocate under bungalows, wallow in own-your-own bathrooms."

"I think I saw Prettyman's to the left," said Honeybody, "it's just that you might just as well sell your little bit and live off the council. Me and Dodo was only talking the other day. Our little house could be joined on to the fish and chips—of course, sir, this isn't official—and made a caff of. The kids are living away and they got these two-roomed flats for old folk and if I aren't old I feel it. And there's Dodo's uncle on the committee. It's progress, sir, can't stand in the way of it."

Elizabeth giggled. Honeybody always restored her to good humour.

The office of Prettyman, Benjamin, Trotter and Cope looked as though things might have been sold there two hundred years ago. Around 1780, thought Harry, and kept up bloody well, the sort of continuous restoration process that costs a packet.

"Perhaps the back entrance," said Honeybody. "I can feel eyes on my arse, pardon me, Elizabeth."

"Okay with me, nunc."

"You start slinking around back entrances in the sticks, comrades," said Harry, "and they're two steps ahead of you or behind, as the Sergeant so charmingly says. Boldly is the ticket."

The Inspector raised his voice. "They might know something about real estate here. Let's try, uncle. Come my dear."

From the corner of his eye he saw a man in a white coat, freezingly hosing before 'F. Smith. Purveyor of Fish and Choice Birds', start like one of his own pheasants in the shooting season.

"It'll be around town in two shakes of a bird's tailfeathers," said Harry, "that the supply of suckers has been renewed."

The outer office held an elderly woman who had been crying. She sniffed and the Inspector gave his best smile and said, "Believe me, I don't want to add to your troubles. I am a police officer and I suppose we should see Mr. Peter Winding."

"I'll phone him." She switched the little intercom panel. "Mr. Winding, it's police, now." A great tear rolled down one cheek.

"I'll be out." The voice was pleasant with rural undertones.

"Look here," said Harry, "this is my wife, Elizabeth. There's a tea shop along the way. I prescribe black coffee and a piece of cake. You won't do any good here."

"I'm Miss Bramble." She was middle-aged and dignified apart from the marks of grief. "It's that swine Redapple and his manner mainly, I think. Thank you, I would like coffee."

Elizabeth looked catlike—her passion for sleuthing was

94

never sufficiently gratified—as she accompanied Miss Bramble to the door.

For some reason the Inspector had thought of Peter Winding as small, clerkly and wizened. As it was he saw a tall, rather disorganised man with a curly shock of grizzled hair and an oddly boyish expression.

"Come in, come in. We're crammed with people, but this is an old barracks—literally in 1800—and full of dismal old rooms. Can't keep all of it up, just the front part." He led the way through a swing door, past two mahogany doors and to a back section which smelled of decay.

"Can't keep the humidity out. Two hundred years of damp. In here."

The room had obviously belonged to a deceased partner. There was an air of Victorian cosiness, the very chairs crowned with anti-macassars and something in the corner that might have been a commode or perhaps a rocking chair by William Morris. Was there a rocking commode, the Inspector thought wildly, among the Victorian comforts? On a massive desk was a curiously contorted oil lamp, but some reticent light came through a small window. The door was draught-proofed by a mouldering bombazine curtain on rings.

"I should say," said Winding, producing a pipe and fumbling it in a pouch in the best tradition of the sport, "that Lord Redapple put the auditors in yesterday and they are faithfully, if unavailingly, seeking felony. He is a proper bastard, in French or ancient Greek."

"Why?" said Harry.

"The Redapple Trust. His lordship wants to break it. It stands at nine million. Redapple's a financier in a big way, always wanting capital. Granted he knows how to use it. He says he'd rather have five hundred thousand cash than his family the interest in perpetuity. The governor didn't see it that way. 'You wait until I'm in my coffin', he said."

Harry looked at him sharply, but the youthful naïveté had not changed. Probably a figure of speech, verbal coinage only, he thought.

"I've a feeling I'll have to put this blasted Estate in my report. Fill me in, please," he said, getting out his notebook.

"Redapple himself appeared around 1818, the first of the

patent-medicine kings. As you know," said Winding with the air of a man on his hobby horse, "the eighteenth-century papers were full of quite bright advertisements for cures for V.D., but Redapple sensed the tide would turn. His universal cure-all never mentioned pox, it was all-embracing, vague, respectable, neatly boxed and advertised and tasted of cinnamon. Kids loved it. Oh, he had a stomach soother made out of opium for empire builders, and a corn cure in an overcrowded market. He died in 1861 leaving nine hundred thousand pounds, not the biggest of its kind, but nice to have when brandy was a bob a bottle."

"Phew!" The Inspector whistled.

"Only the start came out of his bottled filth. He got in on South Wales coal and Cornish tin and financed cargoes to Australia. A lot of ships went down, but those that got there ... oh, boy," said Winding with his strange juvenility, "one needle sold for a bob ... oh, boy! He founded the Trust in fifty-eight, rather an innovation in this country. It specified that the estate should be administered 'at the sole discretion of the trustees for the benefit of my natural children and their legitimate descendants and the natural children of my brother and their legitimate descendants until the end of the world'.

"You see, shockingly vague. Nobody knew he had a brother. He never married, but was an old ram. They traced six bastards he had recognised, four girls and two boys, many others having died in infancy as they did then. One boy, officer in the Guards, God knows how old Redapple wangled that one without actual forgery, died in the Crimea, the girls remained spinsters at Worthing and the other boy was the great-grandfather of the present incumbent.

"Now the whole point was—and is—that the will was idiotic." Winding tamped down his pipe and waved it. "What solicitors did then was to refer it to Chancery for a decision. In the case of big estates with a very dicky sort of will, like this one, proceedings went on until there was literally nowt left. Lovely 'oggings for the lawyers; coachmen, mansions on Muswell Hill, fat red necks in the Athenaeum, but the Prettyman of the day didn't do it. Collapse of the fat lady! He got the known heirs in and explained that if they started complaining they'd be likely to do the lot. Everybody'd scented blood, but with the heirs forming a united front, so to speak, it was no go and the will was probated; it only needed one twopenny-ha'penny legatee—a hundred quid and my second best bed job—to have complained and, bonkers, the nine hundred thousand would have gone to Serjeant this and Sir Herbert that. But it didn't happen.

"Of course, Mr. Prettyman always admitted that overall his family probably made a better thing out of it in the long run than if they had run to Chancery. But now Redapple wants it divvied up. The heirs, known heirs, are three, Redapple, his son and his daughter. The boss wasn't having any.

"It was this 'brother' business that bothered the guv. In 1926 he got the definitive advice, from Sir Val Hebden, as cunning and dirty an old bastard as ever broke a good will. Passed on these many years—they say he found a loophole so that his fellow benchers had to bury him free. But he said any substantiated new heir could not claim retrospectively, but was entitled to an equal share in future income. And Mr. Chas was a very cautious man. He always said that if an heir turned up, the Estate had been managed so conservatively that no shadow of a claim rested against this firm. Hey . . . ."

The Inspector followed Peter Winding's eyes. The curtain covering the door appeared to move slightly. Winding was surprisingly light on his feet. He whipped the curtain back.

"You came in last, Sergeant. You closed this door?"

"I think so," said Honeybody, but with uncertainty in his voice. It was slightly ajar.

"Let me." The Inspector opened it and stepped into the dingy corridor. Possibly nerves, he thought but were there not the faint reverberations of soft, quick footsteps? He hurried along, opening and peering through doors.

The first two were empty and smelled of decaying books, the third disclosed the long, anxious face of Lord Redapple, poised, like a bird about to take off from a telephone wire, over the *Financial Times*, in the next, probably Winding's room, Milton Greenaway faced John Hearman over the desk, jabbing his finger into a file.

"Who's for tennis, chaps?" leered the Inspector and closed the door.

The next—and main—office had four men in it, calling

back to each other from what looked like ledger sheets. One boiled grey eye momentarily flicked over the Inspector.

"Repairs to Tupper outhouse, ninety-four, two, ten," declaimed a nasal voice.

Harry reverently closed the door.

"Nerves plus a wonky door catch and a creaky old building," he said to Winding. "But level, old boy, was Prettyman tickling the peter? Don't worry, it will come out and the quicker the better if so."

Winding smiled wearily. "Why old Redapple is on this caper is that he thinks the *smallest* irregularity would help his case. The bank, the other trustee, sided with the guv. Had to. My late master, sir, was an Edwardian gent with all that it entailed, including *not* tickling the till. Mr. Prettyman and the bank had a three-monthly audit which would make the Bank of England seem a trifle shady by contrast."

"I hear that your late master was a bit of a doer in his time."

"You looked at him and saw a quiet little gent. So he was, but he had lived, sir. I was with him forty years. Not a race meeting on a Saturday he ever missed and always with some old cronies at Ascot and Goodwood. Knew his grub and liked his cellar. At one time he had his seat at every first night."

"A gambler?"

"Oh, sir! Of course he had his account with Ladbroke's and the rails bookies accepted his nod. But he was a once-every-six-meetings sort of bettor, the type the bookies hate. Of course he lost overall, but over the years it cost him very little. Proportionately me and my five bobs have lost far more. No sir, he was a civilised, kind little man, and very formal. He bought a horse once, a nice filly, tail male bred to The Tetrarch, the flying rocking horse. Somebody in his club made a joke about the Trust Funds. He came back to the office white to the lips and told me he was selling her. She subsequently won seven races for the new owner. I reckon that bit of respectability cost him five thou in those days."

"A paragon."

Winding drew himself up with some dignity.

"He was a friend, sir, and a gentleman."

"You are bred to the law," said Harry soberly, "you know policemen cannot *be* gentlemen in the sense you mean it."

"I am sorry," said Winding, suddenly looking much smaller, "but, forty years . . ."

"He had no relatives living?"

"All right," said Winding. "He had a bastard in 1919. He served in Salonica, a place everybody has forgotten about. Got the M.C. but never used it. A leave job. I understand her husband was incurably insane, no annulment possible then. The kid was brought up by relatives in Edinburgh and had no knowledge of his father. Prettyman settled thirty thousand on him, and the boy—man now—is a consultant in surgery in Glasgow. I feel I've betrayed a trust."

"Nonsense," said the Inspector, "we would have found out. Your ex-boss will, metaphorically, be pinned upon our planning board inside a week. His name?"

Winding took out a notebook. "I'll write it. It seems less treacherous." He scribbled.

"You're staying on?"

Winding shrugged. "I told the local police about the will. I'll keep on until the new owner is settled in and maybe find some agency. . . . Our boy is in New Zealand. The wife and I might settle there, though it *is* far away."

"Who is the new trustee?"

"Whoever buys this firm. It should be snapped up."

"Is it not so that the main income derives from the Redapple Estate?"

"About sixty per cent, perhaps more if you take the licensed properties into account."

"So the new owner would want to retain it?"

"Yes." Winding was sweating slightly in the fuggy, damp air, product of never opened windows.

"So to retain the account—forgive me for using that term —the purchaser might side with Lord Redapple regarding the termination of the Trust?"

"You have legal advisers, I'm sure."

"So we have, Mr. Winding. Good day to you! Come, Sergeant!"

"I'd like to know more about that bloke, and that office," said the Inspector. "Both creepy."

"He had a guv for forty years," said Honeybody, "like an old father. When the umbilical cord finally breaks, it's hard . . ."

"And blast your pathology," snapped Harry, "and the hours you spend in forensic. *I* know all about that Cyprus sherry and medicinal alcohol caper."

"In a manner of speaking only, guv," said Honeybody.

"Get the car," said Harry, "I've had this place."

He leaned against the grocer's façade. 'Piggy Wiggy Super', said the red neon sign. He saw Elizabeth shaking hands with Miss Bramble, who walked rapidly back to her office.

"Where was she twenty minutes ago?" He shot the question at his wife as she joined him.

"In the loo, I guess. She made her face look human. Quite a time. Maybe ten minutes or more."

"Back entrance?"

"A clean old place. Specialises in scones. Nice waitress with the sniffs and an old lady with blue hair fumbling round the till. Could be, but why?"

"Somebody might be spying. Or it could be nerves."

"I don't like it," said Elizabeth, "she's a nice woman, but . . . I just don't like it. She did draw me a map of where these clients live. Nearest is the Benting Estate. They're most all mad."

"That makes my day."

Honeybody tooled the enormous car neatly beside them. "All aboard for the conducted tour," he said.

"Tell him where the Benting maniacs subsist," grunted Harry.

Elizabeth did, and then said, "Miss Bramble is the daughter of Mr. Prettyman's father's groom."

"Financial interest?"

"The father was a generous man—encouraged Bramble in little investments, likewise Miss Bramble. She is, well, storm-proofed; little bungalow, etcetera. She was in love with Charles Prettyman of course, but in a dutiful daughter way."

"I don't like this one bit." The Inspector was conscious that they were driving up a muddy side track.

"All right, sir," said Honeybody.

In the foreground gloomy light rested on a chain of glass houses on either side of a grassy strip. Two elderly females bent over bushes with secateurs.

"Better stay in the car," said Harry.

"I want to see any fun."

"All mad as hatters. I don't like it. Lock doors and stay put."

"To hear is to obey, master."

"That's the ticket, train 'em young," said Honeybody, portentously locking the driving door. "'Ere what's this?" Only in moments of utter astonishment or drunkenness did the Sergeant lose his aspirates.

A notice, in forgotten gold-leaf, dimly read: 'The Clive Benting Home for the Reform of Fallen Women'.

It was a stout oak notice supported by a kind of marble tomb.

Elizabeth, through the window, was pointing to it.

"This must be a joke, and I'm getting sick of it," said Harry.

"But the 'ouse is there, through the pines," said Honeybody.

It was a large, indeterminate place, the kind of late Georgian building erected when the Queen Anne original burned down after a drunken party. They trudged through mud to it. The same superscription, this time engraved on worn brass, anointed the door.

A respectable woman in charcoal grey answered their ring.

"We're police," said Harry, "we'd like to see the occupier."

Her face showed no surprise. "Certainly, sir, you want . . ."

"The Reverend Sebastian Rattle." A small stout man appeared from nowhere. He wore an ecclesiastical collar and a great many ecclesiastical ornaments, dotted around him, so that the Inspector never did fathom his denomination.

"Sebastian Rattle, resident Chaplain under the covenant," he said. "Police officers, eh, hum. Come into my, er, pish, sanctum sanctorum."

Which proved to be a littered, smallish room, next door to the cloak-room, filled with old magazines.

"Are the Bentings at home?" asked Harry, watching Honeybody wedge himself in what might have been a valuable but daintyish chair.

"Well," said Mr. Rattle, flushing slightly, "only Lady Edith is, ah, home at the moment. Lord Benting, not to put too fine a point on it, is ah, well deranged in the worst way. He kept following a bishop saying 'God is love'. His lordship was very upset, but fortunately—it was at a house party in aid of North Vietnam—there were two eminent Harley Street men there and, well, it is a delightful little place with very kind staff. I gave him a collection of eighteenth-century sermons and the dear fellow . . . perfectly happy, writes me letters about the Second Coming."

"What's this about fallen women?"

"Well, you see," Mr. Rattle showed signs of becoming businesslike, "in 1870 the tenth Lord Benting willed it so that the Estate became a home for, ar, fallen, um, women from a radius of twenty miles. The ships used to call at Windlesham Port in those days and, well, ar, nobody dreamed of a shortage. The family, one boy and eight girls, were allowed to live on the Estate and enjoy a quarter of the income. But, ar, unfortunately, if the, er, fallen ladies were not accommodated the whole lot went to ease the national debt."

"How many have you got?"

"One," said Mr. Rattle, shamefaced, "and that only by Mr. Prettyman's ingenuity."

"Do you mean that old Prettyman's duties included the provision of superannuated whores?" said Harry.

Honeybody was staring in fascination.

"Miss Gooding is a superior kind of, um . . . you see, it was the only way to preserve the Estate. After all, four hundred thousand pounds or so would scarcely save the economy. You see, sir, they seem to have done pretty well since the war and don't *want* to be saved, and, well, the sailors don't come here now and the police are pretty strict. So Mr. Prettyman took the opinion of Sir Jabeez Lusting who said it was not necessary for the lady to have, ar, practised here. If she was born here and ruined elsewhere, so to speak, it would suffice. The one we had at the time was ninety-six—Mr. Gladstone had remonstrated with her—and obviously, um . . . So we employed detectives —oh, private ones, not your, um, colleagues—and persuaded Miss Gooding to come down from Leeds."

"Is she genuine?" said Harry, scenting fraud.

"Oh, one hundred and twenty-seven convictions. We had, um, photostats. The trouble was that Miss Gooding is quite wealthy. You may have seen her big red Italian car about the village. They say it can, um, do one hundred and fifty miles an hour. We only got her here because her hobby is gardening since she retired and the Benting Gardens are famous. I may say our hollyhocks, um . . . well she and Lady Edith spend most of the day, when fine, in the garden or in the hot houses when wet."

"On Monday," said the Inspector, "were both women here all day? In particular the afternoon?"

"Oh, yes. The ladies had planned to lime wash the apples, but the day was utterly miserable. Fog in London, one is told, but here a fine drizzle all day and a bitter wind from the North Foreland—straight from the North Pole, one believes. So we had a cosy afternoon with crumpets and tea—the cook is excellent which is another reason why Miss Gooding . . . anyway I had my little American organ brought in, Lady Edith played the piano and Miss Gooding sang . . . er, I remember her beautiful rendition of 'Love Divine All Loves Excelling'. It would have been six when we partook of high tea; cook has a way with ham and eggs."

"Could you write down the, uh, the addresses of the other, um, Bentings?" It was catching, thought the Inspector, as Mr. Rattle produced a small address book and delved among the old magazines for pencil and paper.

"There," he said at length.

The Inspector thanked him and walked back to the car.

"Did you see all the fallen women?" asked Elizabeth.

"There's only one, an elderly lady with plenty of money, a desire for tea and crumpets, a fondness for gardening, and cosseted by a first-class cook."

"Don't they have all the luck!" said Elizabeth bitterly.

The Inspector was peering at the list. There were nine Bentings altogether in what the Reverend had termed 'homes' and one in Northern Italy, the annotation primly mentioning 'four able-bodied attendants'. More work, he thought, mournfully.

"Call in at the local station," said Harry. "Let other people do the dirty work."

"Hear, hear," said the Sergeant. "There's an inspector and fourteen men at Windlesham. I looked it up."

While Honeybody and Elizabeth waited in the car the Inspector went in to see the local inspector, named Botting, who greeted him with the usual mixture of camaraderie and suspicion, the latter based upon the possibility of extra work.

"No fears justified," smiled Harry, "I just want to bang something over your teletype."

The local man looked relieved as Harry listed the institutionalised Bentings plus Mr. Prettyman's youthful folly and requested a whereabouts at the time of the murder check.

"Pity about old Prettyman," grunted the Inspector. "A gentleman, not like some of these johnny-come-lately shysters. Redapple had it in for him. I was in the Constitutional Club one night, just quietly by myself in the corner with a pint before getting off home, when I heard Redapple sounding off, not too discreetly, I thought. His point seemed to be that old Prettyman had been battening off the Trust more or less since boyhood. Awful cock-and-bull, of course."

"You seem less than keen about the ennobled apple?"

"Well, people don't like him. In these parts old memories die hard and the progenitor was in trade, and patent pills at that, and all he fathered were bastards. Legend has it that no woman was safe from old Redapple. I must say he did quite a bit for the place; endowed a school for poor children—six-fifty per year today and a fancy great tie! Plus three cottage hospitals that the state took over and the parkland that they're putting the pylons on. The poor bloke's intentions seemed to have come to naught, as they say. Now the Trust may probably go."

"Think he could do it?"

"I was talking to Mr. Briggs—he represents the police when we want a solicitor—and he said probably, if all the current heirs agreed and the trustees did not object. Like breaking an entail, ingenious legal fictions involved. Now is the time. Hew Redapple, he's the son, is due to marry next year and if he has children, well, that makes it more complicated. Redapple's father died in 1950 and Inland Revenue would have a go at claiming estate duty at the rate prevailing then. As old Briggs said, you can't have your cake and eat it with these trusts."

"What I cannot fathom," said Harry, "is why a man who presumably gets the lion's share of the usury on nine million, plus being a big tycoon, wants money."

"These things defeat an honest man," grunted Botting. "It seems (a) Redapple's ambition has no end; (b) his firm are property developers and takeover dealers; (c) his business is like a poker game with no table limit; in certain circumstances a fellow with a bigger bank roll can edge you out. So half a million now is better than what he gets after the income tax have done with him. The trouble with trusts is that in avoiding death duty you run slap into the friendly arms of the income-tax bloke."

"What is young Hew Redapple like?"

"Twenty-three, just finished university. Ineffectual, but damned nice. Loves country life and won't join the old man in the city. There's really nothing the father can do. The boy plans to breed horses; he was quite a protégé of old Prettyman, y'know, and what the old gentleman did not know about bloodstock was not worth knowing."

Harry raised his eyebrows.

"Both Hew and his sister, Marouka—she's twenty-seven—used to stay at Prettyman's when Lord Redapple was abroad, he travels a lot. Lady Redapple died, let's see, fourteen years ago in an air crash. She used to tour a lot, my wife used to say it was to get away from Redapple when the kids were away at school, but you know how women go on."

Harry indicated that he did. "In view of this, I can't understand why they should agree to break the Trust."

Inspector Botting shrugged mournfully. "Money," he said.

"Is the boy at home?"

"Oh, yes, he's got workmen in, building stables; he bought half a dozen yearling fillies at Doncaster in September—they're at Beckhampton meantime. He's got the dream of training them, ruddy fool, but there, it's as good a way of wasting your money as any, although I think women would be my downfall. Oh, the girl's in North Africa. Spends her winters there. She's brainy, supposed to be writing a book of some kind."

Harry thanked him and rejoined the others. "You may repair to the pub, Sergeant, for a very early lunch. I see your thick lips are parched."

"Don't be so hypocritical, Harry James," said Elizabeth. "I never saw a man so sloshed as when you came home after they gave you the police medal."

"It was champagne and stout that night," the Sergeant said reminiscently, "put on by the Commissioner. I kept going round and round in the Inner Circle and you ought to have heard my Dodo, who'd had a hard evening with the fish."

The landlord, with a sly mention of the joys of the bungalow for sale at Frottling, took their order himself. As the Inspector had suspected when he looked around, it was pretentious restaurant French, doubtless cooked by some mournful Maltese, thinking of the sun. The spaghetti with meat sauce had the beginner's folly of too much *moutarde aux fines herbes* and chopped chicken liver; the rich meat and beer taste of *carbonnades flamandes* was messed up, the Inspector thought, by an infusion of thyme and monosodium glutamate. The caramel custard was honest, but almost certainly packaged. The bottle of red Bordeaux had a curious flatness. "Stop it, Harry!" the Inspector admonished himself, it was just one of those days.

"This is muck, ain't it?" Honeybody whispered, spooning a dip made of alleged Caerphilly cheese with distaste. "This is my favourite cheese, outside Stilton, but somebody's been and gorn and mashed it and put soap powder in it."

"Somebody's been reading Auntie Fathead's Continental Tips from Our Model Kitchen," said Elizabeth.

His wife was a bit that way inclined herself, thought the Inspector, but like all women very apt to criticise other people's cuisine.

"It is bloody," he said, "but I've told you about the food in the canteen."

"It's Dame Alice Grittle," said Honeybody. "She says, owing to the balance of trade, nobody should eat more than four pennorth of meat per diem. The Commissioner says we got to set an example so it's cottage pie, not even rissoles. It don't keep soul and soul-case together, Mrs. J. But for Dodo packing me a nice bit of fried Icelandic cod I don't know what I'd do."

"You do well on it!"

The Inspector winced at the bill, assured the publican that he would call for the keys of the bungalow at Frottling, and told Honeybody to drop them at Prettyman's office.

Peter Winding sat in the front office rather morosely eating salmon sandwiches.

"The telephone's been going all day. People wanting to know about the funeral."

"Next week, I would say."

"Redapple finally went home. I gather his auditors held out no hopes of a major deficiency," Winding sounded vicious. "Although they'll be at it for another two weeks."

"You'll still stay in charge?"

"In charge? Under young Mr. Greenaway! I suppose I am also subservient to his clerk!"

The Inspector clucked, feeling his ground. "Dear, dear, I feel sure that Mr. Prettyman would have foreseen . . ."

"He did, including the practice. A firm over at Windlesham have first option; as soon as I heard about the guv'nor I arranged for them to handle the day-to-day stuff. Oh, I and the boy do it, but they sign it. The trouble is the price. If Redapple manages to take the whole caboodle out, well, it's cut down sixty per cent. I suggested there should be some kind of contingency basis and a final arbitration when things have settled, but of course Mr. Greenaway's mighty intellect disdains anything I may say." Winding snorted and looked at his watch. "I sent the typist home, couldn't stand her sniffing away. My assistant's out at the brewery—some business about a tied house—and the gentry from London are obviously stuffing themselves somewhere at poor old Prettyman's expense. The accountants have had to go off this arvo on another job. Redapple was livid."

"Mind if we poke about a bit, getting atmosphere?"

"All you want. I must tell you that one of the boss's peculiarities was that he didn't use the office for personal things. Never wrote a personal letter or made an outgoing personal phone call. Once he scribbled a private postscript on a letter and solemnly put a halfpenny in the stamp box. Oh, he grinned at me, but he used to say that taking your private affairs to work robbed your employer and the Inland Revenue." Winding smiled affectionately at the memory.

"I note he carried travellers' cheques. Unusual?"

"He had his pocket picked in 1931 on Epsom Downs. He'd won sixty-nine quid and as in those days he betted for cash he had his bankroll of eighty pounds. Some light-fingered merchant copped the lot. The boss said 'Never again'. He carried a cigar case, a cutter and matches, wore a wrist watch, and had five-pound travellers' cheques in his wallet. He changed the cheques one at a time, so a pickpocket could never get more than, say, three quid off him. As it fell out he was never robbed again."

"This little book," the Inspector palmed the tiny notebook retrieved from Prettyman's effects. "From 1860 to 1872, various debits or credits." He glanced at Winding.

"I know about that," said Winding. "You see, when Lord Redapple got shirty he started on the maladministration business, the very thing to drive my guv'nor crazy. Mr. Prettyman started going through the ledgers from 1859, when the Trust virtually started. He thought of writing a paper for the Law Society, something like that.

"There were these unusual entries, noted as 'according to original instructions'. Oh, my God, not more than two thou collectively, and that opposed to the nine million that the Prettymans built the estate into. Then the guv started worryin'. Suppose Redapple alleged embezzlement? As far as we could work out—I nearly went blind in the process—they were cash withdrawals by the grandpa Prettyman, grandpa and the dad. And there were the lost secret instructions."

"Lord help me," said the Inspector, "what's this?"

"You know what a traction engine was?"

The Inspector saw Honeybody's face puff with impatience.

"Vaguely," he said, "collector's pieces now, one understands, in every with-it drawing-room, all stoked up."

"Bear with me," said Winding. "My guv was thirty and his dad was a fine fifty-three, sound as an oak log but for his deafness, almost stone-deaf and it was in the ear-trumpet days. He was standing with friends at the bottom of Tanhouse Hill waiting for the hunt—young Mr. Charles as he was then was out that day—might have taken over the Mastership if it hadn't happened. Anyway this blamed machine takes off down the hill, the coroner thought some urchins had sprung the brake, but it wasn't certain. The friends finally see it thundering down and get to the banks on the side of the road. Horace Prettyman stands confused—thinks the hunt's coming. He stands there yelling, 'Where are they drawing?' His friends scream, 'Come up, come up, man!' He stands there smiling and confused and the engine gets him. Finito, of course, strawberry jam. The point is that when Mr. Charles takes over he finds . . . now just a minute . . ." Winding lumbered over to a filing cabinet and unlocked a drawer. Abstracting a file he said, jerking his thumb, "This was one the young master forgot to ask me for the key to. Here."

It was a photostat of sheets written in the conventional Victorian legal orthography. "That one." Winding jabbed his forefinger.

"Certain oral instructions having been given by the said John George Redapple to George Horace Prettyman a trustee of the said Trust it is desired by the said John George Redapple that at sole discretion these instructions be given in perpetuity to one only trustee of the Trust."

Winding sighed. "One of these 'secret of the locked room' jobs, but my boss never got it. I think Redapple suspected; he once offered me a thousand quid—I'm not joking—to tell him if Mr. P. knew. The point was that non-fulfilment might be a factor in an annulment."

"Most of these secret, verbal clauses turn out potty when they get in the light," said Harry. "Like, 'See that Flo, the pretty housemaid, never starves'."

"That's what I always felt," sighed Winding. "He was *such* a ram, was old Redapple, progenitor. God knows what luggage he carried with him mentally."

"One thing, and just for form, what did you do on Monday afternoon, say between mid-day and six?"

"Ate my sandwiches," said Winding, simply, "cold lamb from Sunday, and then locked myself in my office. I told Miss Bramble and the junior I was not in to anybody."

Harry raised his eyebrows.

"The guv'nor had had me in," explained Winding, "about the licensed properties. There had been some kind of offer. In fact they are a nuisance; it might be better for them to be part of a company, shares of which to be held by the Trust. I was to make a complete précis of the position; our rights, our obligations, etcetera. So I locked the door—it was a rainy afternoon, turned up the gas radiator and away I went until six at night."

"The others were gone when you left?" Harry spoke very lightly.

"Oh, yes. They went at five-thirty. The wife and I had a quick meal and went to the flicks at Windlesham. We got home at ten—it was a terrible show—and the police were waiting outside the house."

"Thanks," said Harry. "We'll look around."

The property was probably going to be worth a lot one day, thought the Inspector; fourteen rooms, six above, unused, and eight below, plus stabling at the back, half an acre of land behind, roughly gardened and planted with shrubs, and a path leading from a back door into a country lane.

"Here," Honeybody paused in Winding's office, "you see this?" He reached over and pitched up the window. There were signs of oil on the frame. The Sergeant peered out, exposing a bulging serge-covered posterior. "Shinny out of this and I don't reckon anybody'd see. Get into the old lane and scarper."

"Motive?"

"Tickling, the old tap, as the embezzlers say."

"And he knifed his boss, after forty years, to conceal it!"

"You remember last year?"

Harry did, thirty years of marriage and arsenic to procure the insurance.

"No sentiment in this business, sir."

"Come on," said Harry.

"I am thoroughly sick of sitting in this car, as if one were in permanent attendance at a funeral," announced Elizabeth.

"That is well taken, as Mr. Prettyman might have said, but it's a fine day and I see you are wearing your twenty-five-quid coat, so what about communing with nature and walking the three miles to the Dendles? I am sure Mrs. Jewel has summit tasty round four. If we spot you we'll pick you up."

"Never been picked up in my life," said Elizabeth as she opened the great, heavy door and, mysteriously, made an elegant exit.

"You lie," said Harry. His wife turned and thumbed her nose at him.

Harry watched her strut magnificently away.

"The ancestral estate of the Redapples, I think."

Honeybody consulted the piece of paper that Elizabeth had earlier provided.

"Phew, eight hundred acres, the old homestead, plus prize Friesians and some pigs and glass houses."

"We will cringe and pull forelocks."

Honeybody chuckled and eased the car away.

The drive proved shortish and studded with Spanish oak.

"Staniswy, just a moment, Serge."

It was cunningly done, but amid the trees were ten or twelve small houses. The unpleasant word could have been bungalows, but these were rather nice plain cottages.

"We'll take a look," said Harry.

In the distance stood what was obviously 'the big house', but the vista was cunningly, but not obviously, landscaped. Their feet sank into long, wettish, springy grass. The gardens of the cottages seemed to be so contrived that they ran together but were separated by contoured land and trees.

An elderly gentleman with a small red face was limping under a plane tree. Surprisingly he said, "Hallo, Inspector."

It was without wig and trappings and Harry gawped. The Sergeant, a living camera, murmured, "Justice Lumping."

"Good afternoon, sir," said Harry, standing erect. "I had no idea."

"Not working. Broke my leg, not back until Wednesday week. Redapple rents little places here. We keep one; use of swimming pool when it is usable and his son lets out a hack when you want it."

Mr. Justice Lumping was not a particularly good judge. In fact it was rumoured among the juniors of the profession that counsel, addressing the Appeal Court, had commenced, "My lords, this appeal arises from a judgment by Mr. Justice Lumping. Of course, there are other grounds." Inevitably, as in every generation of judges, there was a 'Mr. Justice Necessity', and in this day it was the unfortunate Justice Lumping who qualified.

The Inspector thought that probably Mr. Lumping, who had written standard books on seventeenth-century legal thought, had become mentally shipwrecked in that fascinating century and was not particularly interested in current happenings. He was a pleasant, shrewd man with a large and comfortable wife who knitted very long scarves.

"Redapple," Lumping said as they walked, "complex man. Descended on the bastard side—wonder why people misuse *bar sinister*? I must not digress. Strong urge to be wealthier than anybody else. You know his companies?—I wish to God I'd put my little bit in them twenty years ago, but come in, come in, Mrs. Lumping brews tea early."

Mr. Justice Lumping's kind heart was well known, if eccentric. It was said that his practice of awarding fourteen years for comparatively small offences was in the belief that the Court of Appeal, appalled, would revamp the sentences to less than that which legal practice required of him. Occasionally, of course, it did not work that way, and the judge was reputed to be extremely perturbed.

"Take a general look around, Honeybody," said the Inspector. "Find out if Lord Redapple is at home."

"Very good, sir."

Mrs. Lumping looked faintly apprehensive. Harry at first thought she might have mistaken him for the very discreet intermediary suggesting retirement on full pension; then he remembered Mr. Justice Lumping's tendency to get caught between floors in lifts, to fall, immersed in some abstruse document, into small pools containing carp, even once, at Devizes, getting his full-bottomed wig caught in the hairpins of the Lord-Lieutenant's lady as he bowed low to hand her from the official car.

"No trouble, my love," said the Judge. "Inspector James, C.I.D., on the Prettyman business."

"Tea's cooking, such a nice little man," said Mrs. Lumping. "Too early for scones, Inspector?"

Refuse a scone and you have an enemy for life, thought Harry with some gloom, but behind a false scone-happy expression. He wondered why judges always smelled rather mouldy, in a decent public school and university way, of course.

"Monday he was killed, I see," said the Judge. "I appreciate your dilemma ... these homicidal killings ..."

"We do not know whether to attribute it to the maniac," said Harry. "There was some trouble, perhaps, of a professional or personal nature."

He saw the judge flinch.

"Bad blood between Prettyman and Redapple?" he pressed.

Mrs. Lumping brought in a tray and busied herself with

ritual. Mr. Justice Lumping fixed his eyes on the ceiling.

"I have to be careful, Inspector, if only because a judge in the witness box is not unheard of, one named Pointing in 1625 gave evidence of simony, not very creditably, one fears, but . . ."

"Let 'em go," thought the Inspector gloomily as he masticated a rather good scone.

"On Monday last," said Justice Lumping, "it was a dreadful rainy day. My surgeon, Mr. Parrot, impresses on me the essential need to walk a mile each afternoon. I must say it reminds me of the old practice of requiring a condemned man to watch his own funeral service. . . ."

"How did you do it, sir?" Harry oozed sympathy.

"He fell down one of those nasty London holes," said Mrs. Lumping. "Walking along reading a White Paper . . . plunged into it . . . notices all around, but no, down he went."

"I do not care to discuss it, my dear." There was a cold ring in Mr. Justice Lumping's voice. He coughed. "This was at noon. I recall hearing twelve strike from St. Nicholas' Church. I was a mile off to the east. My love, get me my ordnance map."

Mrs. Lumping sighed, but obliged.

Lumping pointed.

"Approximately half a mile from this house, which is here, stands a small grove of beech trees at the side of a secondary road. It is on the perimeter of the Redapple Estate. I was walking slowly, thinking of a paper I'm writing—a rather interesting, but never mind—when I saw a small blue car concealed in between the trees. I vaguely recognised it as one of the Redapple cars, the shape, you know."

"The make, sir?"

"I think the small Volkswagen they use for shopping. I stopped, and as I did I saw Lord Redapple get in. I don't know why—atavistic instinct perhaps—but I withdrew behind an elm and heard the car go past. It came out on to the grass, turned and proceeded down a small farm track leading to the road."

"No possibility of error?"

"I am much afraid not."

"What is the local opinion of Redapple?"

"You know I dislike gossip, but"—the Judge gave the conventional gambit of the born gossip—"it's a divided household, one is afraid. The girl, a blue stocking, fancies herself as another Lady Hester Stanhope, rarely in England. The boy, good enough in his way, but has nothing in common with the father. Ah, well . . ."

The Inspector expressed his appreciation for the scone and met Honeybody returning. "Through them trees, sir," said the Sergeant, pointing to a thick stand of elms. "Barracks of a place with turrets all over."

Of the eighteen forties, thought the Inspector, not a bad period, but he wondered who the devil had produced this tessellated and turreted abortion which kept wandering into gothic castle and timidly retreating into Italian lavatory.

"There's a blue Volks somewhere," he said. "Try to find it and see whether there's mud on her."

The Sergeant melted away before a middle-aged woman answered the Inspector's ring at the massive metal door. The Inspector remembered that the original was in Florence. A beautiful thing except that the large porch was, on both sides, decorated by mosaic scenes of English history, all the kings having massive beards.

He handed over a card and with no formality walked along a long hallway smelling of some kind of preservative and into a pleasant long room which culminated in a french window looking out on to one of the largest collections of roses he had ever seen. Wonderful in summer, now fraught with the melancholy of winter.

At close quarters Lord Redapple exhibited the same uneasy nervous energy that the Inspector remembered from the previous evening. He twitched the card between long fingers.

"I suppose it's about Prettyman."

"Yes, sir, as a matter of ordinary procedure we have to ascertain where people who knew him were between noon and seven p.m. on Monday."

"You'll have a job. He knew everybody. It sometimes seemed to me I could not pass a house without seeing him come out." He smiled and Harry noticed with surprise that in repose his face was not only handsome but singularly attractive.

"As for me," said Redapple, "I may as well tell you we are

hardly a united family and rarely dine en famille. In any case I am one of those unfortunates to whom food has little appeal. I regret it when I see my fellow board members tucking into their guinea-fowl. So when I am on a big job I retire to this room with a patent machine which provides, so it seems, infinite coffee, a large plate of ham sandwiches, lock the door and disconnect the telephone."

"Which you did on Monday?"

"I went in here about eleven a.m." He hesitated. "There's no great secret in the circumstances. The P.M. asked me for an opinion regarding future capital investment in South America. The Treasury had boiled the stuff down, but there was nevertheless a small suitcase full of paper. At about ten I saw daylight, went out for a breath of air—it was still raining here. Then I returned, the housekeeper made me a plain omelette and some Ovaltine, and so to bed."

"Fine," said Harry. "I understand your daughter's in Morocco."

"Marrakesh, so I believe."

"And the boy?"

"Hew? He is doubtless supervising the erection of loose-boxes of a new and luxurious design, for the lodging of very expensive four-legged animals." Although Redapple smiled it did not reach his eyes and a nerve twitched in one temple.

"I understood that he was going to have a small stud and train a bit."

Redapple had the air of having something on his chest. "When this business came up I went so far as to talk to a horse trainer who I was introduced to. He surprised me by being a hard business man, originally an accountant in the debt-collecting way. He employs experts in their line. He told me that if you pet a young horse it becomes quite useless for work, and that racehorses must be subjected to a ruthless, even harsh régime, if they are to win. My son is installing central heat in the boxes, he will overfeed them, under-purge them, and as he is constitutionally unable to arise before nine-thirty, his horses —string, I believe is the term—will be exercised later than any others in the kingdom. Oh, well, he's his own master."

"Nice little houses you have to the west. I had tea with old Justice Lumping."

"I'd hate to be up before him," grunted Redapple. "Oh, the houses are nice and don't bother us. In any case as this is destined to be a nest for stable boys I shall retire to my flat in town. If I had power I'd have sold here years ago."

"I do not want to be impertinent, sir, but do you suspect embezzlement?"

"Oh," said Redapple, "I remember I glimpsed you last night. I am sorry if I was discourteous, but . . . you see it was a chance to jump in. No, I doubt that Prettyman or his oafish clerk embezzled—although there were rumours that Prettyman liked a flutter—but I'd like to find some gross error, a fundamental breach of the Act. But if not I'm going to be so damned unpleasant that Prettyman's successor will see it my way. Dammit, it's not as if I won't be generous to vested interests if the thing is wound up!"

His face twitched. "This central heating is up too high. I keep telling them. You see, Inspector, Prettyman was an obstinate little fellow who'd been drawing twelve thousand or more a year from us since Doomsday. And the Prettymans before him. Those houses were his suggestion. You see he would bounce up and state that last year the Trust returned, say, forty thousand more income. But that merely went to taxation, to all intents and purposes. And being conscientious I spend roughly two days a week going into repairs of farm buildings, dwellings, office blocks that return me virtually nothing. But he would or could not see it. And one day such a Trust will be ruled illegal. Only lack of legislative time has so far precluded it; when it occurs we will be worse off than by voluntary dissolution."

"I see. Well, thank you, sir."

It was nastier than usual, thought the Inspector, as he went out to where Honeybody was waiting. About a hundred years since a lord was found guilty of murder. What was his name? He could not remember. It was unlikely that one of the twenty odd of the Queen's Bench judges should have gone off his head —hadn't happened since Victorian days. The Inspector groaned.

"Something bad, sir?"

Harry told him.

"That's just what we wanted," said the Sergeant lugubri-

116

ously. "I found the garage. There was an odd job man cleaning a small blue Volks. I got him talking and scraped a bit of mud unnoticed into my hankie."

"Fine," said Harry. The lab could do wonderful things with mud.

"Five cars altogether. A shooting brake sort of thing, the Volks, a big Austin, a small Bentley and an elderly MG."

"I think the work is going on over there," said Harry. They walked a hundred yards to the right of the house.

There seemed to be fourteen loose-boxes and a double-storey house, rather featureless, being erected.

The master builder, obviously so from his comfortable figure, was talking to a thin young man, who was fingering a blueprint.

"Mr. Redapple?" said Harry, smiling.

"Indeed."

"Scotland Yard. Harry James, Acting Chief Inspector, and Sergeant Honeybody."

"About old Prettyman, no doubt. By the way this is my builder, George Pinkman. I can recommend him."

"It's just that we're checking the whereabouts on Monday of anyone who knew Prettyman."

"I was here all day. A scourge to George."

"Rope round my neck, but he was here, Inspector. He invited me back to the great house for a bite. I left him around eight after we'd gone through things."

"Routine, routine," said Harry, noting from the corner of his eye that Honeybody had scraped an acquaintance with the gang round the cement mixer.

The builder walked away.

"I just had a yarn to your dad," said the Inspector. There was not too much resemblance, he thought, Hew being a foot shorter and broader and darker in his features.

"The woe, the woe," said Mr. Redapple. "Me sins, me sins. You might as well know, in case it involves your thinking, that Dad and I do not agree. If you were the run-of-the-mill son of a famous father you'd know my viewpoint. Same prep school, both at St. Paul's, both at Cambridge. He took all the prizes, I was lucky to scrape a pass. He was even good at cricket; I flunked in when the thirds lacked a man. But I know horses

117

and he doesn't. What do I do, sit at a board table signing things I don't understand? I told him—so did my sister, nice girl but immersed in some dream like me—that we'd agree to his trust-busting if he let us go our way."

"You're going into racing?"

"I tried to take a vetinerary degree, but Dad said no. I've got the books and a crammer, not that I want to dose the animals, but merely to know what happens in their insides and outsides. This stuff," he gestured, "I got the best advice. Dad probably told you he consulted a man who specialises in selling races, makes a lot of money and will end by being warned off. I want a way of life. I have engaged a first-class head lad, which dad would approve of if it wasn't me ..."

"Good luck," said Harry and gestured to Honeybody.

"He was there all day," said the Sergeant. "The men like him."

"Back to the car," said Harry.

He settled himself beside Honeybody. "From the Judge's map—careful old bird to keep these large-scale things by him —you go left about a quarter of a mile and jink left down a secondary. There's a hill about a quarter of a mile before the turn."

"This is it," he said at length. "Pull in at the side, not much two-way traffic." He looked at the trees, dense and vaguely watery, conjuring thoughts of graves.

"That's the bit of track in. Let's get it over."

He fumbled in his breast pocket and produced the shockingly expensive little camera with its flash bulbs, miraculously self-adjusting shutter speed and minute film.

"Tracks here." The Sergeant was bending. "Michelin, correct size, newish. Given rain I'd say four or five hours standing from the time it started. The crate I saw was well shod, not new but a few months old, in Michelin."

The Inspector adjusted the flash bulbs and shot four photographs. "Better get a distance one. Stay where you are for comparison."

"Looks like the old beak was right," said the Sergeant. "Do they still use a silken rope?" The Inspector had the feeling that somebody was watching them through the trees.

"Abolished," said Harry, "just a jury job like Joe Blow.

Maybe a sable top to the loo seat in their cell, special prayers from the Chaplain. Hold still. That'll do. Now to the third estate, Lady Ethelred, that was administered by the late Prettyman."

Lady Ethelred, who quite unconstitutionally contrived to slip 'Lady Mabel' into her title, lived at a fairly unassuming little manor house, beautifully kept up.

Leaving Honeybody to prowl and gossip if possible, he was admitted by a trim maid. Lady Ethelred was in her late sixties and gave the impression of shrewd vigour.

"About poor, dear Charles Prettyman, I suppose?"

The Inspector repeated his formula.

"Easy for me. On Monday at eleven-fifty, more or less, I set out for Deal via Windlesham to visit my only relative, a great-niece, Mrs. Witchford—you may phone her, she's the only one in the book. I left her at six. There were her two maids and her husband, a surgeon, for lunch. In any case Charles was like an elder brother; anything going wrong I flew to him and he never complained or what's more charged any extra. Oh, I'm not so silly as I look"—she had a rather unfortunate simper—"and Sir Tom always said I had a business head, but there are times when a man . . ."

"Quite," said the Inspector, "but this is merely routine. I must emphasise that. Local talk is always undesirable."

"I was driving along the London road, approaching Windlesham, my great-niece living thirty miles along, at forty miles an hour. I know what you men say about old women driving, but my reactions, sight and hearing have not dimmed that much and I keep to the left-hand side. Lord Redapple passed, in the little blue Volks, driving, as my late husband used to say, like a bat out of hell."

"What time was this?"

"My car clock, which is erratic, said twelve-twenty. I wondered what affair of state should impel Alf Redapple to imperil the highway."

An old cobra, thought the Inspector as he disengaged himself. Kind but managing and hating those with more money, like Redapple.

"I saw the little kitchen maid," said Honeybody, avuncularly. "Her ladyship is nice and kind but you do it her way.

119

But nevertheless nice and kind. Monday she went to a niece in Deal, away all day."

"Home, James. I think an afternoon nap is indicated. I fear there might be sleepless nights."

"Ar, one of those," said Honeybody. "But the food's good at the pub. And we share the goose tonight."

6

Cautioning Honeybody, who could move with surprising discretion when necessary, the Inspector, glimpsing his wife through the snug doorway in intimate conversation with Mrs. Jewel, gained the bedroom, removed his outer clothes and crawled into bed.

Somebody tugged his shoulder.

"You've been drinking!"

"Nonsense. Pure as pure. What's the time?"

"Seven. I saw Honeybody sinking a pint with Greenaway—who I like—and Hearman, who is a bit slimy at the edges of the bonhomie."

He always vowed to cut out these afternoon snore-offs, thought Harry, feeling a slight throbbing at his temples.

"I shall shower, but just one thing, did Prettyman's stenog, um . . . ?"

"Miss Bramble? And you are going to ask me if Peter Winding was seen on Monday afternoon," Elizabeth smirked. "You men have obvious minds, as Dame Alice Grittle says, except the P.M. He was in his room, 'Do not disturb for anything'. Actually nothing much ever happened there, not that kind of office. On this afternoon a tenant telephoned and said that water was coming into the cowhouse. A local surveyor looks into that kind of thing and Winding if necessary fixes with a local builder. The London real estate is administered by three firms of agents. Prettyman just wanted a monthly statement of costs from Winding, so if there was embezzlement . . ."

"You should have my job," said the Inspector admiringly.

"I couldn't stand the drinking!" she said, disapproving.

"Tell me, helpmeet, does Winding possess a car?"

"By dint of infinite cunning, and talk about men drivers, I

found that he is a motor cyclist. Not your putt putt man, but a genuine 1100 cc buff, wind and rain in the face and your wheels going sideways. His unfortunate wife, at week-ends, is attached in a side-car which is taken off on Sunday evenings. He was very good at one time, pro standard."

"Take your pretty head down and ogle Honeybody into a gin and tonic. I won't be too long," said the Inspector, taking up a dressing-gown and slippers.

It was eight when he got to the bar. Honeybody was talking to Hearman, Elizabeth was talking to a rather well-built girl, and Greenaway sat looking a trifle sulky in a well-bred way.

"Oh, yes," said Harry to himself, "what was her name, Redding, Barbie Redding, a nice piece engaged to Greenaway."

"Good evening, sirs. Miss Redding your servant, ma'am, and drinks on the constabulary."

"Dry martini, film influence, much thanks. The big boss had six girls in bikinis on Margate Beach, deck chairs and all, and the wind blowing ice-gale force. They've got a filter which cuts out the goose pimples—the poor, dear bitches."

"Do you save fallen women?" enquired Hearman.

"Not for you, dear fellow. Anyway, Mr. S. said I could stay here if I only charged ten bob for b and b, bought my own dinner and got back by nine-fifteen tomorrow, which means hideous risings in the dark."

"I don't know why you troubled," said Greenaway. He gave his sudden smile. "I mean John and I should be immersed in biz, not distracted by lovely woman..." He looked at the Inspector. "I think Barbie had some idea of the local flicks and fish and chips. As it is now it is Mrs. Jewel's T.V. and all girlish with your good wife."

The Inspector grinned and nuzzled his brown ale. Silly girl, he thought, the first thing to learn in the willing bride's almanac is when to leave him be, such as when an ambitious young man thinks he has a break. Sit in the corner, miss, and knit peaceably and brew coffee at hourly intervals with an expression of rueful sympathy. Greenaway did not want her here.

"I've stretched the goose to include your young lady and it's on," said Mrs. Jewel huskily to Greenaway.

They ate in a little private room, candle-lit. It was one of the memories which became, dream-like, embalmed in Harry's

121

memory. There was a clean-tasting anchovy mixture with red wine and garlic, baked into toast, then the goose, simmered in wine, flavoured, egg-and-breadcrumbed and popped into white sauce with small potato cakes, what Mrs. Jewel said was Doboz Torte, layered and with the taste of caramel, and finally, with coffee and brandy, that rare animal, a prime piece of Cheddar, and little rolls tasting very faintly of garlic.

"Mrs. Jewel," questioned Hearman, as she accepted a glass of brandy, "where did you learn to cook like this? What French prince seduced and kept you?"

"Maid of all work in Mr. Redapple's—father of the lord—kitchen for eight years! 'E was English and had Mrs. Braddock, the best plain English cook in the country, and she—beautiful girl, though you wouldn't think it to look at the present lord—was, they said, Rumanian, but I thought she was French, from the way she talked. Anyway the missus had a Frenchman named Henri in the kitchen. Two big ranges, two big pantries, even two wine cellars and deadly rivalry. Old Mrs. Braddock—if you'll excuse me—kept a pepper pot in her stays and she'd try to empty it in whatever was cooking on Moss 'Enri's stove—they're too illiterate to sound the haitch—but he used to wait peeping through the door in his pantry. Threw a duck press one day at her head and they had the police in, but nothing was done. So to speak, I learned a bit of both worlds, writing down what I saw."

"We bless the day you did," said Barbie Redding, sighing with contentment. "It is heaven to eat well."

"A gentleman for you, Inspector." Mr. Jewel, who obviously knew him, nevertheless anonymously ushered in a uniformed policeman.

He saluted. "P.C. Holloway, sir. We got a ticker from London. Superintendent Hawker. I'm to drive you back, urgent, sir."

"I'll pack your bag," said Elizabeth.

"No need, I'll go to the flat. But you might get that grey briefcase, please."

"A brandy, Constable!" Hearman was red-faced and with a host expression.

The constable looked wistfully at the Inspector.

"One, medicinal, for the road, Holloway."

"Excuse me, is it the Inspector?" A pair of reddened eyes looked round the room. It was Peter Winding. "I think I want . . . ." His gaze drifted round the room and he stiffened. "Good night," he shambled out.

"Not a fan of ours," said Hearman, cutting a morsel of Cheddar.

"Is he . . .?" The Inspector raised his eyebrows to the landlady.

"Definitely not," said the landlady, "kind of soft hearted. Anybody dies . . . and Peter's at the age when your friends start going away . . . he has a bit of a wake, like. But he's got a good friend, sober as that ash tray, waiting to run him home. No trouble, sir."

Elizabeth came in with the briefcase and the Inspector kissed her. "I'll phone, luv. Goodbye all. You know what to do, Honeybody?"

"Indeed, sir."

The big green Humber had a built-in tape recorder and the Inspector dictated for forty minutes, detaching the spool. It was a fine night.

"Wake me when we get there, will you, Constable?"

He rarely slept easily in a car and now Lord Redapple incongruously dressed in blue chased him round a racing stable brandishing a lawn mower.

When he arrived he awoke, cloyed in the mouth—these blasted sweet dishes—and went to see Hawker. He passed over the spool of tape and looked around the table to see the jowled face of Superintendent Porterman.

"I started to worry about your story regarding Croucher," said Hawker.

"Unverifiable," said Harry. "He won't talk directly. I know that bastard!"

"Cats and cream," said the old Superintendent. "Mr. Porterman took Croucher red-handed tonight."

"I say!" said Harry. Croucher hadn't been taken for twelve years, since he got out of the Scrubs on his twenty-sixth birthday.

"I know how these tea-leaves think," said Hawker. "This spot check idea of mine, now. A man as bright as Croucher would figure that with virtually all the police in an area checking a couple of blocks, then the place was wide open for a smashing. He spends a lot of time in Spoon's Stockwell Road beanery, so I got a couple of young coppers to go there midday and mention that at seven this evening I was going to blast Kew Gardens and turn it inside out with police from Richmond and as far afield as Wembley.

"That gave him time to think of something. I must admit it was crude, but I calculated that his greed would blind him. Croucher loves a good tickle, one of the most avaricious criminals I have met. So I arranged for two civilian clerks to practically sit on top of Croucher as he took the district train out to Richmond; he mostly travels public transport. They mentioned a big consignment of choice furs. Croucher prefers furs, although he'll take anything that turns over fast. One of the stooges happened to mention that the night watchman was ill, and the other said it didn't matter because it was only for one night.

"Croucher was on their heels as they walked to an old warehouse, owned by one of my few fans. It has Benny Cohen's Fine Furs written up outside, but Benny moved to new premises a couple of years ago and the place is a dead store now. However Croucher didn't know that. He watched the two guys go in. Benny had arranged for a dozen of his workers to be on the premises, walking in and out busily, and also," Hawker mopped his brow, "three thousand quid's worth of skins. I saw my pension going, I can tell you, but it went off perfectly. We had police cars screaming towards Kew. Croucher and four boys are in a van down a side street and as it gets quiet they drive to the warehouse, jemmy the rotten side doors and load up the skins. Then the lights go on and it's Mr. Porterman and a squad of twenty plus cars. A fair cop."

It was a close thing, thought Harry. Agents provocateurs were not, repeat not, used, nor were traps set. Except no one had asked Croucher to listen. 'Upon information received,' Porterman would intone in the box, and no more Croucher for some years.

"His solicitor's outside. Mr. Bird," said Hawker.

Many of the old-time lawyers with criminal clients were characters in their own right. Bird was of a younger generation, school-tied and with a tendency to 'old man' people.

"The van was stolen, a new paint job and false plates. We booked Croucher and the others for receiving it. It won't hold up as far as he's concerned. All right." Hawker opened the door of his little anteroom.

"Come in, sir, do come in," he said with all the geniality of a crocodile.

"Well, well, old man," said Mr. Bird, "I must say I did hope for the committal hearing tomorrow instead of a remand. But as it happens I understand from a colleague that a man named Fern has confessed to stealing the van and asseverates, yes asseverates, that my client was in total ignorance."

"Croucher owns Perce Fern!"

"I know nothing of that, but the other charges, now, my client would plead guilty to trespass."

"What about spitting on the pavement?" Hawker's grin was savage.

"At most breaking and entering."

"How about *conspiracy* to rob?"

The word seemed to drop heavily on to Hawker's desk and Bird dabbed at his lips with a silk handkerchief.

"A conspiracy by five men to rob one of her Majesty's liege subjects, with your client as the mainspring. Fourteen years, perhaps up to twenty."

One could see Mr. Bird's mind working. There was considerable public unease, not only about the Blue Lady murders but about some spectacular warehouse smashings, with admonitory words from the Bench.

"I'm sure my client is willing to co-operate." Mr. Bird advanced his first gambit.

"On the night of September the eighth he saw something over a transom. Why he was there is something I do not care about. I had him brought over an hour ago. Mr. James, take Mr. Bird to the receiving room."

"He seems to want blood," muttered the solicitor as they walked to the lift.

"If Croucher stays mum he will be asseverating in a maximum security gaol for, I'd say, fifteen years, the way they're handing it down now." Harry pressed the button.

"Otherwise?"

"He can't get out of it under three, less good behaviour. Say

125

breaking in with intent and the Super putting in a good word."

They walked in silence to the receiving room where they were met by a hard sardonic little sergeant.

"Mr. Bird to see Croucher. When they have asseverated at each other to sufficiency, over to Mr. Hawker's stockade."

"Aye aye, sir. Prithee come this way, Mr. Bird."

"Well," Porterman was saying as Harry returned, "he's one bastard out of the way for three years. He won't get good behaviour, not on previous form. They caught him on remand in Brixton trying to pinch the lead pipes out of the lavatory. He can't keep his thieving hands off things. Well?"

"Oh, they'll play," said Harry. "Fifteen minutes to preserve the whatsits and then Croucher will talk."

"I phoned the lab," said Hawker, "you better wheel him over personally."

It was precisely fourteen minutes when Croucher was escorted in. Bird looked by far the more nervous of the two. Croucher was a squat man with almond-shaped eyes which looked like polished agate. He had a greasy skin, but he was well-dressed and his movements were neatly co-ordinated.

"Mr. Bird says it's a matter of fifteen or three," he said, calmly. Apart from his lisp his voice was accentless. Harry peered at the dossier. He had won a scholarship to a good grammar school, would probably have gone to university if the army had not claimed him. It was while serving in Malaya that he robbed mess funds of seven hundred and eighty pounds.

"For the record—make a note please, Mr. James—I make no inducement whatever. The nature of the charge is for the Prosecutor's department." Hawker looked righteous.

A rather attractive smile lit Croucher's face. Harry reminded himself that in certain circumstances it would be better to meet a lion than Croucher.

"All right," said Croucher, "I was in a crummy dump named the Morning Star, no questions asked there. That was on the night of September eighth. The partition walls are plywood faked to look like a standard wall. I heard these noises. As you know I'm curious—too much, it seems, for my own good. I should have realised those bods in the Richmond train spoke a bit too much like rote. Anyway I went out, grasped the ledge and peeked through the transom. A man on the bed, thick-set. He was muttering and was waving a knife in each hand. I just hung there. The idea was in my mind that he could open that door and gaff me through the belly like a ruddy salmon. He looked like a man conducting in front of his hi-fi set—you know, dreaming he was Von Karajan. Then he started this noise. I've got an old cat." He sighed. "Remind me to fix it regularly with the neighbour, Mr. Bird, so he gets his grub. When he was a little ball of fur he used to make this cry; a wailing mew, frightening if you didn't know he only weighed in ounces. It was like that, horrible coming from a human being, if he was human....He went on doing this conducting and this mewing. Then he stopped, put the two knives on the blue blanket and started muttering. I guarantee the knives were exactly like the press photos of the Blue Lady shivs, with that forty-five degree point. I dropped down and went to bed. I told a mutual friend to tip you off."

"This muttering." Porterman spoke for the first time. "Was he saying anything?"

"I had the usual seven years French," said Croucher. "Silly old bastards, I can't ask the way to the heads. Not that I was interested, maths and science were my alleys"—Harry thought that he had not known a criminal whose favourite subject was not himself—"but I thought it might be French. Not the Parisian brew, but some argot. Just the soft, nasal intonation, like a drunk Welshman with a heavy cold." He smiled.

"My," thought Harry, "you like yourself." He saw Porterman tense. The big Superintendent disliked uppity crooks. He cut in. "Did he look French?"

"Swarthy, pitted skin, could be a southerner."

"How was he dressed?" asked Harry.

"The dump doesn't run to central heating and you need your clothes on the bed, I tell you. He had a greasy-looking top coat on, kind of fancy light-tan boots."

"What colour were his eyes?" asked Hawker softly.

"God knows."

"But you saw his face, you described his skin."

"I suppose I did." Croucher sounded astonished.

Hawker waved them all down. "Now, Croucher, a man sees

more than he realises. I want you to spend a few hours in a comfortable chair, with your solicitor if need be. There's a thing called identikit."

"Oh, I know all about that," said Croucher with inbuilt arrogance.

"And what you should know," Hawker's voice whipped across like a broken band-saw, "is that I'd like to see you under the big lock, say for sixteen years. Then you'd be fiftyish and the little boys would reach up and tweak your nose. Punch drunk, stir drunk, you've seen 'em. I sometimes give one half a crown. When I've had a good lunch."

"You being your side of the fence, I suppose it's natural," said Croucher very softly.

"Instead," said the Superintendent, "I'm going to speak up for you like a father. What the result will be I cannot anticipate, but I'll bat for you."

"I'll play, Daddy!"

Hawker's face remained without expression.

"Mr. James, you take him over. Sergeant," he glanced at the hard-faced escort, "you follow. Mr. Bird, we have no objection . . ."

"I won't keep you from that red-headed little goodie of yours, Johnny," said Croucher lazily. "See me tomorrow."

The laboratory had an aseptic air about it.

"Looks like a ruddy operating theatre," said Croucher, uneasily.

"In a way it is," said Harry. "Sit down!"

The chair was large and scientifically guaranteed to induce relaxation.

"This is Mr. Trimble." The Inspector nodded to the large, comfortably built man in a white overall.

"That is the room you saw," said Trimble, and suddenly the big white screen flooded with colour. "Taken through the transom," said the scientist, "this afternoon. I put three fellows on to it and they only got it because one engaged the big brute of an owner in an argument about the ethics of Australian pro rugby players. Now sit back and just look. What side of the bed was he seated?"

"The right, halfway down, facing the pillow."

The lights dimmed and Trimble spoke into a throat microphone. Superimposed upon the image of the bed came a figure, a pencilled outline.

"Too tall and he was very broad in the hips. Funny figure, short legs, but long torso getting narrower until the shoulders, then a fattish neck and a perfectly round head."

"Take it easy," said Trimble. "Is that better?"

"Nearer."

It was old stuff to Harry. He sought the canteen and black coffee and read the evening papers. Hawker's suggestion of spot checks had proved that the British public would accept anything. The smug face of Dame Alice Grittle who had insisted on being with the police party at the first check—Tooting of all places—beamed out of page one. An elderly housewife named Aggie Corking had assaulted a sergeant for *not* searching her for knives. "I got me rights, same as them lords and ladies," she had told the press. The T.U.C. was taking it up.

When he got back an hour later Croucher was white-faced and sweating. On one big screen was the picture of a man in half profile. On the one next to it was a face, a moon-face with a pitted cheesy complexion, dark eyes, plumpish cheeks and black, curled hair with a tonsure-like gap on the crown.

"Very co-operative, Inspector," said Trimble, staring at Croucher clinically. The hard-faced sergeant looked on from the shadows.

"He gave me a nice little rendition of the screaming noise he heard, which will go to the doctors. Very much like Olivier having his eyes put out in that Greek thing. But, now, the muttering. You see all language has cadence, rhythm and particularly differentiation in speed. We have five thousand recordings."

"There aren't that number of languages," said Croucher.

"But there are regional dialects," intoned Trimble, pressing a button. After a minute he said, "The first is Spanish spoken in Mexico City, you should have noted the soft, almost lazy intonation; the second strip, fast and staccato, was on a tube station in Madrid. Listen to this...."

"Kraut," said Croucher.

"In fact the late Hitler's last recorded effort. I thought it suitable. Now ..."

Croucher looked puzzled. "You've got me stumped, that's no kind of frog."

"Arabic. Now, listen, I had difficulty in getting this one. It was flown in from Gay Paree half an hour ago."

There was a soft, vague muttering.

"That's it." Croucher was excited.

"The speech was Algerian French," said Trimble. "Oh, the speaker was a terrorist, shot eight years ago. That was his death-bed stuff you heard. All right, that's all. That photo to all stations, and ships—the client thinks he had sea legs—probably a pirate still in practice, heh, heh."

"Please!" said Harry.

"And the press?"

Harry hesitated at this quicksand and scuttled for the dry land. "Please consult the elders of the tribe."

Trimble grinned cynically.

The hard-faced sergeant caught Croucher's arm and the Inspector led the way into the corridor.

"Hey," called Croucher, "a little talk?"

"My room," said Harry.

The sergeant stayed outside. "None of these tapes, eh?" asked Croucher.

"These days there might be," said the Inspector, "but my personal word that there are none."

"Good enough for me, and," Croucher looked cunning, "what you said would be on the tape and any splicing would show."

"And you took science!" said Harry. "There are little blank-it-out buttons. I could be scratching my left knee and rub you out."

"All right." There were beads of sweat on Croucher's swarthy face. "Now I want to come dead clean. Between you and me, my boys sent off a lorry the night of September eighth, but you can't prove it. After a job I use the Morning Star because I'm out of sight, the boss won't talk if I slip him a quid and I never met anybody there I know. There was a lorry with copper wire—a couple of tons of it—going to this American base, but we took the wrong one and eff me if it wasn't full of cans of stew. You know as well as I do that the Fat Chap handles my stuff usually, but there's no market for grub—

except sugar, coffee and tea—apart from Greasy Spoon who pays sweet f.a., but I go to him and get a night's wages. I ask him to tip you off. That was fair, wasn't it?"

"Citizens have an obligation to help the police."

"But not ex-cons. Look, what I want to know is does Hawker mean it, about speaking up for me?"

"Mr. Hawker is not the man I would choose as a father, or, for God's sake, a remote cousin, but if he says he will do something, he does it. You may not know it, but when you're in the dock the judge has your complete dossier before him."

"That's not fair," said Croucher, all astonished virtue.

"Life notoriously isn't. So the dossier will contain, underlined, the words 'prisoner has been of great assistance to the police'. That means you get three years, perhaps two, though that's pushing it. You'll get an easy prison, and the governor will be tipped off that you get an easy run. If you use your head, Croucher, you'll get maximum remissions. Just say 'yes, sir' and keep your nose clean."

"Yes, sir, and bail . . . there are quite a few things."

"I'd put the ill-gotten in a unit trust."

"I like bricks and mortar," said Croucher. "I got seven rows of slums, full of blacks payin' through the nose. Bird looks after it for me. They sign agreements, all legal and shipshape."

"Got a passport?"

Croucher hesitated and his forehead ridged.

"No. . . . I mean, yes, I got four, different names."

"If you run we'll get you. . . . Hawker's a vindictive old swine and you'd never really be out of stir again. Oh, he'll retire, but the word passes on."

"You can trust me," said Croucher huskily, "I'll give them to Mr. Bird to mind."

"All right, better get your kip," said the Inspector and delivered him to the tough sergeant.

He found Superintendent Hawker leaning back in his chair. The old man looked exhausted, but brightened slightly as he saw Harry.

"I said he could get bail."

"Quite right," Hawker sounded indifferent. "We have him, you know."

"Sir?"

131

"Assisting the police. I get the press officer to emphasise that. When he gets out nobody will touch him. Imagine the Fat Chap fencing an informer." Hawker wheezed.

"I see, you've fixed him."

"That is what we are here to do," said the old gentleman showing his teeth. "I shouldn't wonder if he had a nasty accident in the exercise yard. Oh, I'll pass the word for him to be the screws' pet and pride and joy, and the more he protests the less the cons believe him." Hawker laughed. "Many a man has done his lot in an exercise yard." He sobered abruptly. "I heard your Redapple tape. Sir Jabeez'll turn white round his chops. I suppose you can't opt for this clurk Peter Winding? I don't like what you say of him."

"If there is embezzlement it is him, but I feel there has been no fiddling," said the Inspector.

"I'm going home," said Hawker. "Get some sleep yourself. Take this," it was a sheet of paper, "see this cove in Whitehall at eleven-thirty. He's up and coming and was Redapple's runner and scullion during the war. He's a garrulous old cat now and due for his knighthood next time up."

The Inspector went home to a flat which already seemed to smell musty and missed Elizabeth.

7

The bacon remained soggy even after draining and he was suspicious of the egg—should there be that bluish tinge to the white?—and he had left his electric razor in Kent. Thereupon cutting himself twice with the instrument Elizabeth swore by for her legs.

As he was about to go he reminded himself of his wife's horror of dirty washing-up, cursed, removed his coat and did what was necessary and then sat down to do another chore: telephoning the kennels to enquire of the welfare of Mr. Bones.

"Aw. Good, sir, bit three uvver dogs and eats 'is weight in stoo," exclaimed an admiring, juvenile voice.

He then went to Whitehall, where a small gentleman named

Mr. Bessy periodically poked a black fire and talked in nervous gasps.

"Mr. Hawker, delightful character, keeps us in fits at the club, kindness itself."

Harry could only preserve a morose silence and a shrewd pair of brown eyes twisted round from the grate.

"All great men have their eccentricities. Winnie, now. You know he used to say that his greatest cross was the Cross of Lorraine, but he used to add that the second greatest was Alfred Redapple, and that only because the general had the longer neck."

"I dare say, sir."

"Redapple, he was Sir Alfred then, used to lurk in the Map Room. He was not a memo monster, not at all, but he used to treat the Boss to well-chosen words, not that Winnie didn't know how to deal with that sort of thing, none better, but he was sympathetic to all those brilliant fellows who worked sixteen hours a day. But he avoided Redapple all he could."

"I heard that Redapple's judgment was good."

"But narrow, but narrow." Bessy put down a pair of brass-studded bellows of Gladstonian vintage and darted back to his satin-covered chair. "He saw clearly and far, but narrowly. What did Winnie say of Lenin? 'A man going through a crowded warehouse with an immensely strong, narrow-beamed torch'?"

"No idea," said Harry. You could get into trouble discussing Lenin unless you were in the Special Branch.

A bronchial old gentleman in a green uniform brought in strong tea and Marie biscuits.

"Splendid, splendid," said Mr. Bessy. "I hope you get her—this homicide—soon."

"We probably shall."

Mr. Bessy dunked a Marie biscuit and sucked the product with relish. "Everybody here is perturbed; you have no idea the letters one gets, and Dame Alice Grittle on the phone all day . . . although I must say she does rather relish these things; when we put down prostitution she took to her bed with the sulks.

"But Redapple, neurotic, as you may know—twitches a bit and starts at the telephone's ring. Some of the really brainy chaps do. It means nothing. Ambitious, of course. My vis-à-vis at the Treasury says his companies are healthy dollar-earners indeed."

"You worked for him how long?"

"Three years, tore me to the verge of ulcers, but then . . ." Mr. Bessy aged ten years in his face . . ."so many did."

"You see him often?"

Mr. Bessy went and played unavailingly with the coals, opened a cupboard and produced an electric fire with what seemed to be brass cherubs on each corner.

"Damned progress," he muttered, as he bent to put in the plug. "No, sir, there came a day when my Master sent me to Washington. I bade goodbye to Sir Alfred Redapple in four minutes precisely, promised faithfully to brief my successor and left with the impression I never particularly wanted to see the gentleman again. I never have except by chance. He does not know me."

"Scrupulous?"

Mr. Bessy examined something on his blotter.

"I assure you that he is scrupulous in the sense, which one believes is meant, of not gaining advantage from public office. In getting his own way, I believe," he hesitated . . . "Look, it was no picnic. You had to fight for your priority, or else you were stuck on the ground. There was quite a bit of hitting where it hurt most, but . . . well, we're cats, but old, civilised tabbies, and Redapple . . . to coin a phrase he was the most vindictive sod you ever met in your life. He was always right and if you so much as said 'perhaps' he'd get you one way or another. . . . There were people . . . but no matter. It was not a pleasing time for me. I said 'yes, sir', probably two million times. As a reward I have a coal fire that does not work and what is reputed to have been Lloyd George's electric fire, and, of course, an amplitude of strong tea."

Harry went back to the Yard. The big work board showed the photographs of Croucher's recollections. He consulted the sergeant in charge, who shrugged.

"Life's full of big-arsed sailors with small shoulders. You know the tonnage we handle!"

The Inspector did not, but nodded wisely.

Hawker was in Whitehall, allegedly with Sir Jabeez, waiting

in the Cabinet anteroom. Harry made an appointment with a man named Button.

Jobber Button was one of those many men who have some kind of passion for amateur police work. A bachelor, sixtyish and immense and sweaty, but always complaining of the cold, Jobber did not need the modest yearly retainer paid to him through the office of the Director of Public Prosecutions. Over the years he had dealt in annuities, reversions, fag ends of leases, mixed job lots that nobody could bother with. And made a great deal of money. He spent most of his time in the City and Harry was surprised upon phoning to find him at home in his vast, comfortable Highgate flat—the Jobber always said he could not abide small rooms which was why he had always been honest.

He was seated in his great Victorian drawing-room before a blazing fire which supplemented the oppressively high central heating, his fly comfortably unbuttoned at the top, with a small cauldron on the hob with a dipper in it.

"My special punch, try it, and the smoked salmon, table just over there."

The Jobber's was the only place where you got enough smoked salmon, thought the Inspector. Other places provided an ostentatious sandwich or two, but only at the Jobber's had you an unlimited nosh. Similarly the huge man's Christmas party, held on December the first each year, was the only occasion he knew where swift waiters dispensed unlimited vintage champagne until the last guest had staggered off, whereupon the Jobber was reputed to set to and finish the last broken case.

He munched and said the punch was good.

"An old chap I met gave me the recipe. Georgian, he said. I'll bequeath it to you in my will."

"Redapple, the financier, know him?"

"The lordly lord? Merchant banker, he calls himself. Once it was moneylender, then financier, then company promoter, now merchant banker. As soon as you fellows nab a few, the name falls into disrepute and they find a new one. He hates me. After the war he got in quick on the take-over; moribund business, flog the real estate, sell what goodwill there was to a competitor. Well, I knew something he didn't and in those

135

days I raked up seven thou deposit on the Monday, signed
papers on Wednesday and by the middle of next week I'd
turned eleven thou cool profit. By knowing something. Well,
Redapple—it was just before they lorded him—rang me up
and abused me. Said I'd been unethical. Me! Spluttering over
the blower like a gaffed fish. I told him to shove himself. Well,
the time's gone when a big bloke can ruin a medium-sized 'un
for spite, 'specially when he's got my twitching great nose. But
once or twice he's harmed me and cost me a bit. So that declares my interest. A stuck-up swine, but about the fastest man
on figures there is, I'll say that. A great organiser and a bloke
after my own heart in that he never wrote a memo over ten
words in his life. Now his big chance is knocking at his door
and he wants ready cash; of course there are the bankers and
building societies, but they take the cream off and restrict your
movements."

"What's this knocking job?"

"A man named Cy Hoot. Heard of him?"

"Only a car thief named Sam Hooter."

"Cy is a Yank. The family business was chemical engineer-
ing. He got both hands into off-sea oil, now has everything
from insurance to restaurants. He turned down a hotel chain
going cheap because unmarried couples might get in. I met one
of his—Christ, he said he was chief of the stock portfolio
division, what names will they get yet?—anyway he drank
milk all the time on account of his stomach. Hoot is going into
Europe, partly because of tax advantage. Two years ago he
formed a consortium—the names they have, when I was a kid
that would have meant, never mind. . . . It was a kind of trial
marriage, a test run, but next year there are the wedding bells
and the Chancellor carrying the baby to the font." Mr. Button
swilled punch and raised an unlovely voice: " 'When charged
with consorting, he said he was only sporting, with only a bird
and two and two third.' Not my best," he apologised.

"Has he *got* to find money?"

"Not necessarily, but this Hoot wouldn't give you the hard
skin off his feet; the more Redapple puts in, the more he takes
out, and even with capital gains tax he'll sit very pretty."

"Why can't I meet a man like Hoot who says, 'Now Mr. J., I
wish to invest fifty million and you're the man to look after it'."

The Inspector sighed and scooped up more salmon and filled the punch cup.

"No good going out on a day like this," said Button. "I know from experience that there's weather which makes them button their pockets. Not a bob about today. No, you wouldn't suit old Hoot; he won't employ a man who likes his glass—Redapple's TT—or a man who's been involved in divorce—the higher echelons only, what the slaves do he couldn't care less about."

"Doesn't he find it hard to get men?"

"He pays top staff magnificently and the rest very poorly. This chap I met kept his mistress and his private bar over the Canadian border and used a false moustache. That's how he got ulcers."

"I'd like to keep you company, but back to work." Harry struggled into his coat, crammed some salmon into his mouth and waved goodbye. The street was bitter after the over-heated flat.

Redapple lived, not in Park Lane, but a hundred yards away from it in a featureless, expensive building which covered a block. A porter in solemn black moved uneasily around the foyer, which smelled wealthy.

"A tiny police enquiry," said Harry, flashing his warrant card. These things could be the very devil.

"Mr. Blenkinsop," the man in black said, sidling away.

"Who is he?"

"Room with the red notice, over there, manager."

Blenkinsop was old, frail and with an inbuilt fear of things. He recoiled from the warrant as if from a snake.

"This is just routine," said Harry, "I wear a pair of shoes out every two months just plodding. . . ."

There should be a foot club, he thought, as he watched Blenkinsop brighten. "You ought to try running up and around this place at their beck and call. Oh! I know we got lifts and wall-to-wall, but some evenings I have to sit here bathing the trotters before I can limp home. I've got a good man, mind, but he doesn't seem to cut as well as before the national health business. 'Really cut!' I tell him, but he seems remiss, somehow." Blenkinsop brooded for a moment. "They say the razor blades can give you poisoning. Well, what is it?"

"Lord Redapple, Monday last."

Blenkinsop's eyes flickered. "You know what this place is?"

"A haven for the mighty, the wealthy and superior kept women."

"And trouble," said Blenkinsop. "There's somebody, no names no pack drill, on the eighth that's going to fall down the stairwell one day. Four bottles of tonic wine before eleven a.m. And who'll be blamed? Yours truly, o' course."

"Redapple!" said the Inspector.

"Look," Blenkinsop twitched, "this is built through the street, see. The other street entrance does not have a hall porter and the lifts are automatic. The real pricey jobs are the ground floors and maybe first and second up, without too much strain on their old hearts when they toil at 'em."

"Women?"

Blenkinsop shrugged. "Respectable. Oh, we come up in the divorce court a couple of times a year, and then I get a tanning from the chairman—he's from a primitive sect what got their lot out of breweries—but it's discretion they worry over. These rich blokes like creeping around making deals. God knows who goes into Redapple's flat on the ground floor; all the money in the world. Debenture this and debenture that. It's money more than women they want those flats for."

"He must have a servant."

"Now Mr., er, James, I don't want you to think that I don't know everything about the tenants, all seven hundred of 'em. That's why I'm kept on by the boss. The day he rings up and I *don't* know, it's living with my daughter-in-law in Skegness for me. Redapple has a manservant who doubles as chauffeur sometimes. The catering is contracted out, parties, etcetera, to Parkinson's the caterers. But the servant, name of Smithson, is spending the winter in Spain. . . ."

"What the devil . . ." said Harry.

"Been gone three months, arthritis, he said, and Lord Redapple gave him leave. I don't know what the working class is coming to. Foreign parts! Women, no doubt, him being a bachelor. Drink." Blenkinsop shook in nervous rage. "Cheap drink. Champagne, they tell me, is five bob a bottle; lolling on the sands swigging at it, no doubt."

"Has he been with his lordship long?"

"I've been here sixteen years come Christmas and he was here then. One of his lordship's companies owns this place, so they say. Trust him to wangle his rent off the tax."

"Who cleans the flat?"

"Smithson and—so he said—one of those cleaning agencies. I don't know which," Blenkinsop said irascibly, "Smithson kept a close mouth. I met him occasionally over at the pub—always after work, of course," Mr. Blenkinsop glanced fearfully at the telephone, "but he never vouchsafed much. And now there he is with all those Swedish women on the sands. . . ."

"It comes to this, that the flat is closed up?"

"No, sir, oh, no. I go past every door twice a day and occasionally there's a milk bottle outside the tradesmen's entrance. And I've seen his lordship, let's see, four times. Once he nodded."

"Women? He's been a widower for years."

"There was a story about him and an actress once. The usual story, he backed her in a show. The casting couch . . ." said Blenkinsop in naked envy. "To tell you the truth, I was up west a month ago and I thought I glimpsed him in a cab with a pretty brunette bit, but swear, no, sir, I cannot."

Leaving the manager to his gloomy but lecherous cogitation, the Inspector found himself in the gloom of the streets, startlingly like badly-lit stage sets, redolent with sulphur.

Harry felt one of his periodic financial panics coming on— God knows what Elizabeth would get through at Windlesham Parva with Honeybody egging her on—champagne cocktails, no doubt; for a moment he felt like Mr. Blenkinsop. He had noticed a deep-frozen breast of turkey and instant potato in the fridge and he was sure there was cranberry sauce somewhere, so he'd eat at home and perhaps open a bottle. He took a bus, making a note, "tenpence", in his little book.

"Going home early, mister?" said the conductor.

He nodded.

"You're one wise man. Regular old pea soup it'll be."

The Inspector cooked and as usual did not enjoy his own cooking, and treated himself to an hour's nap before the telephone interrupted him.

"Don't get up suddenly," said Hawker's hateful voice, "it can do you an injury."

"I was going through my notes," said the Inspector with what he hoped was outraged dignity.

"Honeybody phoned. The smell of stout came over the wire. He said he'd been lushing the Redapple handyman—God knows what the Auditor-General will say about that—and the fellow, one Cheeseman, said the Volks was not in the garage when he went in there around eleven. The Sergeant then struck up an acquaintance with a Mrs. Sweeting, the cook, heaven only knows what basis he used. I feel like God being reduced to using fallen angels . . ."

"Yes, sir, Almighty," said Harry.

"The upshot was that the master was incommunicado in his library for the day. Honeybody crept and peered, no lord."

"His desk is to the right of the french windows, you could not see."

"There is a ventilator thingamebob that operates in summer. Honeybody sneaked a jobbing ladder, got up and peered. He swears the room was as empty as his head."

The Inspector groaned.

"And just to make your life easier, Mr. James, your wife, who seems to have adopted us, called in at Prettyman's office—taking the lady typist peppermints or some graceful female action—and found that Winding has not been in. His wife phoned, sounding quote agitated unquote and said he was ill."

"I better get down there."

"First you better see Sir Jabeez. I phoned and he is in chambers all afternoon. Check on this Trust caper."

The Inspector put his shoes on, wincing as he did. Peering through the window he dimly saw the other side of the street. He managed to find a bus, an odd route which crept up and down side streets and seemed always to stop near public houses, which deposited him a quarter of a mile from the chambers.

Gloved hands deep in pockets, he walked head-down, on the theory that in fogs you did better to rely on instinct than senses. Near here, he thought. The trappy time when you can just make that wrong turn that inevitably leads to the Elephant and Castle. There was a lamp standard fighting the eddies of fog. Looking up, its fierce, incandescent blaze blinded him.

"Oh, Inspector," a man blundered into the circle of light, "just the job. I was going . . ." and fell on his face.

"Christ, a drunk," just what he wanted. Better get him to his feet. The Inspector bent and saw the knife protruding from the back of the grey tweed overcoat.

"A ship," came a thick voice which ended in a queer sigh. The Inspector peered into the face and staring eyes of Prettyman's clerk, Peter Winding.

Harry fumbled in his inside pocket, heard the expensive little camera tinkle as it hit the ground, and then found the police whistle. He blew three times, repeating it at intervals until there was the sound of pounding feet.

"This bleedin' fog, excuse me, sir."

"He's dead," said the Inspector, and gave his name and rank.

"I've seen you, sir, at the Bailey."

"Stay here. I'll send back what's necessary."

"There's a licensed house a hundred yards on the left, sir."

The Inspector found it and telephoned. A goggle-eyed landlord provided a comfortable little room. "There's no trade, sir, with 'er on the prowl."

Three hours later he was seated there with Hawker and a harassed-looking Superintendent Richman.

"Before your eyes," said Hawker, wearily.

"Within a blanket of fog," said Harry, "and I'm ordering brandy, regulations or not."

"Make it three, large," said Hawker. Presently, he said, "The cordons went out fast, but there are two tube stations within a quarter of a mile. If the murderer had the sense of a louse. . . . The press'll play the coincidence up, master and man."

"These things happen," Richman said as he drank half his brandy in one gulp. "It didn't get out, but the Oval victim was a second cousin to the fellow at Earl's Court, and in the old Ripper days there were—if my memory runs true—family relationships, although prostitution runs in families. . . . But God help us all tomorrow."

"Get sick if you want, Inspector," grunted Hawker. "The 'flu and two weeks in bed. Oh, I'm serious. Heads are going to roll. Myself, Richman here, Porterman, Daventry, the Chief, maybe the head boys in the lab. Enforced retirement. Get to bed and you'll be overlooked."

"I'm damned if I want to be."

Richman gave his rare smile.

"I'm serious," said Hawker. "It won't do any bloody good, but John Bull will have his bucket of blood."

"You're keeping your spot checks?" said Richman, quietly. "I must say I was doubtful, but they've proved reassuring."

"It's this weather . . . checking in fog. The guv'nor thinks it might make us look mugs, so it's called off for today. Look, young James, you hightail it down to Kent. I'll phone if skies drop. Make your depositions back at Records and then British Railways. Go second so you don't get yourself on the Special Travel List that comes up at the meetings."

"Excuse me, sir." No sooner had Harry sat himself in his room and pulled the recorder a trifle nearer, than there came a tap and a long anxious face peered round the door. He groaned inwardly as he recognised Senior Constable (plainclothes) Ernie McWhirter. The Constable, feeling in need of a guide and mentor, had chosen the Inspector, McWhirter was an authority on offences which Harry had never heard of. Uneasily he remembered a question on malfeasance as a prothonotary which he had promised to look up but never had.

He had a kind heart and said, "Take a seat, Constable, I'm sorry about the prothonotary business but I've been away."

"Fascinating, sir, the office dates back to Constantinople, but that's not what I came to consult you on."

It was odd, thought Harry, that McWhirter, with his twenty-twenty vision, gave the impression of wearing green pebble spectacles.

"Mr. August Greasing, sir."

"Who?"

"The publisher. I remembered reading your report that you saw him on Monday."

McWhirter stayed back nights reading any reports he could get his hands on.

"Yes, but nothing to it."

"So I thought," McWhirter nodded. "He fell through his banisters an hour ago, sir, broke his neck, staved in his sconce, broke his back, left leg and sustained multiple injuries."

"He probably feels unwell."

McWhirter goggled. "The Coroner's officer, a charming chap, said he'd never seen anything like it."

"No hint of foul doings?"

"Oh, no, sir." McWhirter was shocked. "He'd spent the morning in the Museum Reading Room. I went round and got the shock of my life. Curiosa he'd been at," McWhirter pursed his lips, which he did when aroused, "some with lewd illustrations. I told the man in charge I had a good mind to close him down without reference back under Section 28 (b) of the Act, it being a public place, but he laughed and said it was for bona fide students. I told him students were the worst, you remember that young fellow I arrested at King's College, in a lecture room with . . ."

"Get to the point, man!"

"Yes, sir." McWhirter was aggrieved. "What would be our definition of a student, sir?"

"One who studies."

"They were all over fifty, sir, obviously been at it for years. One old chap looked a hundred that hadn't worn well. The custodian said he's studying abnormal sex practices among the ancient Assyrians. I can't understand why he hasn't been had up. Lady Whatsername is just spicy if you get somebody to mark the saucy par's and don't have to read the twaddle in between, but I looked over this old man's shoulder and my hair stood on end."

The Inspector surveyed his hair which resembled an unused sandy broom.

"I hope it came down again. Try brilliantine."

"You're making fun of me. Well, Greasing quits at noon and has liver and bacon with prunes and custard as afters at the National Liberal Club. Then to his office, in Great Calcutta Street, off Tottenham Court Road. Perhaps you know the dirty old buildings? He had a repairing lease on the fourth floor of number sixty-two. He had no staff. His reading was called for by various people on piece work, he printed in the north, and had a wholesaler who also warehoused. I found an accountant's report. He was worth eighty thousand apart from his house and goodwill. He had seven of these publishing companies.

143

"Just a dirty little office, sir, one good desk lamp, a little landing with a sink and rotten banisters. A year ago he slipped and half went through, but saved himself. Cracked two ribs. The agent was on to him, but Greasing never could bring himself to spend the money. This time he went down the stairwell."

"Anybody see it?"

McWhirter shook his head. "Rest of the building's a bulk warehouse for a restaurant chain. Chairs, tables, cutlery, sinks, all the spare stuff. Just one man as kind of caretaker. Sits smoking his pipe. A lot of noise outside in that street, deliveries etcetera. He was lying there for some time until the caretaker thinks he'll nip out to gulp a cuppa and trips over him."

"I dare say the Superintendent, accidents division, will welcome all this," said Harry pointedly, but nothing could scar McWhirter's hide.

"On the desk, sir, was a little ditty box. Stamps in it to the value of nine shillings, four and six in pennies, a few printed bits of paper about not wanting unsolicited mss. and this."

He placed a square of glossy white pasteboard on the blotter.

"No discernible prints, sir."

"Inspector Edward Blessings," read Harry aloud and smiled sadly: "Before your time. He retired four years ago. I remember we gave him the usual clock. Poor old Blessings."

"Sir?"

"He was by way of being an expert on traffic accidents—he spotted that fake one in Weymouth that turned out murder. Two weeks after retirement he was in a coach touring Greece. It went over a two-thousand-foot drop. Your pal, the Coroner's officer, would have been captivated. However, old Blessings was a jack-of-all-trades, more or less on permanent relieving jobs. About five years ago we had occasion to see Mr. Greasing quite a lot, he was publishing some rather scabrous stuff of French origin. No doubt Blessings shared the chore."

"Thank you, sir," said McWhirter, "that will round out my report."

"Which will be a masterpiece of irrelevancy," muttered Harry to himself as the door closed.

When the Inspector had finished his reports he thought he could not face eating with anybody, so he went and bought a carton of milk, some ham sandwiches—unfortunately tasting of sawdust—and a very small flask of whisky. He telephoned Honeybody, restrained the Sergeant's garrulousness and instructed that he must be met whatever the hour.

He finished the milk, threw the remainder of the sandwiches in the waste basket and decided to go early to Victoria before anybody could summon him. The journey was as hellishing as he remembered, but more so, as for some reason the trains were crowded, even the branch line to Windlesham Parva, with people apparently suffering from acute bronchitis. Harry wrapped his little bottle in his handkerchief and took little medicinal sucks. He seemed to catch disapproving glances.

He arrived at Windlesham Parva station, devoid of any lights, at two in the morning.

"I laid in a drop of Mrs. Jewel's rum and milk in a thermos, sir," said Honeybody through the murkiness, "and a nice bit of bacon and egg tart."

The Inspector sat thankfully in the back of the old car and ate and drank.

"No talk till tomorrow, sir!" said Honeybody. "I heard the nine o'clock news."

Honeybody had possessed himself of a key and the Inspector crept upstairs and without awakening his wife undressed and crawled into bed.

8

Automatically he awakened at seven-thirty. Elizabeth was putting her face on.

"Breakfast in bed," she said. "Mrs. Jewel advises tea, toast, omelette, kidneys and her grapefruit marmalade."

"Lay it on, hon', but on my feet. I never feel decent eating in bed except on Sundays with the old *News of the World* and the *People*."

"It'll have to be a dressing-gown job in five minutes. The Jewels have put a little room at our disposal. A lot of commercials are booked in, but there's one agency man."

"Keep out of sight, darling," said Harry as he donned his

dressing-gown. "I don't want 'Inspector eats French-cooked goose with luscious wife in luxury pub' headlines."

The room was along the corridor and had a small servery to the corridor. Honeybody was at his inevitable kippers and bottle of light ale. "Papers are all there, boss," he nodded.

Harry glanced with the swiftness of practice, page one and editorial lead. Non-committal, Britons keeping stiff upper lips and ruling the waves, the envy of dagos and others who objected to homicidal mania. On the fence, watching each other's lead, adept at perceiving the movement of the mob before the mob knew it *was* moving. "See the *Express* stop-press," said Honeybody. A thousand residents of Stony Stratford had met to demand assurance from the Watch Committee of their safety.

"There it goes," said Harry, "tomorrow five hundred such meetings. In fifty hours the country will be riddled by them. Ker-ash. Well. Darling, we'll flog the week-end hide-out and get into commerce."

"If you quit, Mr. J.," said Honeybody, "I'll follow. With the few years I have to go, it won't make that difference in the pension; besides I got a doctor friend who'll sign anything. Dodo wants me to help in the fish; says with a small van we could home-deliver so they don't have to leave the telly. Funny, they like cod during the serials, but a nice bit of haddock with the fillums. And chips fall off because if they drop on the floor you can't find 'em."

"Surely . . ." said Elizabeth.

"Duck," said Harry, "the English think that if you replace Mr. Winkie with Mr. Pinkie—the same man but disguised—the nation is saved. I might be spared to become the oldest Inspector to hand visiting dignitaries into their cars, but Hawker etcetera would go. And whatever they felt, the new fellows would feel impelled to move the furniture around with crashing noises."

"Why can't you get it, him or her." Elizabeth pounded on the table.

"We shall," said Harry, "but by chance. Ninety seconds saved him or her on the Walthamstow job, a police car came round the corner. Just like Jack the Ripper: *his* luck was running out when he quit."

146

"Here's your omelette." Elizabeth sounded cross. The food was perfect. Honeybody sharpened a match and picked his teeth, pushing across four quarto sheets of typing. "I borrowed Jewel's old Remington, that's the full report."

"You are sure both Redapple and the car were out?"

"Yes. In the morning and when I checked at four in the afternoon. Then I scarpered. You know . . ."

The Inspector did. You did not tighten the strings on the purse net until the last moment. And you let defence counsel attempt to do the explaining.

"One thing," said the Sergeant. "I'd arranged to have a pot or so with the odd job man, cove named Cheeseman, last evening at nine. Suggested he brought the cook who's a widow. Only him arrived, surly, yeses and nos. I thought he had decided the job was too good to risk. I had a word with Mr. Jewel and he says his lordship pays real handsome, with a pension fund, but must have obedience. He had a cook who absent-mindedly did his toast both sides instead of one, as he likes it, and got the bullet instanter."

"Do you think Cheeseman and the cook will tip off Redapple?"

"He's not the man to welcome the hired help saying"—Honeybody assumed a whine—"'there's bin a fat old copper henquirin' after your lordship'. Cheeseman's the wrong 'un but no guts type. He might screw himself up to black-mail."

"Keep fairly well away from the estate today," said Harry, "keep an eye from afar. According to that ordnance map I saw, the Afforestation people have a hill to the back. Got binoculars?"

"In my case."

"And you, miss," said the Inspector, "no hip-wiggling before the eyes of the press. Read the women's magazines in your room."

"I'm helping Mrs. Jewel in the kitchen. She's been telling me about short cuts, and the left-overs, you've no idea."

"I have watched you put away approximately half a pound of kedgeree and you still look lovely and can talk cooking," said Harry in wonder.

"Talkin' of grub," said Honeybody, "Mrs. J.'s cousin sent

her a lovely little box of oysters, so it'll be her oyster and beef-steak pudding tonight and perhaps fried oysters for tomorrow. I wish I could talk her into peas. Tinned she can't abide and frozen won't have. Could you have a word, sir?" Honeybody looked piteous.

"Under the circumstances I shall take the car," said Harry, "so that by borrowing a bicycle—I am sure there is one attached to the premises—you may work up an appetite."

Here at least the air was pure even if its coldness clawed at your ears and nose, and the Inspector sang as he nursed the great car into Windlesham and stopped in the police station yard.

He had expected a Superintendent, who was indeed there, but there was a nuggety Chief Constable who called him Chief Inspector.

"Bad business," said the Chief, but sympathetically. "Here's what we did. Checked the office, secretary, young man, four accountants peering at books. There are two London fellows who'd knocked off early. Anyhow, the office didn't come into it as far as we could see. Mrs. Winding said they had been married thirty-one years. A son is in New Zealand. Winding had been devoted to old Prettyman, but the night before he was knifed he had a kind of wake—another friend had died in a plane crash. His wife expected it, but didn't worry because he only drank at the Dendles and the landlady always saw that some-body sober within the Act took him home. He arrived home, stunned as a fish, at eleven. It was his habit to take off his shoes and outer clothing, crawl into bed and go out like a light, so that he could not be roused.

"Not so this evening. He sat, red-eyed, in an armchair and muttered to himself. All she could understand was something about Sir Jabeez. She's a tiny, meek ineffectual little lady. Finally she went to bed and was aroused at seven in the dark. She put the light on and Winding was dressed in his best suit and shaven. He told her to phone the office that he was ill and more or less bolted.

"After worrying for a bit she got up. It is a very large bunga-low with a huge living-room. There were the remains of a huge pot of instant black coffee, a few books strewn on the floor which she put back. She thought some paper had been burned on top of the coke ashes in the grate. At nine-thirty she phoned his office as ordered."

He paused.

"What were the books?" asked Harry.

The Superintendent shrugged beefy shoulders and spoke in a gravelly, resigned voice. "Deceased was a paper hoarder. The place is festooned with shelves, presses, horrid old cupboards. There are two hundred and forty copies of the 'Dick Turpin Library', thousands of the tuppenny comics they sold in his day, old newspapers and mags—my God, all those 'Happy Mags' —and several thousand books, all those second-hand, in no kind of order. His adult taste was non-fiction, Victorian stuff mostly—*Works of Swedenborg, Animal Magnetism.* Mrs. Winding says he at least glanced through each one, but his favourites were true-life adventures. Then, letters, circulars, etc., greetings cards were placed on the mantelpiece until his little wife did say something, whereupon he gathered them into a bunch and stuffed them."

"Stuffed them?" said Harry, feeling the onset of one of his headaches.

"Under the bath, in the airing cupboard, behind the lawn mower in the potting shed, behind her preserves in the larder, under the bed and once in the spin dryer. In short, when she picked up a book she just looked about for a spot where another could cram in. I got six men on the muck; it will take them two weeks. Crikey, what a game!"

"My own small contribution," said the Chief, "was to realise that there is a nine a.m. from Windlesham to Victoria, scheduled in at eleven-ten. For the superior commuters, the hoi polloi go by the seven o'clock. I stress Windlesham. Unlike Parva we have a flourishing passenger traffic plus goods from the light industries. A bus leaves the bottom of Winding's road and totters along to catch these trains. A ticket collector, occasional drinking companion of Winding over the years, remembers him taking a second to Victoria. The train was two hours late owing to fog, which makes the time factor jell. His motor bike is parked by the side of Prettyman's office. He never drove when he intended drinking."

"You've done a lot," said Harry. "A mixture of much booze on top of shock can produce a hallucinatory state. I had a

149

case where a man killed somebody in his car—not his fault—but he afterwards drank a bottle of gin and two days later was found in Aberdeen with some vague idea he was to meet his boss there."

"H'm." The Chief had the air of having left the disagreeable until last. "About Redapple. If you want—Hawker has left it to you—we will give him complete surveillance twenty-four hours a day."

It was a wonderful offer, thought Harry; when the whips were cracking you rallied round, one of the reasons he remained in the game.

"I think not, sir, not at the moment. I'll let him run loose. London will check his official movements there; his office is in Throgmorton Street and he is on the board of eight companies with city addresses. But we might require a bit of confirmation this end."

"I don't like this backstairs business," said the Chief, "but one of the brighter young men is having what I gather is a hottish affair, view marriage so I suggested sternly, with Redapple's assistant cook, a saucy little red-head. The cook is a nasty old woman who learned in the school of hard knocks, seven bob a week and keep in the old Duke's kitchens, and cooks magnificently. The assistant is the new school, two years' training in Paris, looks more like a high-class whore than a lady chef, good family." He sighed. "I wish we were in a world where female cooks looked like female cooks. However if we have to I'll get the boy to enlist her."

"Redapple keeps it up quite feudally!"

"Of course, it comes out of the Estate to some extent, but he has an army of retainers, most of whom are fed, plus when he used to entertain there were twenty-odd guests. A lot of work. Of course you know the family origins—not that I care," said the Chief in the some-of-my-best-friends-are-negroes manner, "but in the country there is some, uh, reserve, and I suppose he feels, uh, obliged to keep it up."

"I found it a little difficult to place Redapple—oh, I know, the money and distinguished financier—but as a bloke."

"I meet him occasionally, socially. Always lectures you on your subject. Police to me, of course, schemes for T.V. plus helicopters. When I ask him about the monetary side he takes no notice. But nervous, you expect him to shy, neigh and gallop off. An uncomfortable man. Needs somebody comfortable to look after him."

"Thank you, sirs. Anything from the paper litter of Winding would be gratefully received."

"I doubt it," said the Superintendent.

As Harry left he had a puzzling memory of their facial expressions. He suddenly remembered having, in the old days, seen it on the faces of the dock attendants as the judge put the little black square of silk on top of his wig.

He called in at Prettyman's. The typist whose name he could never remember, ah, yes, Miss Bramble, was more tear-stained than he had imagined a person could be.

"I am so sorry," he said gently.

"Poor Peter, he was so *gentle*," she said.

"Did you take Mrs. Winding's call?"

"Oh, yes, she sounded upset, as . . ." Miss Bramble stopped abruptly.

"As . . .?"

Miss Bramble flushed. "Oh, well, it doesn't matter. Peter was not a drunk, but if anything ghastly happened—a friend dying or something—he'd be drunk every night for a week. Then he'd stay in bed for a day, barley water and slops. Ethel got upset, but then it was perhaps once a year. He controlled himself when Mr. Prettyman passed away, but then a friend died in an air crash, so, well I thought Peter must have so over indulged that . . ."

"I see. Just one little thing. We suffer from curiosity as an occupational disease. I notice that Mr. Winding's office window had been recently very liberally oiled."

"Oh," she managed a little smile. "He fancied himself as a handyman. He wasn't, but, there, he was always writing away for things. He brought some new oil in one day and started oiling things in the lunch hour, until I found he had slopped oil over my brief-sized typewriter—that's one with almost a two-foolscap-sheet-size carriage. I was furious; it had to be dismantled and cleaned, so poor Peter stopped oiling."

He thanked her and wandered through the old building. In Mr. Prettyman's office the accountants droned to each other. Winding's office was occupied by the junior—Pilling, Harry

151

remembered—who with lugubrious mien was piling things into stacks.

"Morning sir, dreadful business."

"Your excavations have indicated nothing with any bearing on his death?"

"I thought it was the Blue Lady, sir."

"Of course," said Harry, "of course, but our job is to seal up every possibility."

"There'll be nothing here, sir. Peter was a fair slummock at home, but in the office shipshape. Mr. Prettyman would never countenance anything personal here. 'If you want to write a letter'—it was one lunch hour when he caught me—'go to the P.O. and do it', that's what he told me."

"Ah, thanks." He found Milton Greenaway and John Hearman drinking coffee.

"Can we interest you in the instant?" asked Hearman.

"I think it's an alcoholic beverage day," said Harry, "but not until lunch."

"That poor old Winding," said Greenaway, "fair knocked me for six. We got it on the ten o'clock news."

"I didn't have much to do with him," said the Inspector.

"Neither did we, but he was, if you'll excuse me, John, a proper subservient old clerk—one of those ghastly Dickens characters, old Bob Scratchit kind of thing, 'don't spare the lash, dear master'."

Hearman gave his engaging grin—a man with the girls, thought Harry. "Don't mind me, Milton, but the same old servitor got five thousand nicker, a car and a bungalow. What will Sir Jabeez leave me? His second-hand copy of *Snidby on Torts*. Winding was a good clerk, beautifully accurate on conveyancing, which is what the business was, you know."

"Well, he gave me good advice about flogging the business to some dreary old firm in Windlesham," said Greenaway. "Four old men who never heard of drip-dry, and two young 'uns waiting for them to pass away. We saw 'em yesterday afternoon."

"I gathered from Winding that you had spurned his advice."

"Good God, no. But he dotted his t's, told me how to draw up a contract, explained to me elementary law regarding sales involving goodwill and contingency, so I choked him off. Wish I hadn't, of course."

"Nothing sinister?" asked Harry.

"Whistle clean. Prettyman left things all apple-pie as far as his own stuff, eh, John?"

"A model of his kind," said Hearman, "and not so avaricious as most. He did things the cheaper way, unlike some I could name."

"He was rather like that Dickens character who left cryptic notes for himself," said Greenaway, rather dourly. "Look at this." It was an exercise book marked 'Cash payments made to C. G. Blucher by C. Prettyman'.

Amused, Harry took it. It covered a period of seven years, the last item being one hundred and twenty pounds two weeks previously.

"Only Blucher I know won at Waterloo, or so my landlady who comes from that part of the world always tells me," said Hearman.

"Mr. Prettyman undertook the divorce of friends and members of the peerage, so one understands," said Harry. "C. Guy Blucher is one of the most adept practitioners of peering through bedroom windows. You may have seen his advertisements, 'retired police detective of utmost discretion'. Slanderously, he was a sergeant who was supported by seven street bookmakers, two madams and a dubious club. It was touch and go, but he was allowed to resign."

"Doesn't sound like Prettyman's cuppa."

"Oh, C. Guy Blucher has several levels, as the critics like to say. The top one is like a bank manager crossed with some discreet old abortionist. Down the mine shaft you find rather loathsome things, like blackmail, collusion, and fake evidence."

"Thanks, Inspector. We'll let old Redapple pay for the greater part of the audit. I tried to phone him yesterday, but he was unavailable. But everything is as sweet as a nut. I'll swear it, or almost. I'm going to have a spot percentage check made of the properties—any hidden payments—but I'd drop down in a faint if they found it."

"Talking of dropping, your Mr. Greasing dropped down his stairwell."

"Christ!" said Greenaway, "I can't take much more of this."

"His own fault," said Harry, "too mean to get a carpenter to shore up the banisters."

"Where will our fun come from nowadays?" asked Hearman. "All those naughties. Remember last year, Inspector, a series of famous classics with photographic illustrations. *The Golden Ass* was the case in point. Old Justice Maple said, 'Are you thinking of including any Trollopes in the series, Mr. Greasing?' Old Greasing turned not a hair, just said, 'I congratulate your worship on your taste.' I was holding the fort for old Margits. You had no chance, you know, not with Sir Henry leading the defence, all teeth and sympathy, and the headmistress of an experimental girls' school as his leading witness."

"We're padding things out," said Greenaway slowly. "Might as well make a week of it. Damned if I even like the thought of London."

"How's your Miss Redding?"

"At Margate, might return tomorrow night."

Hearman chuckled. "Her boss wants these wretched girls bikinied and sent out on a trawler. The fishermen are wearing four jerseys and two sets of long underwear. He wants the girls playing with lobster pots."

"Noshing back at the pub?"

Greenaway shook his head. "The two senior partners of Grubb, Bundleham, Goch and Potter entertain us at their club. Both florid and obviously know drink if not food."

"Plus two quid on our expense accounts," said Hearman.

"A venial man, I fear, Inspector," said Greenaway, not quite smiling.

Harry went back to the Dendles, to find Elizabeth a trifle floury and flushed, make-up awry, gloating over professional secrets and planning a meal to knock the eyeballs out of her dearest friend, who had put in six months under a blue-haired cookery lady with a French name which Elizabeth, after a third gin, alleged was assumed.

They ate in the private room and Harry was just suggesting they start, quoting the old Chinese proverb 'Better that a man should wait for his meal than the meal should wait for the man', when Honeybody, beaming, and exuding a smell of stout, entered.

154

"Holy mackerel," said Harry.

"Disguise, fading into the yokel background, sir."

The Sergeant's great stomach perilously rested on the upper edge of riding breeches, spread taut against vast thighs. Riding boots, polished bright, encased the size twelve feet. A checked shirt with a red cravat and a vast Harris tweed jacket with patch pockets completed the picture.

"Packed 'em for needs be. One thing about riding boots, you can keep bottles in 'em so the space isn't wasted. Of course, I got two sets of underwear on."

Knowing the Sergeant's ideas of country life were strange, the Inspector merely said, "I didn't know you were equestrian, Sergeant."

"Two years before the war, sir. Took a course for horse duty, you should see the marks I still got. They used to send us out to bash the unemployed and people what didn't like old Hitler when they demonstrated, but I got tired of it."

"It's coming up," said Elizabeth, "no talking."

Harry ate his way through leek and potato soup, ham with lentils, and, to avoid a scene with Elizabeth, meringue tarts with a strange-flavoured ice-cream.

"Passion fruit," said Elizabeth, aggressively defensive.

"Fruit, eh?" said Honeybody. "When I was a boy it was Spanish fly they swore by."

"It's a climbing vine that grows in Australia," snapped Elizabeth.

"I wouldn't wonder, but I'm too old for it," said Honeybody, pushing his plate away and reaching for the cheeseboard.

Seeing the battle-light in his wife's eyes, Harry whipped over a change of bowling. "How was Greenaway's girl friend, the well-stacked Redding?"

"She's charming and oddly shy and madly in love with Greenaway, of whom she's worth six. She even put off their wedding so she could save, paste-sandwiches-for-lunch stuff. She won't be here tonight. Maybe tomorrow. I shall take her in hand. They should marry next month. She should bash some stuffing into that very indeterminate young man, if necessary insisting that he should get a job which pays money."

"H'm, married bliss all round."

"Talking of that, sir," said Honeybody, drinking coffee and

looking wistfully about for signs of liquor, "who d'you think I saw?"

"How the hell should I know?" The Inspector relented. "Liz, go down and order two double brandies and a light ale for me."

"Thank you, sir," said Honeybody as Elizabeth left, "a morning spent in tightified trousers and two pair of coms gives one a thirst somehow. Well, I'm on the hill watching through the glasses where that old Volks of his lordship was hidden and do you know what I saw?"

"For God's sake," said Harry, "I told you, how the hell . . ."

"A car, sir."

"Not a camel, not a dromedary, not a . . . oh, well."

"It stopped."

"They put the goddamned brake on."

"And got out," said Honeybody imperturbably. "One being C. Guy Blucher; the other one of the little sharpies he has working for him, Soho scum that want to lie low for a time. They talk for a bit, much head shaking, and then Blucher drives off. I could see the smirk he wears when he hears a fiver rustle. His man walks into the copse and comes out with one of those titty little bikes with a one-horse engine. Now I hired a bike from Mr. Jewel, the one he keeps for his pigman, and I haven't ever known a push bike to stink before. I've got it in *my* trees, so as he putt-putts off I keep a hundred yards behind. He draws away, of course, but . . . oh, thank you ma'am."

"I bought two brandies each for the Sergeant and me and a quart of light ale for you."

Harry poured. "Go on, Honeybody."

"Luckily there's this hill. I don't reckon a bike ever went so fast, and me with no knowledge of the brakes, but at the bottom I saw his bike outside a pub. . . ."

"It would be," said Harry.

The Sergeant ignored him. "It's called The Traveller's Rest, snuggish little place with a few rooms and two bars plus jug-and-bottle. I have a stout in the public. You can more or less look into the little saloon. The man's ordering a meal—shouldn't think the grub's good, bought pies, that kind of stuff—and it's apparent he's staying in the house. The landlord says is he in a hurry, and the man says, no, he won't be going

156

out until six. About all. I managed to find a lorry driver who brings me and the bike home for ten bob." Honeybody finished his first brandy. "Only other thing is that the driver had to stop to deliver a crate near the P.O. I phoned the Redapple mansion and said I was the Press Association and had his lordship any comment on Mr. Winding's death. A man with a voice like a whelk in heat said he would enquire. In two minutes, even colder, he said his lordship had no comment."

"An excellent job, Sergeant."

"We better have a squint at him this evening, sir. Say we get to the pub at five-thirty."

It was inevitable, thought Harry. "All right," he said, "and I know I've been trapped."

"All in the line of duty, therein lies its beauty," soothed Honeybody, "and to tell you the truth, me getting on a bit and lying in that copse this morning, I feel like a bit of a snore-off."

"I shall be in my room writing reports, and, Honeybody, perhaps you'd revert to your usual disguise of a seedy traveller in the wine and spirit trade who is paid in kind. Elizabeth, you will no doubt help Mrs. Jewel." He thought he made rather a good exit.

At a quarter to five Elizabeth, initiated in some arts of puff pastry, found him sleeping.

"Must have dozed off, my love."

"Do you customarily report in bed, in underpants, with the electric blanket turned on?"

"Except in summer when I lie nude on my rubber Li-lo."

Wincing at the cold as he dressed, the Inspector put on a pullover under his suit-coat, and donned his overcoat.

"I hammered at Honeybody's door until the horrible snoring stopped and he said 'Aw right, Dodo, love'," said Elizabeth.

"Pearl of inflation," said Harry. "God knows how long we'll be, but await to welcome us and persuade Mrs. Jewel to leave some stewy soup on the gas stove."

"She says they're fatal. She uses a slow combustion stove. I suppose, Harry, we couldn't . . ."

"No." The Inspector fled, encountering Honeybody, smelling of liniment, on the stairway.

"Nothing like the old Sloan's when you've been lyin' in the undergrowth. My Dodo . . ."

"Come on, man, my woman is talking of new kitchen equipment."

As Honeybody had said, the pub served decent liquor but did not look promising for food. From his position in the public the Inspector glimpsed, gracing the saloon, a large glass jar of yellowish preserved hard-boiled eggs and the most vinegary brand of pickle in a slopped-over jar.

The place was packed. "There he is, red-faced little bastard, with the green pork pie," breathed Honeybody.

Harry, who had been thinking of food, started, but finally saw the hat adorning a small apple face with eyes that constantly moved. You saw men like it topping up fruit on barrows, making fake bids at fake auctions, sidling up to visiting firemen with suggestions of pleasure. He knew better than to underestimate such a man, bred God knows where, seemingly bereft of education, a child originally of the streets, wits sharpened on the hard pavements.

"Look over there," hissed Honeybody. Cautiously Harry slid his eyes sideways and with a groan recognised the profile, large slightly reddened nose flanked narrowly by small brown eyes, thick lips and a mass of greasy black hair above a bull-like neck.

It was one Jack Nippet, of a family of rural gangsters, poachers, petty peculators, sneak thieves, seducers of innocent —well inexperienced—rural maidens, sneakers of small articles from unlocked cars, adepts at screwing money out of the welfare state. Harry, thinking the game was up, stood gloomily cataloguing what a garrulous local sergeant had once told him. Nippet even got a new pair of glasses each month, not that he needed them, but he could flog the frames for four quid. Where he, an Inspector and a righteous man, could not get a painful—well, annoying—cyst taken off the sole of his foot.

Oh, well, better attack than wait for Nippet's sly weasely approach, half blackmail and wholly false and untrustworthy.

"Well, Jack," he said, "how's Nippet tricks?"

The small eyes looked at Harry gloomily. With something of

a shock the Inspector saw a certain sleazy respectability about Nippet. The bucolic carelessness, a poacher's pocket and a faint smell of horse manure, a two-day stubble and an egg-stained but open shirt, was gone.

"Hullo." Even the rich, beery voice was lifeless.

"Not been ill, Jack?"

"You mean, lookin' like a pox doctor's clerk?"

"If you put it that way."

Nippet looked down at his blue serge trousers with distaste. "They got me, got me down and kicked me."

"Who?"

"The effing welfare state, the effing income tax, and me never done a tap in me life. I was sittin' in the kitching with a drop of brown ale and the effing *Sportin' Life*, reading Gussie Dalrymple, when 'e walked in, knee high to a sparrow. 'Now,' 'e says, 'I've got you down at a two 'undred tax a year since 1956. Why,' 'e says, 'the four pheasants that the farmer reckons you take a month is worth three quid, then there's the glasses frames'—the optician 'ad been talkin', couldn't work out 'ow I smashed so many—'and the lead from empty 'ouses, the rabbits, the car wirelesses, and the quid Lily Trotwin gives you every time you introduce a Yankee tourist to her, plus the bits on flag days'—I shouldn't be sayin' this, but I might as well be in quad as what I am now. He knew it all. 'E said, even if it is dishonest Callaghan wants it."

Harry signalled for another pint and watched the great nose delve into the tankard.

"What are you doing about it?"

"In the jam factory, Joy o' Kent brand. They buy damaged stuff from Italy and process it. The smell turns you up. I did ask the man—labour welfare counsellor he called 'imself—for a sardine factory, to which tins I'm partial—but 'e said we don't do 'em which shows Teddy is right about there bein' little 'ope of economic recovery. I count the cases, thirteen nicker, and seven quid off to the tax each week.

"I told this little man that Mum supported me from 'er charring, but it didn't work."

The Inspector knew that Jack's mum, one of the wealthier Nippets, did not char but subsisted on the rents of various rural slums which represented thirty-eight years of picking the pockets of such elderly male visitors to Broadstairs as allowed her to sit on their laps.

"I voted for 'Arold, but in future it's Teddy. Arter all, 'e's a local boy and we think alike, stands to reason."

Fascinated, the Inspector watched the protuberant Nippet Adam's apple wobble as the pint disappeared with a slight gurgling noise.

"What are yew doin' 'ere?" There was the flicker of cunning in Nippet's yokel face.

"I got a car outside," said Harry. "Let's talk out there. Come to think of it, there's a quartern of whisky in the glove box."

Nippet drained his pint.

"Now, Jack," said the Inspector in the car, filling a tooth glass with spirit, "if I said a word to that income-tax chap you'd be in that factory until you died. I'd see to it."

"Not the old-age?" quavered Nippet, afraid of the unknown.

"The old-age for tax evaders? You're joking! And all you Nippets kicked out of the council houses. And the kids taken into homes, if I say the word and which I *will* if you blow it about that I'm a busy. One word and I see Callaghan in the morning when he makes out his lists as he does each day with the head of the income tax."

"Now look, guv," said Nippet huskily, beginning to smell musky.

"Now listen to me. Have you got a relative that pays the income tax?"

"The old mum she do pay the tax," said Jack, "but she's controlled."

"Controlled?"

"Nineteen thirty-nine rents. The Member patted 'er 'ead in public and said she was a rare patriot. She'd gone because 'is missus was giving away meat pies and free tea. But," Nippet looked perplexed, and stopped abruptly.

"Now, come clean, Jack," admonished Harry.

"Well, there do be a bit on the side, in cash like," said Nippet huskily. "Like my uncle Aubrey what 'as got the pig-manure contract."

"Say that again?"

"Well you wouldn't want half a ton of pig-manure dumped against the front door by mistake like. Downright un'ealthy.

Or there's my bruvver Dave, 'e can make a cesspit pack up in the dead of night. Or the windows get broke and people keep peeing through the 'oles when you are out. Downright un'ealthy. So they do give the old mum a bit of dropsy to keep the old girl sweet. No tax on that. Say fifteen notes a week it comes to, though Uncle Aubrey charges when we use his manure cart."

"A rural Rachman."

"Eh?"

"Never mind. What you want, my man, is bankruptcy."

Fear crept across Jack Nippet's face. "I wouldn't want to meddle with that."

"Then you're in the jam factory for good. And if the old mum leaves you a bit, they'll have it off you before she's cold."

"'Ow do I go about it?"

"In the classified pages of the telephone book are listed accountants. I'll scrawl you out a bit of a screed to take. But first get rid of your possessions to somebody you can trust."

"What possessions?" asked Nippet, with infinite wariness.

"You got guns!"

"Two, no, I'll be frank, it's kind of complicated. You see I 'ave a friend who comes home early, and, well, they dew jump out o' the window, fierce-looking fellow he is, and leave their luggage be'ind. This tourist 'ad matched shotguns, and, well, my friend did ask me to mind 'em."

"It's known as the badger game," snarled Harry.

"Not many badgers about," said Nippet, "but they do say that my great-auntie Flo, over at Canterbury, bought her li'l pub off the proceeds. 'Er 'usband Ned always dressed up as a chorister and had a Bible in 'is 'and."

"Just shut up," said Harry. "Go bankrupt and live with your mum. You must never get credit without disclosing you're bankrupt."

"Nobody gives us Nippets credit, not even the washing machines," said Jack simply.

"Describe yourself as an odd job man living off your mum. Don't take cheques, keep everything in your pocket in cash and you'll live happy ever after."

"You mean this is going on?"

"I do!" The Inspector found his unofficial notebook—as opposed to the numbered, official book with the inbuilt penalty for removing pages—and wrote. Accountancy had been the Inspector's first love and he felt his tongue loll between his teeth, sure sign of engrossment, as he sketched out Nippet's dilemma and possible cure. He handed the sheets over, and was conscious of Honeybody's heavy, disapproving stare through the window.

"While you were blathering, he scarpered, not on his bike, which foxed me, but into a car with C. Guy Blucher driving. Fifty yards down the road. I couldn't do anything."

"In trouble?" Nippet sounded as grateful as he was capable of, which was little.

"Oh, well," said Harry, "a little red-faced bloke in a green hat."

"What's he done?"

"Oh, white slavery!"

"Me gran used to do that," said Nippet reflectively. "Parlour maids in Bonos Ires she used to tell 'em and the gentleman paid her four gold sovereigns a go. It came easy those days when the Liberals were in, more's the pity they ain't at the 'ead of things. But that li'l feller, been here a munce. I dunno there's girls'd fall for that these days, the way they always ask about the money. Anyway he hangs about in Windlesham. I see 'im late when I work overtime—keep that dark, this li'l income tax don't know about that."

"Trust him to," said Harry, "but he's saving it up."

"Another glast, governor," begged Nippet and accepted it with a slight tremor which Harry thought was not entirely alcoholic in origin.

"This man in the green hat hangs around Sir Charles Dilke Street, the posh part of Windlesham. Here, give us the notebook and the ball-point. It's at the bottom of the valley, with what they call booticks and little shops with Polish ham. Here," Nippet drew like a man who rarely handled a pen. "There ... hanging around ... I suppose it's worth something, guv?"

Harry got out his wallet and handed over two pounds. "You're an ungrateful hound."

"All us Nippets is, but my lips are hereby sealed, guv." He

opened the door and sidled past the menacing, impassive Honeybody.

"I'd've put my knee where it hurt, Mr. James." The Sergeant was definitely huffed as he got in.

"And you would not have got a map out of him."

"Lying bastard made it up."

"We'll see. There's a map of Windlesham in the glove box. We want Sir Charles Dilke Street, must have been a Liberal enclave down this way."

"Sir?"

"Just do the guidance."

The planners had bent their beards over Sir Charles Dilke Street quite recently, so that it was a curious concrete ravine, with undulating blocks of flats with smart little shops acting as navels. A longish hill ran down to it, named William Ewart Gladstone Road. Before the intersection Harry braked and pulled back the big hand-brake. "No problem. Leave this great bus here and foot-snoop."

They got out. "Better lock it," said Honeybody, "these posh places are full of crooks."

In recalling the incident the Inspector thinks that the faint pressure of the key was the straw that broke the ancient camel. The car magisterially commenced to move down the remaining ten yards of hill.

"Hang on," yelled Harry, but the observation mirror on the right wing snapped in his hand. At the same time he glimpsed Honeybody sprawled on his face and the disappearing backside of the car. Honeybody reached his knees and said "My God!"

The monstrous car waddled majestically across the intersection, its momentum carrying it up two steps, before plunging down three, and—so the Inspector swears—nuzzling open a double door. At that moment he and the Sergeant were sprinting after it, through the shattered portals and to where the car was bogged into a kind of pool, goldfish swimming hopefully around the windows. On the wall was a life-size reproduction of 'The Rape of the Sabine Women', with a gilded inscription: 'This shall never happen here. Signed President Alice Grittle, League of Modest Maidens.'

"Bludgeons, girls," said a contralto, "the Beast is among us."

There seemed to be a lot of women in abbreviated pants lying on Dunlopillo mats who scrambled to their feet.

"Now ladies," said Honeybody's reassuring voice, and "Police here," said Harry, far less reassuringly.

"More than likely," said the contralto, who was small and lively and seemed to the Inspector to be an alarming but diminutive edition of his wife. He glanced at the car, from the bowels of which steam seemed to be arising, and produced his warrant card.

"Police," he squeaked.

"Caution, girls, weapons at the ready, the Blue Lady has many guises. Stay quite still, this is our judo instructor," she indicated a middle-aged woman with muscles.

"Could she instruct me?" asked Honeybody, bovinely, and the instructor blushed. Some of the women giggled and the contralto, with political sense that she was losing her audience, grabbed the warrant card.

"Why this intrusion, Inspector?"

"Now," said Honeybody, "I'm a grandpa. The Inspector hasn't been married long, so you'll excuse me if I speak, as all you young ladies embarrass him."

It was hateful, thought Harry, to see that while some of them showed irritation or amusement, the majority looked sympathetically at Honeybody, his vast, two-combinationed figure some kind of male god-image. The contralto, whom the Inspector guessed was a paid organiser and doing well, hopped readily on to the bandwagon.

"We are on the side of the police, Sergeant." She ignored Harry. "The Dame herself has made that clear. With our bludgeons we patrol Windlesham until the early hours. You see us at our joyous strength calisthenics which will be followed by our joy through dancing."

"Ah," said the Sergeant, "the handbrake failed and it rolled in the door."

"There will be compensation." The contralto was on to it like a bone.

"Now I dare say, miss," Honeybody avoided looking at the wedding ring. "If you'll show me the telephone, I'll get the station to tow the old creature away."

The contralto led the Sergeant into a side office.

"How long, Inspector, shall we have to endure this fiend," said a very masterful and craggy old lady, arising from her cushion with a dexterity that Harry, feeling his rheumatic stiffness, frankly envied.

"We do our best." Inspiration hit him. "We have so many sinister ones to keep an eye on, which impels me to ask have you seen a small red-faced man around in a green pork-pie hat?"

There was a babble of voices and the Inspector realised that he had struck a jackpot.

"Pray be silent," said the craggy lady. The Inspector thought she might be the principal local landlady. "The paid secretary of this nest—that is what we call our local branches—has, by order of Dame Alice Grittle, received descriptions of any sinister strangers. The man with the green hat, sometimes accompanied by a stout man clad in galoshes, has been seen lurking outside the Robert Menzies Mansions." She saw the Inspector look dazed. "We are naming them after the lord wardens, except the one that was executed by mistake. But opposite the Menzies is a shop which displays Italian corsetry. In the entrance of this the two men have been seen hanging about. Our worthy paid secretary informed the local constable, a young man of no great perception in my opinion . . ."

There were choruses of 'yeses'.

"Told me they were upright and harmless citizens. It may be my duty to inform the Chief Constable."

"This Menzies Mansions," said Harry, "which way is it?"

"Going out," said the craggy lady, "it is a hundred yards on the right. You cannot mistake it because of the fourteenth-century reproduction tower. The manager," she pursed her lips, "has long hair. I fear that he is *avant garde*, or so they say in the library. The committee were quite put out by the titles he put in the suggestion box; in fact they removed it."

Honeybody returned with the contralto rather on the fawning side, or at any rate to the extent of receiving an admonitory glance from the craggy lady.

With his susceptibility to atmosphere, the Sergeant disengaged himself. "In two shakes of a lamb's tail, miss, the breakdown car will be along, plus two blokes to fix the door, temporary like."

"'Ell to pay about that old crate," said Honeybody, as they gained the front of Sir Charles Dilke Street. "Two dozen forms, I reckon, and the enquiry."

"Leave that to the day," grunted Harry sourly, "if anybody's there to conduct or attend."

The massive bulk of Menzies Mansions, flanked by Churchill Close and Birkenhead Retreat, was faced on the other side of the road by smaller business buildings mounted upon rows of shops.

"That's them," the Sergeant, who had a hawk's eyesight, nodded to what the Inspector merely noted as two glowing cigarette butts. They strolled across the road and caught C. Guy Blucher in his expensive overcoat and his pork-pied myrmidon in a much cheaper one.

"James of the Yard," said Harry. "You know me, Mr. Blucher."

"Know you both," said Blucher with resignation but no enthusiasm, "and goodbye."

"I'll put it straight," said Harry. "What are you on?"

"Client's bus." Blucher had a trick of sounding innocently offended. "A man on the beat asked me a week ago. Me and Percy produced our credentials and he said all right."

"We're on a murder trip."

"I read it, old solicitor and 'is clurk, both by the Blue Lady. They said crool things about me, Mr. J., but I didn't have no blue women on my beat; mine were always fly, eh?"

The assistant grinned dutifully.

"Come on." Harry led the way over the road.

"I'd like to punch that bastard," said Honeybody.

"He knows when to fight and when to run away," said Harry, "and particularly when the stakes are big enough to justify a risk."

"I've been thinking," said the Sergeant, "the little fellow is Blucher's son-in-law. Haven't seen him for ten years—used to have an off-licence—but he could be the same fellow. And Blucher himself on the job. He doesn't catch his death of cold hanging round the building any more."

"It stinks of blackmail," muttered Harry as they entered the dignified portals of Menzies Mansions. There was a man behind a desk with a switchboard, a discreet man in grey knee-breeches and a cutaway coat, and a harassed-looking and rather seedy man at the junction of the two lifts

The man in grey knee-breeches, competence itself, took him to the manager's flat, where a large, untidy young man named Jones opened the door. The two rooms seemed festooned with piles of typed paper.

"Thank you, Snodbury, come in, sir. Come in, Sergeant. Perhaps a cheap sherry, but definitely Spanish, if perhaps a trifle shady in origin, not quite received in decent company."

"I don't mind if I do, sir," answered Honeybody quickly. The room they settled into was sparsely but decently furnished.

"You're the manager, sir?" asked the Inspector.

"In title. Snodbury runs it. His name has held him back. Some kind of Yorkshire obstinacy made him keep it. But de facto he manages. I, well they wanted an old Etonian, I'm writing a book and my mother's sister was married to Redapple—the Estate owns it."

"A writer, eh?" said Harry to gain time to think.

"Unpublished," sighed Jones. "I thought of taking the lid off a block of flats, all the pot-smoking, wife-swapping, knifing in the back, but they're a shocking dull lot. They just nod at each other and scuttle off. Snodbury does his best, but all he has found out has been a lot of drinking and that the couple in 273 are probably unbenefited by clergy. But she's sixty-fivish and every afternoon a man comes to wheel *him* around in a bath chair. I've had to invent my own block where everybody's raping when they aren't flogging people with electric flex. Should sell when it's done, but I prefer drawing from real life. Still, this keeps me meantime, and Snodbury does all the work really."

The Inspector could see no other way than directness.

"There's a private detective named Blucher, sixtyish, plump, with violet eyes. He has . . ."

"Yes, oh, yes, Snodbury headed him off and told him to call back. Snodbury is nobody's fool and the man that Blucher—odd name, what?—was asking about was Redapple himself. I told Snodbury to answer Blucher as if it were about a stranger—try lying and you find the mess is apt to be worse"—Jones was no fool, Harry thought. "As a matter of fact Snodbury could truthfully say he had not ever seen Redapple enter the flats. Our contact was that nice chap, Peter Winding, and the managing agents. A private eye, mind you, is no rarity, but it's always in connection with credit, some of the bright young things haven't got the money you might think. Blucher asked about Redapple and the tenant in four-o-eight. He did not believe Snodbury when he said that Redapple definitely never came near the place."

"Pray who lives in four-o-eight, Mr. Jones?"

The manager massaged his longish hair. Not the type he liked, thought the Inspector, but maybe having his points. The sherry, in an outsize *copita*, wasn't too bad, either, probably one of the unblended *montillas* really.

"Well, now," said Jones, "a lady, whose name shall not be mentioned in this mess. If you want to know, you'll have to snoop. I should explain that my mother exists on a small annuity and Redapple has been good to her—a little house for free, hampers of goodies on feast days, nice cheque at Christmas. I must admit I'm not of a grateful generation, we old angry young men aren't, but I'm a good judge of bread and butter. I rang Redapple, mentioning Blucher as vaguely as I could."

"His reaction?" asked Harry as the young man refilled the glasses.

"Just thanked me in that nervous high-pitched voice of his. He is so twitchy, is Redapple, that you can't tell *what* he's thinking."

"You might as well tell me the person's name, having come so far."

"The point is," said Jones, "that when I lose your company I shall fly to the blower and peach to Redapple. I shall tell him truthfully I mentioned no names. He might wangle me more pay."

"Ah, well," said Harry, "we've had a passable sherry."

"I think so. There's a curious cavity under the back seat of my girl friend's old car. We found it by chance. When we have our seven days of sun I bring four gallons, near enough, concealed there in one of those wicker-over-glass carboys. But I don't want ever to have it said I impeded you fellows, so here goes. A well-preserved forty-eight, brunette, rather plump for my taste, well-bred. I would type her as 'comfortable and calm'.

168

Separated from her husband who is a frightful brute of whom I never heard anything good. But his mother was a daughter of the old Duke, which gets him a certain amount of social acceptance, the swine. A bully, a man who has had dozens of partners and robbed them. If ever there's a fixed race you may be sure he's got fifty quid on the winner."

"You sound personal."

"He is the main reason why my father died broke."

"Fair enough." The Inspector drained the sherry. "Is there a back entrance?"

"Of course, and balconies around the back of the flats for the tradesmen, leading down into the garage area. If you like, ask Snodbury to show you."

As they left a typewriter began to tap.

"No bottom, these lads," said Honeybody, "lack of leadership. Writing books!"

"He does all right," said Harry, "although I admit in a parasitical way."

"The back entrance, by permission of Mr. Jones," the Inspector told Snodbury, who silently led them along carpeted hallways.

"By the way, who's in four-o-eight?" asked Harry.

"So many people here, sir, I lose check," said Snodbury, face wooden in the pinkish wall-lighting. The Inspector essayed a wink, but the smooth face remained without expression.

"Here, sir," Snodbury opened a door. The large area was brilliantly lit. "Tradesmen's staircase runs to balconies extending round the flats, sir. And garages over there. Three ramps, sir," the structure looked like a fabulous beehive, "all double garages, sir, most of the tenants having two vehicles." His side glance at Harry was tinged with the contempt habitual to high-class manservants when addressing the lower middle class.

"And yet some don't stump up so quick for the bills, eh?" Honeybody inserted his penny and received a freezing glance.

"Their affairs are their affairs, sir," said Snodbury.

"Thank you. Is there an attendant?" asked the Inspector.

"Of course. Alfred!" Snodbury raised his voice.

A chunky man, lame in one leg but walking fast, appeared from somewhere. Ex-N.C.O., Harry thought. The man sketched a salute. "All quiet and right, Mr. Snodbury.'

"Seen four-o-eight?" asked the Inspector.

"That will do, Alfred." Snodbury's voice was quietly authoritative and the chunky man receded into the shadows. "The exit, sir, for vehicles and tradesmen is straight across. Good night to *you*."

The door clicked softly.

"I'd like to meet him on the outside," Honeybody sounded perturbed, "drunk and assaulting the police and his uppers smashed."

"Come on," the Inspector said, in no mood to discuss ethics. "What the hell does Redapple take Blucher for? There'll be a man outside."

They walked across two hundred yards of concrete and through the double concrete pillars.

"On your right," said Honeybody. Sedately parked was a van with 'Plus Electric Repairs. Phone 4325'.

They strolled over and passed it. The back door was un-locked and with a jerk the Inspector opened it. From the inside came the faint steely whiff of mechanical equipment. A small red-headed man, with the indefinable aura of toughness, turned round and peered through the darkness.

"All right, Toothy," said Harry, wearily.

Toothy, presumably so-called because of the remarkable way in which his front teeth protruded, was almost an institution. A brilliant photographer technically, although devoid of artistic power, he did most of the divorce work requir-ing photographs. In addition he freelanced for newspapers, photographed surgery with bored aplomb, and very occasion-ally, when staff was short, worked for the C.I.D. at cut rates. The latter was important because counsel could refer to it when Toothy was in the witness box and introduce a witness of absolute integrity, which, as far as Harry was aware, was truly the case.

"Oh, yus"—Toothy had an unfortunate accent which he said when drunk had precluded him from a good marriage— "h'it's the Inspector, and, bless my soul, my old guzzlin' frien' Cedric Honeybody. Gawd it's cold. The guv wouldn't let me 'ave my little paraffin 'eater because the stink would cause notice."

"A stake-out?"

"Yus, one of the Blucher efforts. He makes a nuisance of 'imself out front and they scuttle out the back. Sounds better in court."

"Give us the strong of it, Toothy," said the Inspector.

"Ain't they comical, tryin' to trick Blucher? Rabbits and the stoat. 'Is technick now is picture and sound—'e got the idea from somethink they do in French castles, sun ett lumer he says, means somethink dirty, no doubt. A complete picture story, the lot, plus tapes. It's a money job when the injured party gets paid and hopes to make a good profit. They look, 'ear, blush, reach for the ol' cheque book and it just goes through as an or'nary undefended."

"Where are they shacked?"

"King 'Arold Court, three 'undred yards away. To the left down Lloyd George Street. Not posh like these. What they call stoodio flats, studies from life"—Toothy leered; it was impossible for a man in his way of life not to leer occasionally, thought Harry, although the teeth did make it unfortunate.

"What number?"

"Six. Ground floor. There's no liftmen or porters, just a super and cleaners. Blucher got to the super and there's a man there who looks like an electrician. Matter of fac' he is. It's 'im wot put the bug be'ind the built-in bar."

"Thanks, Toothy. Do a bit for you sometime."

"Quite all right, I'm sure."

King Harold Court was a rather good example of a certain quality in planning. Here were not the two-car garages of Menzies Mansions, but one-car ports and an arrangement of bars to support scooters. And the boutique did not hold Italian raffia-work handbags, but fish and chips. Harry was in favour.

They—or rather Honeybody's massive forearms—raised the electrician, dungareed, festooned with more tools, coils of wire than an electrician should have outside a film, off his knees beside a junction box in which rested earphones.

The Inspector flashed his warrant, and said, "I saw Blucher and Toothy and nobody wants trouble. Are they in?"

"Been on the nest, sir," said the man, "now dressed and discussin' how to buy the husbind orf. He says he'll go to fifty thousan'. Can you imaging payin' fifty thousan' for it? I tell my ol' duck she's lucky to get the eight nicker house-keepin' for keeping us all."

"I want two quick questions," said the Inspector, "and God help you if you cross me. Were you here on Monday or yesterday?"

The man scratched his left eyebrow. "We come from London each day, except Mr. B.'s son-in-law. Monday and yesterday, what with the fog and plenty of jobs in the West End we didn't come down, although I think old B. charged . . ."

He broke off abruptly. C. Guy Blucher walked with silent tread.

"Don't say any more. Why are you meddling with my men, Inspector? I'll see what my member, Dame Alice Grittle, makes of it!"

"Do that. And as a matter of interest what did you pay for him, scurfy eyebrows and all?"

"Look, Mr. B.," said the man, "I seen his warrant card. . . ."

"No lip," said Blucher. "I know me rights. Righto, Len, you come along with me."

He walked towards the entrance, Len following with apprehensive backward glances.

"Stay here, Sergeant," said the Inspector as he walked towards flat six. There was a delay of perhaps two minutes after he pressed the button of the doorbell, which was one of the kind he detested. It played the first four bars of 'John Peel'.

The long, serious face of Lord Redapple looked out.

"Inspector," he double-took, "you here!"

"I think I must come in, Lord Redapple."

Redapple stood aside. The studio apartment was one large room, basically shoddily furnished, apart from some added pieces. There were two rugs which the Inspector, who knew something of such matters, recognised as valuable.

"Look, Inspector, I think you should see me tomorrow. I have to attend the Chancellor in the afternoon, but, say at nine in the morning?"

"I am sorry to find a person of your position, my lord, unwilling to assist the police."

That nearly always pulled them up.

"All right," Lord Redapple said sulkily, "I suppose you'd better sit down."

"One minute."

The built-in bar bore horrible lamination. In the dimmish, arty light the images looked like dead frogs mixed with turnips. Harry ran his hand behind a bit that jutted out, observing that the decanters and glasses were fine crystal.

"Here," he extended his hand to Lord Redapple. "A quarter the size of a match box, but as powerful a mike as you'll get. They import them from the U.S., though I believe the Russkis have better ones."

The Inspector looked around. There were what he thought to be some rather good water-colours scattered around.

"You always get two mikes," he said, wearily, "the Russians have a 'without limitation' sort of theory, mikes in the glasses, in the cushions, baked into those little pies they love to nosh."

"Surely this is not political?" gasped Lord Redapple.

"Ah, here," the Inspector removed a water-colour and from behind it another microphone. "This should be the end. You see, sir, you are an amateur in adultery. Most people are. I would not oppose you in high finance, but when you start hiding little cars in trees, capering around the back entrances of flats, you are plain silly."

"It's nothing to do with the police."

"Who said it was? I am probably beyond my duty in telling you that a private detective, with his men, has been tape-recording and photographing you for some time; driving you like a fox from his covert, so cunning that the huntsmen can hardly stop their laughter."

Redapple's dignity asserted itself in adversity. "I have been a fool, in other words!"

"A human being. This detective is filth personified; you would need to be what you aren't to combat him. What I want to know is where you were Monday afternoon and yesterday afternoon. The hounds rested in London."

"I . . . Good God, what is this?"

"I am required by law," said the Inspector, feeling tired, "to explain to you that I do not suspect you of the deaths of Messrs. Prettyman and Winding, but that I believe you had animosity towards both."

"I was here, both afternoons and part of the evening. Time?

173

Well," he smiled faintly, "there are times when even a business man does not count it. One minute."

He rose without hurry and opened one of the two doors. The kitchen, the Inspector thought.

"Sit down, my dear, you have heard the conversation?"

The woman sat and looked at Harry out of great, black eyes. Whilst it was true there was a certain meatiness about her, it was the well-preserved muscle of the athlete who has perforce wandered to the quieter fields of life. Her magnolia skin glowed. Only the professional training he had endured made Harry place her in the mid-forties.

"No need to bring in this lady's name?" asked Redapple.

"I don't even want to hear it."

"Lord Redapple," she had a rich contralto, "was here on Monday and on yesterday afternoon." There was a kind of luxuriant silence about her, a kind of calm in which Redapple patently relaxed.

"Then that clears it up," said the Inspector.

"I should say," said Redapple, "that this lady has been long estranged from her husband, and I have long been a widower. We wish to marry."

"We have a very competent extortion and blackmail branch," Harry saw Redapple bridle. "I refer to the detective, a man named Blucher, who is always suspect by us. Should he approach you, telephone me. Good night."

He went quickly to the door.

Honeybody smelled of gin, but said quickly, "Take this card, sir, I nipped up and copied the name plate on her door."

Harry looked and whistled.

"In the line of duty, sir, I nicked into the pub along the way. Decorated after Louis Quince, so the bloke said, with a commode in the corner. I'd oppose his licence, but it's not my business. She's out of the top drawer, sir, pitchers in the old gravure mags and nearly an Olympic swimmer. Big girl, crush you like a walnut."

About four gins, thought the Inspector. "Did you take a look at the car?"

Honeybody looked apprehensive, as well he might, because the hirer of the ancient machine, Jas. Cockling, materialised from the night.

"Ar, concealing the fack you was a busybody, getting the val'able machine from me an' wreckin' it in some kind of assault on a lot of innocent wimming. If I had known . . ."

"Silence!" said the Inspector.

"What the . . ."

Harry looked at the garage proprietor. The years, as they wore on, were giving him queer powers of *looking*.

"Awry," said Cockling, "but the insurance . . ."

"Letting a car out with inadequate brakes. I might be magnanimous. I'll see. Tomorrow you get on the phone to the Inspector at Windlesham. He'll send you a Buff Form B.3. Fill in and return."

"You're getting hard, guv." There was nothing but measured appreciation in Honeybody's voice as Cockling vanished into the gloom.

"About getting back," said Harry. "I don't want to know any more about that effing old car."

"Sir, sir," said Honeybody, "in the Goose and Feathers—that's the local rubbidy-dub, I met a nice fellow named Woodcock, in the earth-moving business, but a little of the car hirin'. If we went back and had one I'm sure he'd oblige."

"You have four minutes, Sergeant, to get Woodcock and his vehicle here at the ready, thus missing a disciplinary board."

"Sir, sir, sir!" Harry grinned as Honeybody disappeared. But you could not beat him. It was twelve minutes, and with talk of getting petrol, before the Sergeant got very formally out of a rather smart car, driven by a very red-faced man who smelled of cloves, and insisted on saluting as the Inspector got in. One more gin, Harry thought, quickly consumed.

They reached the Dendles at ten-thirty.

"There," said Mrs. Jewel, attended by Elizabeth, "I said ten-thirty. That's when the men think of their bellies."

"I've learned how to keep a pudding without it getting hard," announced Elizabeth. "In three minutes."

The Inspector grunted, and was forestalled by Honeybody at the bathroom. Presently he admitted that the mulligatawny had indeed been followed by a superb steak and oyster pudding. He ordered black coffee to finish with.

Mellowed, he told Elizabeth that the hired car had inter-

175

rupted a chapter meeting of the League of Modest Maidens.

"Good job the Dame wasn't there," she said. "She'd have had your uniform. But she's up organising the Liverpool branches into patrols with bludgeons. Bet you ten bob she gets the Blue Lady before you do."

"You're on."

"I thought you might like a drop of Calvados," said Mrs. Jewel. "My uncle, being sea-faring, brings us a drop."

As she poured, she said, "Somebody in the bar said he heard of a case where a P.C. was doing it, though he strangled them. No offence meant."

"In fact it was a sergeant."

"Gawd!" said Mrs. Jewel.

"In a short story, by a man named Aumonier as far as I remember."

"Writing!" said Mrs. Jewel with contempt as she piled dirty dishes into the serving hatch.

"My researches," said the Inspector with a sense of well-being and a spiteful look which caused Honeybody to draw back the arm which was snaking towards the Calvados bottle, "revealed that I erred in asking my clerk, who has a literal mind, about getting to Windlesham Parva. One can, but it is three times as long as taking an express direct to Windlesham and catching a bus."

"Fancy you not knowing that," said the landlady, preparing to depart. "Bus leaves at six-thirty at the stop. Train at seven, all the city gents in it. Breakfast?"

"I'll feed him in the kitchen," said Elizabeth.

"Use the bacon at the back of the fridge, dear, the stuff in front is kept for the commercials," said Mrs. Jewel before shutting the door.

"You better stay, Honeybody, for a couple of days, just in case you can get an identification of Redapple for Monday and yesterday. Borrow one of the local blokes. It's an outside chance. And no drinking."

"Might have to be a little, sir, in the way of duty."

"I'll check on him," said Elizabeth.

Harry raised his eyebrows.

"I'll stay a couple of days, dear, if you don't mind. Barbie Redding is taking two days off—her naked girls rebelled at the weather off Margate and they might be taking a working party to Spain on sardine boats. She's perplexed. She should get married this year."

"Ar," said Honeybody, and Elizabeth transfixed him with a dagger look.

"In that," she said, "she finds the long engagement hard."

"But *you* didn't, love," said Harry.

"That was different." Elizabeth looked at her most matronly.

"You see, sir," Honeybody had prepared to be heavily avuncular, "one time I was on exchange to Cardiff and . . ."

"Good night all." Harry collared the bathroom first.

9

At C.I.D. Headquarters there is an office run by an elderly inspector and a youngish sergeant, the latter becoming more dyspeptic as the years go by. They work in close association with the Special Branch and keep their files in a large safe of which only they and a Commander know the combination. To them, orally, are reported the tidbits of scandal concerning the great persons 'in society'. Sometimes there is some discreet investigation; occasionally a very fashionable trial. Generally its value is more oblique, concerning the apprehension of that most slippery of crooks, the blackmailer.

To this office Harry at ten a.m. next morning took the piece of paper upon which Honeybody had written the name of Redapple's mistress.

The nature of his work, or natural inclination, had made the elderly inspector melancholy. A little dismal light came through a small window to reinforce a desk lamp; but the impression was one of slight decay.

He looked at the piece of paper.

"Them! They'll be at it at eighty."

"Plural?" asked Harry.

The gloomy man was not to be hurried. He took an antacid tablet from a tin and said: "He's of very good family is the Captain and such a nice fellow that a lot of people never believe what they hear of him. Handsome fellow of fifty. It's more or less been bogus business, with the partner's money flying out of the window. Oh, the Captain has a first-class snide accountant who knows his law. It's forces beyond the Captain's control, mysterious third parties, that stuff. You can't touch him, though I think a couple of times he's settled civil suits out of court. Then there are dogs and horses; when there's the occasional 'boat race' the Captain's *in*. But he's a compulsive gambler. Every bookie and casino owner raises his titfer when the Captain passes. God knows what he's lost over thirty years."

"I see." The lugubrious atmosphere was contagious and Harry felt gloom descend on him.

"I wonder if you do? In her twenties she was one of the best-looking women in the world. Could have had a tiara. Instead she gets this fellow. Clever girl, knows when to hold her tongue. Twitchy industrialists are her marks. Ostensibly she's been separated from the gallant Captain for fifteen years; they've got a week-ender at Weston-super-Mare. Our old friend Blucher does the work, and the Captain says she can divorce him quietly if the money's right. Then, when the cash is paid, the lady changes her mind. We have eight cases on record— one of Blucher's men is an informer."

"How did you manage that?" asked Harry, admiringly. Blucher could smell a rat at a hundred paces.

"Getting him brought on my second ulcer attack, but it's basically six quid a week regular. I keep getting the please-explains from audit and only last week the Auditor-General wanted to know whether we deducted tax at source. I think I'll have another of these tablets. They ease it for a few minutes. I can't eat cheese any more. You'll come to it," he brightened at the thought.

"Can't we get the Captain?" Payment to informers was a permanent headache, tacitly not discussed, and Harry thought his gloomy colleague had displayed bad taste.

"Nothing you can prove. If anybody came to court they'd come with dirty hands. No, Mr. James, there's nothing, but just for my little book, who's he got the fangs into now?"

"Lord Redapple."

"Pride and joy of the Establishment, but the Captain's mark, nevertheless. Not quite the thing in the County; bastard de-

178

scent from a pill pusher. Of the two they'd believe the Captain. The Specials might nab him one day."

"You mean ...?"

"A man who'd flog his missus'll flog anything. Now, if you don't mind ..."

It was impossible at this time of the year, but as Harry left he imagined he heard the faint drawl of a blow-fly.

Hawker, blank-faced, said he had listened to the Inspector's taped report. "I had heard of the gallant Captain, as it happens, when he got a bit too near the doping of race-horses. Nasty fellow, received in the best circles. Prettyman would act for him in this case because of the noble relatives. That's the lay. Innocent, respectable solicitor who has no idea of what's going on. C. Guy Blucher and the confidential offer through some intermediary to let him have the lady for a cash settlement. Fool-proof. What's she like?" The Superintendent had his share of human curiosity.

"Athlete gone a bit to seed, like Honeybody."

"My Gawd, you mean ...?"

"She started out five stone to Honeybody's seventeen. No grossness. Fine figure of a woman, beautiful features."

"I can't see Redapple doing both jobs," said Hawker.

"One followed the other. With the need to pay off the Captain he wants money even more. He kills Prettyman. Winding suspects and gets his too."

"Only thing," said Hawker, "is that I cannot see the lady backing him in an alibi ... unless, unless," spatulate fingers caressed the old desk, "she is going to take him for his last penny. We'll put it back to the boys in Kent and have the Finance Squad watch. If Redapple starts pawning his gold plate we'll move in fast. Just a minute," the red light had flashed upon the intercom.

Hawker put down the receiver. "Briefing room, all ranks above Inspector." He glanced at Harry. "Come my worm, Acting Chief art thou and thus admitted to the Holies."

The briefing room is large, with a porous ceiling which absorbs sound, chairs and a raised platform at the end. A harassed, red-faced man stood before the microphone. Harry took a chair beside Hawker and watched the Old Guard, tired and a little seamed around the face, come in. He felt a tingle of pride that he was the youngest present. It was an unusual gathering: the last, he had heard, was when Christie was on the run.

"All right, close the doors. This is to brief you against any, repeat any, enquiry. At seven-ten a.m. a Percy Buttershaw, a shift worker, was returning to his home in Clarence Street, Liverpool. It has many intersections. He says quote he had a prickling in the back of his neck and looked round, seeing a man with a knife unquote. Coincidentally two P.C.s, off duty, turned the corner. The man with the knife ran in an opposite direction and," the red-faced man sneezed into his handkerchief, "he encountered seven ladies, led by Dame Alice Grittle, who fell upon him. One was an ex-Empire Games javelin thrower and she was twisting his head while the ladies applied their bludgeons. The constables managed to rescue him with only slight concussion and a dislocated shoulder.

"He is Bertrand Mesnil, aged forty-seven, employed as a cook upon the tramp steamer Loire, based on Marseilles, a very dirty erratic little boat. She delivered olive oil at London Pool four months ago and has been on the coastal trade since, waiting, her skipper says, to get a substantial cargo back to France. Mesnil was a small Moroccan farmer, dispossessed without compensation, so he says. He worked it out that if the English had not supported De Gaulle it would never have happened, so it occurred to him to kill one English-speaking person per ten thousand francs of his valuation of the worth of his farm. Mad as a hatter! Our alienists are getting there now, but the local men say he has a long history of brain damage caused by a childhood disease. His powers of speech are rapidly going. They anticipate that in a few days he will have reached a motionless, catatonic state, with death a few months off. Unfit to plead. He is talking incoherently, but on the ship the local authorities found seven sharpened knives, a diary written by the same hand as the letters to the Sun, and three hanks of hair. Preliminary lab reports state that they could belong to the Walthamstow, Kennington, and Baker Street victims, but exhumation will be necessary. Gentlemen, in any statement to press or public, emphasise that the two constables would have got him and that the ladies' presence was fortuitous. There is no need to mention that the constables were off duty. They have, incidentally, been promoted as sergeants and you might use their new rank."

The soundproof roof ate the small babel of comment.

"One question." Hawker's six foot three, slightly stooping, made him look like a dyspeptic old vulture as he stood. Some glances were not too friendly. "Does he admit the killing of Prettyman and Winding?"

"He admits everything and anything, unfortunately. He could of course easily have made the journey in spite of the fog. This boat is a kind of outlaw, goes anywhere, does anything. They prefer to give the crew a small sum to fend for themselves ashore rather than feed them on board, if a few days are involved. Mesnil was known to be nutty; never talked except to mutter to himself. But he could cook rather well, stews and French muck, and he was on rock-bottom pay. Did not drink or smoke, no amusements. Any more questions?"

There were none.

"Catatonic," sniffled little Mr. Middle, the Treasury junior, as he trotted beside Hawker to the lift. "Have to be carried into the box; always causes an outcry. There was that man with no legs who strangled his mother-in-law—she'd bent over his wheel-chair—just after Munich. The Government felt they had to discourage crimes of violence, so he was hanged. A great deal of unfortunate comment and a meeting in Trafalgar Square with Sir Stafford and the others. Mounted police out. Dear, oh dear, and the hangman. Understand," Mr. Middle puffed beside the old Superintendent's huge strides, "that it's difficult to hang a man without his legs unless he co-operates. This fellow was a Welshman and wouldn't and the hangman demanded double money, which Mr. C. said he could not justify because of what was needed for the armaments. Oh, dear!"

The Superintendent bent over momentarily and soothed him. "It's different now. Go and see Sir Jabeez. . . ."

"Gout," said Mr. Middle. "He couldn't come." He scuttled away in his double-breasted overcoat.

"All over," said Hawker to Harry James, "except the P.R.O. job. Get that sergeant of yours back and take three days off. There's some more warehouse-smashing jobs I want you on to."

Harry relaxed in his chair. It had been an unpleasant wood

and he was glad to be out of it. He looked at the telephone. Might leave Elizabeth a couple of days, not answer calls and perhaps look up some of his old acquaintances of whom she disapproved.

The door opened and the melancholy face of Constable McWhirter appeared.

Harry was experiencing the sense of well-being that came of a closed file. He had remembered a blonde divorcee from his bachelor days and was wondering if he should ring her.

"Sit down, McWhirter, and tell uncle."

"A very funny thing, sir, I stayed back last night . . ." McWhirter went on and on.

An hour later, Harry said, "I think we should do some research, Constable. It might, probably will if successful, get you a step up."

"Sir, all night if necessary."

Harry momentarily saw his days of ambition, and perhaps of incompetence.

He phoned Hawker.

"Oh, God," said the Superintendent. "Even I have heard of McWhirter; he'll end up Commissioner by sheer attrition. Can you cope? I've got to go to see the Big Feller. There are crowds of women carrying posters demanding that the Dame be appointed Home Secretary."

"God help us!" said Harry, reverently.

"But he's fast on his feet and as soon as he got the news from Liverpool he phoned and offered the Ambassadorship to Paris. But she said they drank and fornicated. So he thought quick and made it Plenipotentiary Extraordinary to Peking, which she snatched."

"I thought the Chinese drank a lot," said Harry, "on dock duty they're often found tight."

"The Dame said *that* was different, friendly libations between the working class; she didn't mention the other. She gets on a plane in forty-eight hours, thank God! But they're putting me on T.V., all teeth and reassurance. Take care of your end, Inspector, with my full backing."

Which was fine, thought Harry, except what you needed really was forty-eight hours of cogitation. And time was running out. He shrugged and dialled Personnel. There were fifteen plain-clothes men back from influenzic leave. Masterfully he ordered the services of ten of them. At the end of a nation-wide campaign like the one just ended you felt flat as hell, devoid of energy or ambition; throughout the country there would be thousands of policemen with dead batteries. Better get ten post-influenzics.

"Now," he said to McWhirter, seated grimly stroking serge-covered thighs, "here's what I want you to do . . ."

Later, he telephoned the Dendles. Honeybody was in—in the bar, in fact—but, as he explained, in the way of duty.

"Your wife is out, sir, with Miss Barbie Redding, all giggling and the League of Modest Maidens. I'm faithfully at work, sir."

"Now, listen," said the Inspector.

"Cor," said Honeybody when he had finished, "makes me feel like retiring to the fish."

"I'm sending a teletype to the Chief Constable that you get all assistance needed. Tell Lizzie she might as well stay on. I'll be sleeping here, more than likely."

10

Two days later the Inspector sat gloomily in a Humber bearing him to Windlesham. Not but that the Acting Chief Inspectorship, although acting, was not of some worth. Beside him sat P.C. McWhirter and a younger, more burly constable, chewing gum. Beside the driver sat the youngest inspector with a barely concealed air of excitement.

"You never taken anybody in for murder?" asked Harry.

"Never, sir, that M.P. in Hyde Park was my biggest case. But do you think you can persuade Lord Redapple to come with us?"

"Your guess is as good as mine," said Harry, deathly tired after about five hours' sleep in two days. "I phoned and made an appointment. Were I him I should fly to the lawyers. Better stop in Windlesham, please driver, so I can phone the pub."

Elizabeth, in company with Milton Greenaway, John Hearman and Barbara Redding, teeveed, watched the triumphant exit from London Airport of Dame Alice Grittle, supported by huge mobs.

"Honeybody isn't here, dear," she said. "He's been hanging round with that young clerk at Prettyman's who is a crack darts player. Did you know the Sergeant is first class at it?"

"When he can see the board. He got into the *News of the World* series one time, and needed double twelve with his third dart, but overcome by the pints he saw fit to implant it in the left buttock of a large lady representing a trade magazine." He realised he was talking to put off an evil hour. "Be seeing you in an hour. Love."

"Just a minute, my sweet. Barbie and Milton are getting married tomorrow, special licence—I wonder how you get one?—at a Register Office. I persuaded them, and we must see about a present. I thought money, but . . ."

"In one hour or so, my precious pet." Dexterously the Inspector hung up and returned to the police car.

The youngest inspector looked chagrined as Harry assured him that he did not want help in seeing Lord Redapple. They parked outside the great house and Harry was away for nearly an hour. He looked dead tired as he finally appeared through the front door and with premonition the youngest inspector wondered if he should have accepted the offer of a junior partnership in his father-in-law's ironmongery shop.

"Drive slowly," said Harry. "He's putting his coat on. His chauffeur will drive him. Keep your eye through the back window, McWhirter."

"Aye," said the P.C., grimly, but as they neared the road the big grey car came through the trees.

In a few minutes both cars had parked outside the Dendles.

"Into the snug, please," said Harry. Milton Greenaway, John Hearman, Elizabeth and Barbara Redding looked up. The Inspector said quickly, "Let me introduce you to a remote cousin, Lord Redapple. This is Barbara Redding."

Lord Redapple gave his brief charming smile. "You'd better call me Alfred." He took a seat. "If what the Chief Inspector says is true—and I have no reason to doubt it—you will share in the Trust. I want to impress upon you that neither I nor my children will bear you the slightest ill-will." He smiled again. "Not from altruism—we are not an altruistic family—

but because the tax position makes it so that another one, or half a dozen, would hardly alter the individual net share. Anyway, you'll want a solicitor and perhaps you'll allow me to arrange it."

"Certainly," said Barbara, humbly, "but I don't understand. . . ."

"My dear," said Redapple, laughing, "do you know you are the spitting image of my daughter? Funny thing, heredity."

"What happened, Miss Redding," said Harry formally, "was that the original Redapple founded a trust for descendants of his children and those of his only brother, a shadowy figure, none of whose children had descendants as far as are not represented by the present line. But there was one, the eldest, Ferdinand Redapple. After the Trust was founded he got into bad trouble. After crawling through ancient police archives I think it was a City fraud and that his uncle provided four thousand pounds to buy him out of it. But he was sent to Australia. There he married and had one son. Ferdinand followed the profession of being a 'leg', as they called crooked gamblers.

"The Sydney police did a wonderful job. He was sued quite often for misrepresentation and was found not guilty twice of fraud. This is surmise, but I fancy the founding Redapple verbally told the head trustee, the Prettyman of his day, not to tell Ferdinand of the Trust. Should he or his heirs return, well and good, they should have their rights, but if not, then let it lie. Ferdinand's son, William, legally changed the name to Redding, presumably to rid himself of his father's reputation. He prospered as a gold buyer and became quite a civic figure, on the board of a hospital, etcetera. He was your grandfather, Miss Redding. He had one son and the fortunes declined. Your father enlisted in the Australian Air Force, came to England and married a Scots lass and was shot down and killed in 1944. Your mother died three years ago. To round it off, I may say that this Australian business was not passed on to the late Mr. Prettyman, his father while hale and hearty being trampled to death by a traction engine."

"I suspected as much," said Redapple.

"Meantime, let me congratulate you on your good fortune."

"Oh," she said, as if in some dream. "Milton and I are to marry in the morning."

"Dear Barbie," said Greenaway, "this puts a different complexion on it. You are a near millionaire."

"It makes no atom of difference," said Barbara.

A spasm of disapprobation wrinkled Redapple's cheeks but he held his tongue.

Harry nodded his head.

"Milton Oswald Greenaway and John Hearman," said the youngest inspector with relish, "I must take you to London for interrogation upon the murder of the late Charles Prettyman, of which I suspect you. Anything you say may be used in evidence and"—obviously savouring the moment—"as gentlemen bred to the law you will know that you need answer no questions."

It was Hearman who dived for the door and McWhirter who tripped him, dragged him to his feet and propelled him outside. Greenaway sat, his face a molten red.

"Get cracking," said Harry, and the youngest inspector put an arm round his waist and dragged him slowly to and through the door.

There was a long silence. They heard the police car move off and Harry noticed sadly that two large tears were trickling down his wife's cheeks. Then Mrs. Jewel came bustling in with a small tray.

"Listened outside the door," she said crisply. "Brandy, on the house."

"Thank you very much," said Redapple, astonished at the thought of being given anything.

"A pleasure." The landlady left.

"I must know," said Barbara, "or I shall never sleep again."

"Are you sure?" said Elizabeth quickly.

"Sure," said the dull voice.

"Very well," said Harry. "To relieve your mind I will say that three killings, Prettyman, poor bumbling Winding and Greasing, a publisher, were done by Hearman, being the dominant partner."

"I have always known Milton was weak, but . . ."

"I was always puzzled," said the Inspector wearily, "by the relationship between the two. Hearman's dominance was odd.

186

The two seemed curiously lacking in scruples, although I thought that was affectation. And Hearman seemed to have expensive tastes. But, there, a lot of people have just that little bit of private means to add the jam. In fact, Hearman was a juvenile delinquent of singularly vicious character; on police records but no convictions, too cunning. He used to try to influence somebody else to act as 'front'. Then he realised there was only gaol ahead, so he turned 'honest', studied nights.

"It's not easy to get legal advice on how to be a crook. If you think up some scheme to defraud the public and go into the office of Basil, Saffron and Mace and pop the question you will be ejected."

"The question never occurred to me," said Redapple primly.

Oh well, thought Harry, the creaky old thing was due to be taken for fifty thou by his girl friend; so he smiled.

"A lot of people desire such services, and these Master Hearman provided to a great range of people. Oh, in police work once we get the end of the string we always unravel the mess. It is getting the end that presents the trouble. In this case the end was a close-grinding Scot named McWhirter. Mr. Greasing fell through his banisters, pushed through by Hearman masquerading as an inspector of police. My surmise is that he found out exactly what old Greasing had seen, asked him to come round to the Yard and poked him through the banisters. But Greasing had popped the card into a little box on his desk. It had belonged to an inspector long retired and in fact dead. He was a kind of maid of all work; anybody fell sick he took over. His name was Edward Blessings, a punctilious old gent of the old school, always presented his card first, even if he was taking you in.

"It meant nothing at all to me, but McWhirter spent an evening going through old Blessings' work sheets—they're kept—and he could not find that during his five years as an inspector Blessings had gone near Greasing. But he had visited Sir Jabeez Lusting regarding that gentleman's car which had been pinched. So off trots McWhirter to the laboratory and on the back of the card, erased but visible under radioscopic examination, was written 'Could I have a few words re the stolen car, please?'

"So that set me off putting men on to both Hearman and,

I'm afraid, Greenaway. We got a woman into Hearman's bed-sitter—the landlady detests him. Nothing there except some evidence of his legal advice sideline and a bank statement showing a credit of twelve hundred pounds. So we saw Sir Jabeez, who co-operated. In the vault containing old briefs we found a complete summary of Miss Redding's descent. Most of it came from an enquiry agency in Sydney. It was not too hard a task; they destroyed the convict records in 1902, but rosters of the voluntary migrants persist. The report recorded Miss Redding's father's arrival here in the R.A.A.F. and after that Hearman was capable of taking it over himself. That was two and a half years ago. When did you meet Greenaway?"

"Two years and three months ago," she said sadly.

"Hearman heard of the Redapple Trust and he smelt money. He probably thought of forging documents for a false claimant—a Tichbourne sort of thing. These things stare one in the face in retrospect. I should have faced the obvious fact that Hearman was at home in these parts. He had struck up an acquaintance with Prettyman's young clerk; the youth was flattered to have such a dashing acquaintance. Oh, yes, they frequently discussed the Redapple Estate, and Hearman expressed great interest in the set of figures which Prettyman had dug out. But Hearman was quicker. He realised that the first entry 'Orion 25' referred to a ship. In fact twenty-five pounds bought you a deck cabin to Sydney, though I'd hate to have done the trip. The remaining sums, top being thirty-five pounds, represented the begging letters that Ferdinand Redapple sent his uncle and, later, Prettyman, the original solicitor. Not wanting him back they doled it out small.

"I fancy that Hearman and Greenaway, a penniless young man, might have had a few 'transactions'. In any case Hearman had sense enough to know that a girl like you would see little in him. So . . . Greenaway . . . did he pick you up?"

"We collided on a corner."

"A charming young barrister!"

"I used to lie awake at night worrying," said Barbara. "I had the odd feeling sometimes that deep down he disliked me. Oh, mostly he was so, so nice. But then I got the impression at times I scraped his nerves. I'm sorry . . ."

"You have no relatives except a distant aunt of your mother. I rather fear you've had a bit of an escape. Remember that."

"My God, I will have a brandy!"

"It was your amazing resemblance to Marouka Redapple, his lordship's daughter, that upset the apple cart, to make a fearsome pun. You had put off the wedding . . . subconscious eh?"

"I suppose so," said Barbara, "though I don't really know."

"Old Prettyman must have seen you with Greenaway a few months ago. He'd have thought 'Marouka Redapple' and then remembered she was in Morocco. She used to send him little letters regularly. It was easy for him to investigate and to find you were the orphan of an Australian flying officer. Then the significance of the 'Orion 25' entry hit him. He got in touch with a Sydney firm of solicitors who produced the story we have talked about. The Sydney police cabled us the substance of the report; Prettyman must have destroyed the original. After due process of thought I think he telephoned Greenaway, very discreetly, but enough to panic both young men.

"It was easy enough for Hearman to announce on the Monday morning that Prettyman had phoned for an appointment. In fact no call was made by Prettyman from his hotel. I think the appointment was made earlier, that Greenaway suggested picking Prettyman up outside Hentrotts Hotel at three-ish—it never occurred to me to ask the time he left the hotel until yesterday—so that they could talk in the car.

"Now the weather was pretty bad—all the forecasts being fog, cold and misery. And the other barristers, if unengaged, were well known to get off home or to a cosy club on such occasions. Hearman therefore suggests in the afternoon, after the others have gone, that Greenaway brings the old chap back to chambers, thereby giving him confidence everything was above board and that he, Hearman, would be in the offing, if needed.

"At two-forty p.m. we have an identification; a blue Volks standing thirty feet from Hentrotts. The hotel van had been unable to get through to Billingsgate so the proprietress despatched a boy to scour fishmongers for a turbot. He is prepared to identify the driver as Greenaway."

Barbara momentarily pressed a broad palm over her eyes.

"Don't worry too much. He's an unprepossessing boy, acned,

shifty and of dubious morals for a sixteen-year-older. We are afraid counsel will destroy his testimony. Now I surmise that Prettyman, without witness, was pretty forthright. Surely Greenaway realised his fiancée was a Redapple! What was Hearman doing pumping his junior clerk? Greenaway must have sweated despite the cold. He may have been able to convince you, Miss Redding, but not Sir Jabeez. He would have been asked to leave his chambers, thus losing his profession—and its worldly standing—that he prized. He parked the car near chambers, opened the door and Prettyman came out. Hearman emerged from the fog-reeking shadows and knifed him in the back."

The room was strangely silent for an instant until Barbara Redding's laboured breathing started again.

"Again, a guess. He said, 'I'll put him in the waiting-room, Milton, just keep the door open as you would do and discover him when calm.'

"He's got muscles, has Hearman, did a bit of weight lifting in his tough days. He took Prettyman upstairs. That was Greenaway's moment of truth, I guess. He should have screamed for help. As it was, he stood in the doorway of the chambers.

"He said no word and from then on was in it hock deep, knowing it well as a barrister. He probably had the briefest few words with Hearman and then carried on his charade. Look at the appointment book, look at clock, etcetera. He was in a state of shock when the doctor arrived; he wondered why a healthy young man should be so reduced, so he told me yesterday.

"He stood there in the fog while Hearman took up frail little Prettyman and carried him to the waiting-room. From the doorway he saw old Greasing pass. Thereafter he went to his room and embarked upon this terrible farce, eventually 'discovering' the poor old devil in the waiting-room. Hearman, of course, had nicked off home. His evilly disposed landlady declares there is a raincoat of his missing.

"The next day was the usual hurried, guilty whisperings in corners; and of course the suggestion they should come down to Windlesham Parva, which must have come as a dreadful blow. Refusal was more dangerous than acceptance."

The Inspector poured himself another brandy. Honeybody's face was that of a small boy watching a Punch and Judy show. Redapple's jaw was slightly slack.

"But you see," said Harry, "*I didn't know*. Why should anybody tell me, really, that Hearman was an old habitué of Windlesham Parva? Miss Redapple has been largely abroad for four years and in any case why should mention be made to me that she is the spitting image of Barbara here? They assumed I knew it. So there we are, except that poor old Peter Winding, blundering in after his wake, sees Barbara. He double takes for an instant, but he knows that Miss Redapple is in Marrakesh. . . ."

"She used to send him a postcard occasionally," said Redapple, in a faraway voice.

"The penny finally fell," said Harry. " 'Orion £25'. There had been talk in the bar about Mr. Greenaway's young lady. The Sergeant enquired and somebody remembered that Mrs. Jewel, quite innocently, said she was of an Australian father. At home, amid his junky stuff, Winding had *The History of Anglo-Australian Trade and Navigation* by Charles Smith, published 1903! We found it in his great collection of books. Winding was not a *smart* man; dour and honest and a little drunken. It ended in his vague intention of going to London and consulting somebody in Sir Jabeez's chambers.

"Of course, our smart cookie Hearman knew what had happened. He had seen Winding's face. He spent the night in Greenaway's car a hundred yards from Winding's home; we have an identification. Oh, once we get the end of the ball of string we can unravel it." He looked at Redapple.

"The point I did not know—sheer carelessness—was the fast Windlesham-Victoria service. Hearman beat the train to Sevenoaks: the fog was closing in and he ended with a clear fifteen minutes. He parked the car in a garage; he would have done better leaving it in a side street, but, as usual, they overelaborate. He caught the train; no difficulty to follow vague, troubled old Winding. A nervy young fellow with better eyesight than I have, although I *was* under a lamp. He stabbed Winding dexterously. Then, with the usual passion for tying up loose ends—never do that"—the Inspector grinned savagely around.

. . ."I won't," said Redapple, apparently seriously.

. . ."Then he called in to old Greasing who worked alone, produced an old C.I.D. card—he was a collector of potentially useful documents—and found that Greasing had indeed seen something which disturbed him, more than one figure in the fog, something odd. He was like that, hugging things to his chest, keeping out of everything unless he saw money; but of course in this case he could see none. But he was cautious and admitted the facts to Hearman, who asked him to accompany him to the Yard and hurled him down the stairwell.

"Oh, no! Miss Redding, your young man was genuinely shocked. I should have seen it. He was lead horse to a killer."

"Have I got money?" Barbara was sweating in the gas-fired heat.

"I will advance anything within reason," said Redapple, magisterially.

"Can money get him—I suppose both—off?" she demanded.

It was the old question and the Inspector gave the old answer. "I do not believe that innocent men are convicted because of bad representation, but some guilty persons are convicted when a first class counsel could get them off."

"I'll pay." She was high and mighty.

"I imagine," said Harry, "that both know the ropes. Perhaps, Lord Redapple . . ."

"Come, my dear," said his lordship. "We'll put you up. To-morrow we'll see."

"Thank you," said Barbara, and allowed herself to be taken by the arm. "Thank you Betty, and . . . even . . . you Inspector." She followed Redapple to the door.

"Life!" said Honeybody as the door closed.

"Beastly!" said Elizabeth, finishing her brandy.

"The landlady's got meat balls in sour cream sauce," said Honeybody, "learned it from a Frenchman, up to no good no doubt, but nice grub so she says. No purpose complaining, it was years ago."

"The building superintendent sent on a letter," said Elizabeth. "Mr. Grunting says he will remove the soft growth from your left foot at four-thirty next Wednesday."

They stared at Harry whilst he laughed.